D1295603

# PAYBACK

# PAYBACK

## RUSSELL JAMES

A FOUL PLAY PRESS BOOK

THE COUNTRYMAN PRESS

WOODSTOCK, VERMONT

*For Charles and Edna*

This edition published by The Countryman Press in 1993
Copyright © 1991 by Russell James

All rights reserved. No part of this book may be reproduced in any form by
any mechanical or electronic means including information storage and
retrieval systems without the publisher's express written permission, except
by a reviewer who may quote brief passages.

**Library of Congress Cataloging-in-Publication Data**
James, Russell.
    Payback: a novel of suspense/Russell James.
        p.      cm.
    "A Foul Play Press book."
    ISBN 0-88150-267-7
    1. Brothers—England—London—Fiction.   2. Murder—England—
London—Fiction.   3. London (England)—Fiction.   I. Title.
PR6060.A473P38    1993
823'.914—dc20                                                          93–29903
                                                                            CIP

A Foul Play Press Book
The Countryman Press, Inc.
Woodstock, Vermont 05091

Printed in the United States of America on recycled paper

The body has been laid out in the dining room. Someone spread a red fire-blanket across the table, and they rested the coffin on that. Inside, my brother Albie lies on his back wearing a dark blue suit. He is in a striped shirt with collar and tie, and has his eyes closed. His hair needs a wash.

It always did. His dirty blond hair is streaked with dark strands, above a face still scarred from measles he caught as a teenager. Pitted skin and greasy hair. Although the undertaker has cleaned him up and dressed him in the blue suit, Albie looks like a mechanic lying beneath a car.

I glance down at his hands to see if there is dirt beneath the fingernails. There is not. On the third finger of his right hand he wears a gold signet ring, and he'll be buried with it. No, cremated. Before they tip him into the fire, I guess they'll slip that ring off his finger. No sense wasting it.

'We got a pine coffin,' Ludo says. 'Real pine.'

He stands huge and helpless beside me, hunched inside an old green sweater. His eyes have the sorrowful look of a bloodhound with a head cold, and he fidgets while he works out what to say. Then he runs his fingers through his wiry red hair and says, 'I'm glad your plane was on time, Floyd. Not like last time.'

It isn't a criticism: he is just glad to see me. Losing Albie was a shock to him, and the last three days have been lonely. It is the first time that Ludo has been left on his own for so long. For a few hours he can cope, but come evening he needs someone to fix supper and send him to bed.

I cross to the window at the back of the room and move the brown curtain. Outside, April sunshine blazes down from a blue sky. The back lawn needs cutting. The flowerbeds look overgrown. On the stone patio stands an empty cardboard box, blown in from somewhere. A cat sniffs at it and walks away.

I let the curtain drop across the daylight, and turn back into the room. 'Where's Uncle Paul?' I ask.

'Well,' Ludo says slowly. 'He went out to buy some cigarettes.'

'Has he been staying in the house?'

'No. He goes home.'

'Who gets your meals and clothes?'

'I can manage, Floyd. I can do that.'

'Good.'

'Albie taught me how to work the cooker. And the washing machine.'

I smile at him encouragingly. In these last ten years I have seen him twice. I didn't expect him to have changed, but I was wrong. Even in his early thirties he is developing. Ludo has grown up slowly, that's all.

'Do you want a cup of tea?' he asks. 'I make a good cup of tea, Floyd.'

We leave the room.

Since last I was here they have repainted the kitchen. It is a pale yellow colour now, garish in the spring sunlight streaming through the back window. Confidently, Ludo makes tea. He waits till the kettle is boiling vigorously, then before the temperature drops, he pours the water quickly on to the tea leaves. 'Milk and sugar?' he asks.

'I take it black.'

He fetches down a decorated tin from the wall-cupboard and shakes biscuits on to a plate. Then we sit at the kitchen table. 'Uncle Paul did stay last night,' Ludo says. 'Because of the body, you know?'

I sip some tea. 'You wouldn't want to be alone with it.'

'I'm not afraid of Albie's body, Floyd. It just makes me sad.'

'You're gonna miss him.'

'Yes.'

He wants to add something, to explain how he feels, but he finds it difficult. So he frowns and drinks some tea. 'Will you be staying long, after the funeral?' he asks me.

I don't reply. For ten years I have kept away from here, lived my own life. I am not back to stay.

'What will you do?' Ludo asks.

'I can sleep in my old room.'

'I mean, what will you do about Albie? Are you going to get them for doing it?'

I knew someone would ask. I knew in the first minute, after I read the telegram. 'Albie killed in street accident,' it said. A street accident. Albie didn't have accidents. Nothing happened to him by chance.

But I don't say this to Ludo. 'It was an accident,' I say.

'It was a hit and run.'

2

'People get scared. Someone walks in front of their car. They can't stop. It's late at night, they've had a drink or two, no one's watching. They drive away, keep out of trouble.'

He lets me finish. Both of his big hands are clasped around his warm teacup, and his brown eyes gaze into mine. 'It happened in daytime.'

I shrug. 'Accidents can happen in daytime.'

He shakes his head and takes another slurp of tea.

'It wasn't . . .' he mumbles.

'Wasn't what?'

'Well, I saw it, didn't I, Floyd? I saw the car hit him. The car chased him, on the pavement.'

'The pavement? What did the cops say?'

'Well,' Ludo sighs, and peers into the bottom of his teacup. 'I don't know.'

'Did you tell them?'

'Of course.' He puts down his cup and looks at me angrily. 'They didn't listen. No one listens to me.'

'But you told them?'

'Yes.' He looks indignant that I should ask.

'What did they say?'

'They said it was an accident.'


After Albie is cremated, the line of cars drags back to the house. Before we went, Paul and Vera put out drinks and food. Vera must have spent the whole morning back in her kitchen making plates of triangular sandwiches, squashed and glistening under transparent film. She made jellies too. Paul's job was the drinks: whisky, port and crates of beer. They made a proper funeral.

Hired glasses stand on the sideboard beside film-wrapped dishes of extra sandwiches. As the guests creep into the room Uncle Paul presses drinks on them. Vera dispenses sandwiches. Her food is arranged on the same dining table where Albie's coffin lay this morning. She has replaced the red fire-blanket with a white tablecloth.

Twenty people cram into our dining room to collect a plate and a glass. I offer to help hand things out but am shooed away. They say it isn't right that I do things at my brother's funeral: I have my grief. So Ludo and I stand awkwardly in the centre of the room while people slink up to pay respects. In my left hand I hold a plate of cold food, and I use my right to shake with the guests. I don't try to eat. Whenever I touch a sandwich someone comes to shake my hand.

3

I suppose I recognise about half the faces. They give condolences and move away, watching me warily. They are not comfortable with me – partly because I am the bereaved, and partly because I am a stranger now. With Ludo they can be natural: they can lay a reassuring hand on his arm. He is undemanding for them to talk to. With Ludo, all they have to do is talk at him, and he will stand nodding, agreeing with them. For the funeral, he has dug out an old black suit a size too small, and an awful tie. His red hair has dried where he slicked it down, leaving tufts sticking up from the top of his head like fur on an angry cat.

I follow Uncle Paul into the front parlour. He wears a dark suit with stripes, and a cheerful tie. Since I last saw him, his hair has thinned and turned silver. I tell him that I am grateful for the way he handled things. It's family, he says. We can talk about it later when the people have gone. I guess he means we will talk about the funeral costs.

Paul turns away from me. 'How do you think our Floyd looks?' he demands heartily of the room in general. 'Seen a lot more sun than we get in London, hasn't he? D'you like his tan?'

They all smile at me. The men have that South London grey look, and the women have painted skin.

'You're looking well, Floyd,' a thin man says. 'Fancy suit.'

'Just foreign, that's all.'

'The clothes in *our* shops are foreign nowadays, Floyd. Where'd you get it?'

'Nowhere special. On holiday in Naples.'

'Oh, Naples!' an old woman laughs. 'Is that all?'

I take one of my untouched sandwiches and raise it towards my mouth.

'I had a holiday there once,' the thin man says. 'Sorrento. You been there, Floyd?'

I say that I have. My sandwich buckles in my hand and I put it down.

'You've been everywhere, I suppose,' says the old woman with a laugh. 'Nice suit, Floyd, anyway, wherever you got it. What you going to do with yourself now – are you coming back?'

'I live in Germany now.'

'He only came home for some decent clothes.'

People joke about my suit because it is safe territory. They include me in the conversation because this is my family's house, and it is my brother who died. But no one knows what to say to me. They are no longer sure who I am.

We wear polite faces. Guests say appropriate words to me, mostly about the funeral, and they tell Ludo that if he needs anything he only has to ask. Then they talk among themselves. I drift uncomfortably among them, unsure what to say. I can't relax here. I don't belong.

Another old woman plants herself in front of me and asks if I remember her. I say I do. 'You're nice and brown,' she says. 'Though you don't look English any more, if you don't mind me saying.'

I smile.

'You always were the good-looking one, Floyd. Perhaps you should have taken Albie with you. Bit of sun would have done him good.'

Beside us, people stop talking, as if at Albie's funeral you should not mention his name.

'I did ask him once,' I tell her. 'When I opened the gym in Germany. But he said he preferred living here.'

'He knew where he was in London,' she says. 'Shouldn't think he could handle things abroad.'

An old man that I assume to be her husband takes her arm. 'You're running on again,' he says. 'Come on.'

When he tries to lead her away, she shakes him off. 'You'll be staying now, I suppose?'

'I'm afraid not.'

'Won't you have to look after Albie's business?'

'Did he have one?'

'He always had a business. You know Albie.'

She grins knowingly at me, but I just smile and drift away.

'I'm sorry there weren't more people, son. 'Cos we let everybody know.'

Uncle Paul sits in the armchair facing me. We each hold a glass of Scotch. 'Of course, a lot have moved away. It would be a long journey for some of them.'

'It doesn't matter, Paul. Really.'

The sun has slipped behind the houses, leaving the front room cool in the April evening. Through the window I can see early leaves on a small tree in the street. They quiver in the breeze.

'And Albie did upset people. Well, I don't need to tell *you*, do I?'

'That's over and past.'

'I didn't want you to think they stayed away because of you, Floyd.'

I sip my Scotch. 'It was Albie's funeral, not mine.'

From the back of the house come the sounds of Vera and Ludo

washing up. She chatters and laughs. Ludo tries to keep up. Dishes and cutlery clink, and tap water runs.

'People blame you for the bust-up,' Paul says suddenly. 'They say you left him in the lurch.'

'I just left, that's all.'

'Ah, it was easy for you. You left Albie with the problems.'

'Ten years, Paul.'

'A long time.'

And now I am settled in Germany. I run a gymnasium in Munich with two friends. Rolf handles the finance, Gerhard the equipment and catering, I look after the gym. I give people their fitness programmes, help get rid of their flab. But I don't box any more.

Paul says, 'People do harbour grudges, Floyd. It's all they have to think about, some people.'

'They feel like that about me?'

'I don't know. Maybe not.'

We sit in silence and finish our whiskies. Paul's thinning hair shows that ten years have passed. I have aged as well. I wonder if he is right that people have these memories. After ten years the past should be dead.

'Ludo seems to be coping well,' I say. 'Perhaps Albie's death hasn't sunk in yet.'

'Of course it's sunk in. Ludo's not stupid. You've been away too long, Floyd. You don't give him credit.'

'I expect you're right.'

'I know I'm right. Ludo's not an infant, you know. He has a mental age about twelve, doctors say. Well, twelve year olds are quite bright, especially in London. They have to be. They get around on buses and trains, do a bit of shopping, cook simple meals. In the old days kids used to go out to work at twelve.'

'When *you* were young, eh, Paul?'

'Still the joker, aren't you? Well, what *are* you going to do, Floyd? I heard everybody asking you. Will you come back and take over from Albie? He looked after Ludo very well after your dad died. Though Ludo's no trouble. Not when you know him.'

'Ludo's my brother.'

'Me and Vera could keep an eye, of course.'

'That's kind of you, Paul, but he's my responsibility. I've done nothing for him these last ten years.'

Paul reaches forward from his armchair and pats my knee. 'That's what I like to hear. Families should stick together, shouldn't they?'

# 2

Jamie Farrant lives in a flat on Malpas Road. By his standards, Malpas Road is a comedown. It isn't even in Deptford; it's in New Cross, next door. He lives a hundred yards from where the railway line passes on its way down from New Cross station to Forest Hill, then on to Sydenham and Crystal Palace. With his window open, he'll hear a murmur of traffic, and trains passing.

Jamie has always lived around here. When we were kids, we went to different schools. He went to Grove Street, I went to Clyde. But around his twelfth birthday he stopped going. He decided he had learnt all that school could teach him. Anything else he would learn on the streets.

Later, while I tried to get somewhere boxing, Jamie skipped through a string of jobs. He was a bus conductor, a dustman, parks attendant, even a street-lamp attendant. For this he had to walk round Deptford early in the morning before the sun came up, and check the lamps to see which tubes needed replacing. That was a great job. It lasted six months.

Sometimes I'd walk his beat with him. On a fine dry morning we'd wander in the dark through the empty streets, chatting and laughing. We'd pass directly underneath street-lamps that weren't working, but he wouldn't put them in his notebook. With the light out he couldn't write.

Some rainy mornings he didn't get up. With luck, he might have done half his territory the night before, strolling from pub to pub, noting faulty lamps along the way. Or he would create a morning's report by taking a ride on a 188 bus. And on the days he did walk the route, if he collected over his quota of lamp-outs he would leave some out of his report, for the following day. Then he could take a lie in bed.

I admired Jamie. Everyone else around our manor admired my older brother Albie – the fly guy – but I liked Jamie. He made me laugh. He had a cockeyed view of life that I found easy to string along with. Compared to Albie, Jamie was pure and straight. He did each of his humdrum jobs till they bored him, then he quit. Next week he'd do something else. He only did things that he liked.

But he liked most things.

*

I reach Malpas Road at eleven a.m. and ring Jamie's bell.

He appears yawning in his dressing-gown as if he had come down to fetch the milk. He shows no more surprise at seeing me than if we met every week at the pub. 'Right then,' he says, grinning sleepily. 'Been on a sunbed, have we?' We climb the stairs.

His flat has the drab feel of Malpas Road itself, but it doesn't affect Jamie. He potters in the kitchenette making coffee, whistling a tune from Victorian music hall. He is perky. Just as I remember him.

'You want a spot of brandy in this?' he calls across to me. 'Being from the continent as you are.'

'Why not?'

Jamie has dark hair, almost black, and a heavy lock at the front flops down across his forehead. It always did. When we were younger, girls liked to touch that lock of hair. They'd try to smooth it into place. He was good looking. They would run their fingers down his cheek.

We are both older now. Approaching forty. That hank of hair just hangs there, limp and lifeless. It is flecked with grey. The laugh-lines in Jamie's cheeks are furrows now.

'Nice funeral, was it? Many come?'

'About twenty.'

'Oh, people turned you down, did they? Tut, tut. I'd have thought they would come to make sure he was dead.'

'You never liked Albie, did you?'

'I liked him well enough.'

Jamie sits down heavily on a sagging sofa. He waves me to the only decent chair. 'You ain't gone soft on him now he's dead, Floyd? Decided he weren't such a bad 'un after all?'

I shrug. 'I hardly saw Albie these last ten years.'

'That was the idea, wasn't it? That's why you went away.'

I drink some coffee. 'And what have *you* been doing, Jamie? Fill me in.'

I should not have asked. A glance around his room tells it all. Jamie and his surroundings have grown seedier, sadder. He seems stifled, repressed – shrivelled already into middle age. Something inside has given up.

He sits on his shabby sofa, telling me how he spends his days. Though he does drag up a quip or two, he has forgotten how to make them funny. All the time Jamie talks, he ducks and jabs with his head, like a loser in the ring.

I get up and skulk around the room. At the window, I stare down to the street below. When Jamie says how he envies the life I lead, I scowl through the glass. I do not want to hear him talk like this.

'You got something, Floyd, you know that? Something I never had. I can't put my finger on it.'

Jamie hasn't left London for three years, he says. The last time he went abroad was five years ago, when he took a girl to Spain.

'What happened to her?'

'They come, they go.'

'Another holiday would do you good.'

He laughs. His life *is* a holiday; why should he go away? I say there is more to life.

'More than this flat, you mean? Yeah, it's crummy. But this is just where I doss out. I've got the whole of London out there, Floyd. I don't need no fancy flat or foreign hotel. Everything I need is here.'

'Is that right?'

'What've these foreign dumps got that London ain't?'

When I stare out of Jamie's window I miss the sun. 'Do you know the guy in a blue anorak,' I ask, 'over there against the wall?'

The man slumps against the brickwork, resting on one leg. His other leg is bent, the foot flat against the wall. He looks bored.

Jamie joins me at the window. 'Friend of yours, is he?'

'He got on the bus at the same stop I did. Got off at the same stop too.'

'We better have a word with him,' Jamie says.

As Jamie moves away from the window, the man in the anorak looks up. Our eyes meet. I drift casually away from the glass.

'He just saw me. Come on.'

We nip out of Jamie's flat and down the stairs. When we emerge into the street we find him gone.

'There he goes,' Jamie says. He points down Malpas Road. The anorak is pumping off towards Brockley Cross. He rounds the corner and does not look back.

We walk down to the Cross. Fresh air brings colour to Jamie's cheeks. I ask who he thinks might want to follow me.

'Whoever it was that done for Albie.'

'*Done* for him? It was an accident, wasn't it?'

'No one believes that, do they? Even the bleeding paper didn't call it an accident. "Hit and Run" was what they said.'

So Jamie doesn't believe it was an accident either. No one believes it, he said. Now that we have reached the corner, we squint up and down all five roads off Brockley Cross.

9

'We could try the station,' I suggest, pointing down to where Brockley Road dips beneath the grey metal railway bridge.

'Brockley? He wouldn't go there. He could sit half an hour waiting for a train. Maybe he cut up to New Cross Gate.'

We round the corner into Shardeloes, which runs back in a fork almost parallel to Malpas Road, but he is not there. Shardeloes Road stretches a hundred yards before it bends away, and looks the same as when I last saw it a decade ago: mean houses, cramped terraces, two up, two down. We stroll along the left-hand side of the road in the shade, Jamie plucking at weeds that grow from cracks in the high concrete wall, me kicking at cider bottles in the gutter.

'You really think he was following you?'

'He was on my bus.'

Jamie purses his lips. 'Geezer's learnt my address, hasn't he? Think he'll call on me again?'

'Are you worried?'

Jamie shrugs. 'He could think I'm working for you.'

'Doing what?'

He gives me his old sly look from beneath that loose coil of black hair. 'Dunno yet, do I?'

'I only came for the funeral, Jamie.'

'Come off it. We know you Carters better than that.'

I sigh. 'That was Albie. Not me.'

'Oh yeah? Come on, Floyd, you two were as bad as each other. You had your differences, but you stuck like Araldite. Am I right?'

I don't reply. He is right about the old Floyd Carter, not the new.

'And on top of that, with Albie gone so sudden like, leaving all the ends untied, I think you might want to take over his patch.'

I shake my head. My brother is dead, yet I'm still not free of him. I should have asked the priest for an exorcism.


# 3


'I'll have a Saint Clements,' Ludo says.

'Is that a drink?'

The bar is crowded, and it isn't easy to attract the barman's attention. There are two of them. Nowadays, barmen pull cocktails instead of pints. It takes longer.

The one nearest us is manufacturing a round for six, every one different. He serves a red one, a pink, two ambers that aren't beer, and two beers that aren't amber.

'A Saint Clements,' I tell the barman. 'D'you know what that is?'

'Sure.' He fetches a bottle of orange juice and another of bitter lemon and he tips them into a glass. 'Ice and slice?'

'Sounds right.'

'Oranges and lemons,' chants Ludo softly in my ear, 'say the bells of Saint Clements.'

'I'll have a pint,' I tell the barman. 'From the pump.'

We move away with our drinks and stand among the crowd. All the tables are taken.

'Cheers!' I say.

'How's your beer?'

I sip it. 'Not bad. At least some things don't change.'

'They had to bring back real ale,' Ludo tells me knowledgeably. 'People wouldn't drink that other stuff.'

I glance up at him. Here in the pub he looks less awkward. He stands glowing at the bar with the soft drink lost in his massive fist, like any other thirty year old relaxing with a drink. Except he is bigger.

'Which beer do you drink?' I ask.

'I don't drink beer.'

'What do you like – apart from Saint Clements?'

'Well. I like lemonade. But in pubs they serve it flat.'

'What else?'

'Oh, most things really. Bitter lemon, grapefruit juice, Coke. They serve Coke flat too.'

'Nothing stronger?'

Ludo examines the contents of his glass, decides he is getting through it too quickly, and puts the glass down on someone's table. 'I don't like – um – alcohol much. It doesn't agree with me. I can drink it, but I don't like it.'

Ludo is an undemanding guy to drink with. He doesn't open a conversation, but responds to whatever I say like an acquaintance agreeing about the weather. He is improving. In the old days I had to wait impatiently while he constructed things to say. When he was a kid, he would trail around behind me and Albie, lean and gangling, an embarrassment. We didn't want him with us. We could have sent him into care; it was recommended. There was only Dad to look after the three of us, and Ludo was difficult.

But we didn't think of it. We didn't think Ludo was stupid enough or trouble enough to send away, so he stayed with us. At school he had remedial classes, which he struggled with. But because he was big, he was not taunted in the playground. He grew up friendly; slow but likeable. He trusted people. Sometimes his slowness was exasperating, but we made allowances. Because he tried hard, we would wait.

Ludo stands wiping his finger round the bottom of his glass, then he licks at what he has found. I swallow the rest of my pint and ask if he wants another Saint Clements.

'I'll get it,' he says, grabbing my glass. 'Let me.'

That he has money in his pocket surprises me. I still think of him as a child. I will have to stop behaving like an uncle on a treat.

The bar is still crowded. Ludo doesn't use his strength to muscle his way to the counter, but when he appears behind people, they melt away. He stoops over the bar with his wiry hair erect, and he places his big hands on the counter.

'Yes, sir?' the barman asks. Respectfully.

London streets at night are cold and dirty. Few people walk in them. I have grown used to the easy pleasures of warmer countries, where people stroll in the balmy evenings and take the air. I have forgotten how the British lock themselves indoors.

A few kids are out. They lurch along the pavements, kicking cans. They shout. They laugh. They are bored.

The streets get quieter as we walk along.

In a car at the end of our road the men are waiting. I guess they tried the house, found we were out, and hung around. It could be worse. They could have waited for us inside.

They slide out of the car as we approach it. Ludo doesn't notice. He plods innocently towards them, assuming that men might step out of cars at any time. But I see the expression on their faces. I touch his elbow.

'You the Carter boys?' a voice begins. He knows we are.

Ludo nods. 'Yes,' he says pleasantly. 'That's right.'

'We got a message.'

There are four of these hulks – three whites and a black. They wear casual clothes and hard shoes. Two have their hands in their pockets. One does the talking.

'It's about your brother Albie.'

'I'm afraid he's dead,' says Ludo.

'Shame about that, ain't it, chum?'

Ludo frowns.

'Your brother Albie died owing some money.'

Ludo is about to speak again, but I squeeze his arm. The spieler notices. He directs his next words to me. 'Taking over the business, are you, Floyd?'

I guess he wants to show that he knows my name. I don't say anything. I wait.

'Then you also take his debts. Did Albie tell you how much it was – before he passed away?'

'No,' says Ludo.

The spieler smiles. It is not a friendly smile. 'Then I will, chum. Albie owes us ten thousand quid, and we want it paid back.'

'Ten thousand?' Ludo queries.

'That's right, chum. Didn't he tell you?'

'No.' Ludo sounds genuinely surprised. So am I.

The black guy decides that he should say something too. 'I bet him told you where he put that delivery though, right?'

I nudge Ludo, but he answers 'No'.

'Come on, man, you his brother. You help him do things, right?'

Ludo's expression shows that he does not grasp what is going on. The black guy does not grasp things either. He does not seem to realise that it may not be wise to jab Ludo in the chest. 'You understanding English, or what?'

I ease a step to the left. Ludo may need some room. As I move, I say, 'You can whistle for your money.'

The first spieler addresses me. 'We want our ten grand, or the whole lot back.'

'And if not?'

'We're gonna show you.'

The third man steps towards me. He has a crew cut. I know that his first blow will be a low one, so I block it. When he swings his right fist toward my ribs, I step inside. It thumps my elbow. I jab my right into his solar plexus, my left in his ribs, and put my right again beneath his jaw. He sits down hard.

For a moment, no one moves. A breeze blows. Then the black takes a poke at Ludo, misses, and gets Ludo's big fist smack in the centre of his face. He retires.

Two of the four men are now sitting on the pavement.

The other pair think it is time to even the odds. Knives slip out of their pockets as if spring-loaded. The men inch forward.

Each of us waits for someone else to make the first real move. Ludo faces the talkative one, I have his friend. Both men hold their blades high, like plasterers' palette knives. There is a pause. The breeze blows again in the damp night air.

Ludo reaches across and takes the spieler's wrist. Though he does it quickly, he doesn't seem to hurry. He simply stretches for the knife as he might reach to catch a cricket ball. It takes just a moment. Then Ludo reaches across with his other hand, opens the guy's fingers, and removes the knife. The spieler's eyes bulge. Ludo looks at the knife and throws it away.

I grin.

Then I fold up. But not from laughing. I fold because that slob with the crew cut who was nursing his guts on the pavement has suddenly slammed his fist up between my legs. Gasping, I sink to one knee. Down at Crewcut's level, I crunch my fist into his face. As he falls away, a green wave of nausea fills my throat. My head reels.

Now the second knifeman has grabbed my hair. He has lain the point of his steel blade just below my eye. It lies so close that if I blinked, my eyelashes would touch the blade. The knife and his hand are out of focus. I don't move.

He speaks to Ludo. 'Drop him or I blind your brother.'

Ludo releases the spieler and starts walking toward us. He is told to stop.

Crewcut clambers to his feet. So does the black guy, clutching what used to be a white handkerchief to his face to soak the blood from where Ludo hit him. While the black guy walks across the pavement to retrieve the knife, the spieler flicks his fingers at the wounded black man. 'Get in the car,' he says.

Ludo moves toward it.

'Not you, idiot.'

Ludo stops. The only man moving is the black guy, still holding his Arsenal handkerchief to his face. He climbs into the car and starts it up. Ludo waits alone on the pavement, unsure what to do. The spieler leans towards me. 'We oughta take your eye out for this, chum.'

I am kneeling on the cold pavement with the knifeman's blade flat against my cheek. Its point pricks against that little sack beneath my eye. From the blow that Crewcut slammed between my legs, my stomach feels trodden on by a bull. I may throw up.

'Shall we take your brother's eye out?'

Ludo mumbles something, but the spieler interrupts. 'You start walking down that street, big feller, and we might not do it. Understand?'

For several long seconds, Ludo doesn't do anything. Then he says, 'No.'

'What d'you mean "No"?'

'I mean no, I don't understand. What do you want? Shall I walk down the street or not?'

14

I cut in. 'Just walk away, Ludo. Otherwise they cut out my eye.'

He hesitates, shuffles his feet, and frowns at me. Then he turns reluctantly and walks away. Crewcut steps well aside to let him pass.

'Good boy,' the spieler says. Then he places his face close to mine. 'Now, have you got the message, Carter? You got three days to find ten grand. Otherwise you're a dead man. Is that clear?'

I don't nod my head, because I can't. The knifeman still has his blade pressed against my eye. He has his fingers twisted in my hair. 'I hear you,' I reply.

The spieler looks along the street. 'Keep walking, big feller.'

The knife blade remains against my cheek. It has lost its coolness, but not its threat. The spieler walks to where the car purrs at the kerbside and he opens a door. He glances at the mean-looking white guy with the crew cut, standing spare, then he glances back at me. Crewcut looks at me too. He thinks he owes me one.

'Make sure Carter got the message,' the spieler says. Then he ducks inside the car.

The knifeman's fingers tighten in my hair. The knife blade stays. Across the pavement, Crewcut wipes a smear of blood off his upper lip. Then he comes towards me. Without breaking his stride, he swings his leg. I take his kick full in my face.

I sit very still in the kitchen, my eyes closed and a wet flannel against my face. My heads feels as if I am holding it too close to a roaring fire. My tongue keeps straying to my loosened teeth.

Ludo replaces the water in the bowl. The sound of splashing water seems strangely loud. He starts pacing around the kitchen table, trying to work out what else to do. When I tell him to sit down, my words come jumbled. He can't understand what I am trying to say.

After twenty minutes, the blood stops dripping from my cheek. My jaw feels as if it has cement in it, and I suspect I will lose two teeth.

Speaking each word slowly and carefully, I tell Ludo to telephone for a taxi.

# 4

At Greenwich Hospital I am examined briefly by a young nurse with tired eyes. She says I must sit down and wait. There are more urgent cases.

For nearly an hour Ludo and I wait on vinyl chairs in the desolate waiting area. Maybe it would look more cheerful in daylight, but I doubt it. I suggest to Ludo that he buy himself a coffee, but he says no, he will stay with me. He sits hunched on the little chair, his elbows on his thighs, his hands fidgeting between his knees. He looks so damn guilty you'd think that he was the one who hit me.

Minutes tick slowly past. The pain in my face has become a part of me, like chronic toothache. By the time a doctor gets around to stitching this cut on my cheek he'll have to re-open the wound. It has stopped bleeding and begun to heal of its own accord. Maybe that's the idea. If they leave me sitting here long enough I'll get bored and go away.

When the sister calls for Carter, I unfold myself from the hard chair and stand to follow her. Then I stop – because she has her hand on my shoulder. She gazes into my battered face.

'Floyd Carter! What have you done to yourself?'

'I fell off a bus—'

I begin before I recognise her. Suzie Peters. I try to smile.

'Sit down,' she says.

Suzie looks older, but don't we all? She wears a pale blue and white uniform, with a watch on her bosom and two pens in the pocket. The blonde has faded from her hair, and she wears it scraped back. She has green eyes. I remember them now. The lines around her eyes are new, but at this time of night I'm no teenager myself. Suzie's full figure, trimmed and belted behind her white starched apron, looks in fine shape for a woman of – what is she now? – thirty-eight. When she gives me a smile, she loses ten years.

'You look a mess, boy.' She shakes her head.

Ludo tells her that I fell over.

'Fell over what – London Bridge?'

I move another chair a little closer, so she can sit. But she shakes her head.

'I'm on duty.' Then she reaches out softly to touch the rip along my jaw. 'You want my personal assessment?'

I nod.

'Don't try a comeback for the championship.' She grins. 'Are you staying long, now you're back?'

I shrug.

'Oh, I forgot,' she cries. 'I'm sorry about Albie.'

'Yeah.'

'He was run over,' Ludo says.

'Yes, I heard. I'm truly sorry.' Suzie looks at me coolly. 'So, Floyd, you've been in a fight. How long have you been back?'

'Couple of days.'

'And in trouble already.'

'It's a long story. Do you want to hear it?'

Suzie smiles. 'Now is not the time, boy. Tomorrow I'll be free.' She leans forward and touches my hair. A stabbing pain shoots across my scalp, and I wince. When Suzie removes her hand, she sees a smear of red on her fingertips.

'That looks nasty.'

I try to grin. 'I'm OK from the neck down.'

'They always told you not to lead with your chin.'

I sleep uneasily. When I am not lying awake, staring into the dark, I dream fitful dreams. All the threads in my unconsciousness become tangled and confused. I see Ludo hit by a car. Albie appears at the funeral, arm in arm with Suzie, and they keep laughing. I don't know why. Someone opens the coffin and it is full of banknotes. Ludo climbs out of an open grave and slams a shovel into my mouth. I wander out into empty streets till I find Jamie. He is counting street-lamps. Jamie says he will take me to a dentist, but though we wander for hours we can't find a surgery. It's a bad night.

As I watch the darkness fade to grey, I hear the sounds of neighbours waking up: voices at first, front doors, some cars. Gradually, the sound of traffic becomes a continual murmuring background. The sun shines through the curtain. I hear Ludo come out of his room, go downstairs, and make tinkling noises in the kitchen. The tap runs. I fall asleep.

At ten o'clock I awake with a jump. It is several seconds before I remember where I am. I stare at the faded wallpaper as if I have not seen its pattern before. Against the wall, the wardrobe has never looked so ugly. It must have been glued together in the Second World War. The chest of drawers comes from the same period, and is finished in the same thick dark brown, the colour of varnished horse chestnut.

Sometime while I have been asleep, Ludo has placed my breakfast on the bedside cabinet – toast and marmalade, a glass of lemon squash, two aspirin. I need more than aspirin. And the toast is cold.

When I creak over on to my side to swallow the pills, my mouth feels as if I have been chewing a rusty pole. I gulp down the pills with the squash, and collapse back on to the pillows. They feel hard as a folded jacket. I ease myself up again, plump the pillows and sink back.

For ten seconds I lie on my back with my eyes closed. Then I open them, and breathe out.

I swing my legs over the side of the bed, and get up.

'Did Albie ever talk to you about business, Ludo?'

'Um, business? I don't think so.'

'Were you part of it? Do any jobs for him?'

'Well.' Ludo frowns as he pours out my tea. He slides the cup across the kitchen table and says, 'Yes, in a way.'

I leave my cup untouched. 'What sort of way?'

'I used to buy things.'

'Like what?'

'Well, Cigarettes, you know, from the shop on the corner. The *Evening Standard*. And I did the food shopping sometimes. Albie used to give me a list.'

I explain that these are not the kind of purchases I had in mind. When I explain what it is I do mean, Ludo sticks out his lip. 'Albie wouldn't let me do things like that.'

'But did you know what he was up to?'

'Well.' His brow wrinkles again. Then his face unfolds into a mischievous grin. He looks like an overgrown kid in the corner of the classroom. 'I knew he was – you know – everyone knew Albie was – people said he was a bit of a lad.'

'Yeah, he was that.'

'Yes.' Ludo rubs his cheek. 'He was a good laugh, Albie.'

I can see Ludo remembering his rogue of a brother. But he doesn't understand what Albie was up to, he doesn't know why he was killed, nor why he and I were attacked last night. I reach across and pat his hand. 'Don't worry. We'll sort it out.'

'You and me, Floyd. We'll show them, eh?'

'Sure, Ludo, sure.'

For another half minute we sip our tea in silence. Then Ludo stands up and carries the crockery to the sink. He runs the tap.

When I push back my chair he tells me to stay sitting. He will deal with the breakfast things. It's his job.

I watch him plunge his big hands into the hot soapy water. I watch the way he removes one item at a time, studies it, and wipes it all over with the wet cloth. I watch him think.

'I wish we'd caught those guys,' he says.

'Last night?'

'Yes. I shouldn't have walked away, should I?'

'You had no choice.'

'I ended up too far away to stop them.'

'You did all you could.'

When he did come pounding back along that pavement last night, they did not wait till he arrived. The car tore itself away from the kerbside with two of them clambering inside and the doors still open. Ludo lunged at it as it passed. He would have chased it. But he knelt down by me instead.

Now he glances around the kitchen for anything else he can wash up. There is nothing. He empties the plastic bowl into the sink. He dries his hands. 'D'you know what I think?' he says suddenly. 'Those men – I bet they're from the same gang that killed Albie. And we let them go.'

'They didn't kill Albie.'

'You don't think *anyone* did, do you, Floyd? Not on purpose.'

He looks across at me indignantly. I look down. I don't want to believe that Albie was murdered. I don't want to know anything about him. I am not interested in the life he led.

Eventually I say, 'Those guys last night said he owed them ten thousand quid. Why should they kill him? If they killed him they couldn't get paid.'

Ludo thinks about this. 'So who did?'

I shrug. 'This place is full of villains, and Albie mixed with most of them. It could be anyone. Maybe he deserved it.'

'Come on, Floyd. Albie was our brother.'

'And a villain. He was more than "a bit of a lad", Ludo. He was bad news.'

Ludo looks hurt. 'He always looked after me. I liked him. You didn't really know Albie, because you weren't here.'

'If someone did kill him, it was because two villains fell out. What are we supposed to do – start a vendetta? Will that cure things?'

Ludo doesn't try to answer this. He just looks at me. I expect him to say that his brother Albie would have reacted differently, would have gone to get these guys, would have shown them who was boss.

But he doesn't. He says, 'I think we should leave Deptford, start somewhere else. I think I will, anyway.'

I study him with interest. This is not a thought that has just occurred to him. He has been thinking about it. I ask where he would go.

'I don't know, really.' He sits down. 'I mean, I'd like to go. I don't want to live in this house without Albie.'

'Should we sell it?'

He nods deliberately. On the tabletop he draws an imaginary doodle with his finger. 'Who would get the money?' he asks. 'I mean, if we sold the house, who would get Albie's money?'

'Albie had no money. This house wasn't his. It belongs to the family.'

'Oh.' Ludo pauses again. 'That means you and me, right?'

'Well, you really, Ludo. I don't live here.'

Ludo casts an eye around the pale yellow walls of the kitchen. 'So this is my house?'

'I guess so.'

'I could sell it, couldn't I? Buy somewhere else?'

'If you want to. Is that what you'd like?'

For five slow seconds we maintain eye-contact over the kitchen table. Then he looks away. 'Not really,' he says.

'It's your choice, Ludo.'

Ludo nods, still thinking.

'I could come to Germany with you.'

'They speak German there, Ludo. You'd get lonely. You belong in London.'

'I suppose so. But where do *you* belong, Floyd? Are you going back to – um – Munich?'

'I have to.'

'So what will happen to *me*?'

# 5

I invite Jamie into the Duke of Edinburgh across the street and pour a Scotch inside him. He knocks it back the way he'd eat an oyster: the whole thing in one shot, rolled around the mouth, savoured on the tongue, swallowed down. He beams at me.

'My round,' he says.

'Leave it to me.'

'Are you flush?'

'You can buy the next.'

These little English spirit-measures hardly wet the glass. It is not worth leaving the counter before our second. Like oysters again: the way to eat them is to stay at the bar, half a dozen on a platter, the drink of your choice beside your plate on the marble slab.

But you won't get oysters here.

The old man serving behind the bar shuffles to the optics to refill our glasses. He wears jeans, slippers, and what looks like his pyjama top. Behind the three-sided island bar in the centre of the dark saloon he is comfortable. The idea is that we should feel comfortable too.

Jamie and I turn to lean our backs against the counter. In the corner of the room stands an upright piano, closed, and two stools, for duets. A large wooden-framed mirror hangs above. When I catch my reflection I see that I am beginning to look British again. I wear older clothes. My hair is tousled. I have a strip of plaster below my cheek and a bruised lip. My tan looks paler. Maybe it's the light. Maybe Deptford is absorbing me back into its inner-city grey.

'You want another?' Jamie asks.

'Yeah, with peanuts.'

I stroll to a small table between the door and the gas fire. From in front of it, a rubber carpet leads to the dartboard. No one plays. The air is drowsy. On a wet dark evening this is a pub where I could grow slowly and benignly drunk.

I sit down.

Jamie brings the two whiskies and puts them down. When he breaks open the cellophane packet he spills peanuts across the table. 'Help yourself,' he says.

A few customers sip their lunchtime drinks, exchanging muttered conversation. Two men sit alone. One reads the *Mirror*, the other stares at his nails. I ask Jamie if he has seen the man who followed me yesterday.

'The gyp with the anorak? No. You sure he was tagging you?'

'Yeah.'

'He ducked out quick enough.'

'You've seen no one since?'

'No one that I don't know.'

I take a drink. I eat a peanut. 'You think it had to do with Albie's death?'

He pulls a face. 'I hope not. Are you sure he wasn't one of them that clobbered you and Ludo last night?'

'No. He wasn't one of them.'

Jamie finishes his Scotch. 'If I was in your shoes, sunshine, I wouldn't walk out alone. Especially night-time. Guys like them last night don't believe in fair fights. They mean to do you. They don't fight to Queensberry rules.'

'I can look after myself.'

'Wait till next time. I tell you, this ain't a sporting match, Floyd. You are not boxing now.'

'I haven't boxed for years.'

'Too old, ain't ya?' Jamie grins. 'I ain't knocking you, Floyd, I'm concerned. You ain't used to this kind of fighting. What d'you think they wanted from you?'

'They were getting back on account of Albie.'

'Been giving them hassle, had he?'

'They were mixed up in something together.'

I let this hang, to see what he'll make of it.

'He was always mixed up in something, your brother.'

I stay silent. Maybe Jamie can tell me what that something was.

'Could have been anything,' he says. I nod. Jamie grins his sly grin. 'But you got a pretty good idea what it was already, haven't ya, Floyd?'

'How d'you mean?'

'Well.' He pushes a lank curl of black hair off his forehead. 'You were a part of it, weren't you?'

I buy the fourth whisky and some sandwiches. Stretching our feet by the low gas fire, we talk quietly. Someone comes in. A couple goes out.

'I want to know what I'm supposed to have been a part of.'

Jamie tells me. And from the sound of it, Albie spun some tales. Maybe it was because he was slipping down in the world. Maybe he needed to talk. Time was, when I lived here with him, Albie was looked up to. He was somebody.

He was two years older than me, and he made a lot of it. When Dad's health started to fade, Albie wanted to show that he was the one who would take over. I remember the way he'd strut around the house like a buck reindeer, stomping around the territory to oust the old male from the pack. Being eldest. Albie should have started favourite, but he didn't. Not with Dad. Maybe he would have been favourite with Ma, if she had lived. But she died long ago, when we were kids. We grew up without her.

Albie was trouble as a teenager, and trouble as a man. But he kept it outside the family. For us, he liked to be the breadwinner: he made money easily, and he always brought it home. Around the house he stashed away odd pots and boxes with loose notes stuffed inside. Albie said that with him around, we would never run short. He said it lots of times. It made Dad angry.

Maybe Dad was wrong about Albie, because when Dad died, Albie really did take over. He took over the house, he took over Ludo. He did it properly.

By then, of course, there were just the two of them. When Dad died, I had been gone six years.

'Albie had his good side,' I tell Jamie.

'I know that, sunshine. I saw him look after Ludo, I saw him care for your Dad when he took sick. But Albie had two sides to him, you know that.'

'Sure I do.'

'What did you two fall out about – a woman?'

'Yeah.'

'Which one?'

I shrug.

'Oh, that one,' Jamie says with a chuckle. 'Did Albie make a pass at her? Come on, Floyd, it's been ten years.'

'Albie's dead.'

'All the more reason.'

I just smile. Some stories you never tell. I don't tell him how I finished early, went round to her flat, let myself in. She was not alone. Albie lay in her bed with a cigarette in his mouth, grinning at the ceiling. 'Can't trust nobody, can yer?'

Jamie says, 'Albie liked to pretend he owned the manor.'

'No one would believe that.'

Jamie shrugs. 'You Carters have a reputation, like the Richardsons. Know what I mean?'

'They still around?'

Jamie eyes me curiously. 'Are you that out of touch?'

'I've been away.'

'I reckon you have. Well, Tod Richardson's still around. Sam's inside. Frank is dead. But the gang's still dealing. They have the name, don't they?'

'Did Albie have anything to do with them?'

'That's how it seemed.'

'Who knew this?'

'Customers.'

'What did he supply these customers?'

On Jamie's face lurks the suggestion of a smile. He looks me full in the eyes, trying to read what I am thinking.

'Well, he was into import and distribution, you know?'

'Importing what?'

'I wouldn't know, Floyd, would I?'

Jamie grins.

# 6

Suzie's house is a slate-roofed two up two down, opening on to the pavement. It is painted white. The door is green. Kids play in the sreet here, because around Crofton Park is a family area. Two little girls run down the pavement, hauling a rickety buggy made from a wooden box mounted on an old pram chassis. Inside is a toddler. He grips tight on to both walls of the box and he screams with laughter. I stand aside to let them pass.

When I turn to ring the bell again, the door opens. Suzie wears a pale blue housecoat. Her blonde hair is down. She says, 'Well, well. It's Pretty Boy Floyd the Outlaw.'

I point to the sticking plaster on my injured jaw. 'I'm a sick man.'

'At least you didn't pick at your dressing.'

We pass along the narrow hall into the warm kitchen at the rear. On a little pine table two places have been laid. A kettle on the gas has started whistling. The grill is on.

I watch Suzie's loose flowing figure as she glides around her kitchen. She has aged well. Ten years at school we were kids together. We became teenagers. We grew up. Once upon a time we started a short affair, but nothing came of it. We were twelve, as I remember.

I sniff the air. 'The toast is done.'

She whips the tray from beneath the flame. 'You've spoilt my timing,' she says with a laugh. 'Are you staying, or did you eat already? It's scrambled eggs.'

'I'm staying.'

'Keep an eye on that.' On to the gas she slides a saucepan. She drops a pat of butter in it, then as she slips away from me at the cooker she squeezes my arm. From the kitchen door she calls up the stairs, 'I'm putting the eggs on. Come down and say hallo.'

I check the saucepan. The butter has started sizzling, so I reach for a wooden spoon.

'Sit down out of my way,' she says.

'Shall I lay a third place?'

'That's my boy.'

Suzie removes the saucepan from the flame while she cracks another pair of eggs into the jug. Then she beats them all together lightly, adds more pepper and salt, and tips the mixture splat into the bottom of the pan. I lay my place at the table.

More toast cooks beneath the grill while she stirs the eggs. My plate joins the two already there to be warmed. I pour cups of tea.

'Both with milk?' I ask.

'How else?'

Way back in my first year abroad, I gave up taking milk in my tea. Now I drink it black. Suzie begins to serve the eggs on to warm plates. Without leaving her place beside the cooker, she calls, 'It's ready.'

I hear feet on the stairs, running down.

I remember who it is.

Shortly before Suzie left school she began going out with Tom Peters. He was new, and had joined our class. People talked, of course, and her parents played up: Suzie was too young to be going steady, and with Tom it wasn't right.

None of that stopped Suzie. She wouldn't give him up just because her parents didn't want her dating a black boy – though things were different then. Those were the days when the government said we had too many blacks already. They passed laws to stop them coming in. People had to have family here, like Tom had, to squeeze through. Immigrants were not welcome. There was bad feeling. Whether the government reacted to public feeling, or whether the public reacted to government discrimination, I don't know. I was a teenager. In Deptford we already had so many people of every colour and religion that we saw things differently. Half of us weren't English anyway.

Eventually, Suzie became pregnant – maybe on purpose – and declared she would have to marry him. The two families must make the best of it. Well, I went to the wedding, and it was a joyful day. Both families smiled all the time and afterwards got on fine. Tom and Suzie's baby was born a few months later. A little girl. They called her Tamsin.

That little girl must have been about seven years old at the time I went abroad. I don't remember too clearly. One hasty day I just packed a bag and left.

Tom and Suzie were among my closest friends, but we lost touch. Years passed. Then about three years ago, Tom fell off some scaffolding at work and was killed outright. I didn't hear about his death for six months. If I had known, of course, I would have come for his funeral, but by that time all I could do was send a note.

I guess the only times I come home are for funerals. First it was Dad. Now it is Albie. The other time would have been for Tom.

In the kitchen doorway, Tamsin appears.

She pauses with one hand on the upright, and she glances at me across the room. She wears a long cream sweatshirt over tight blue jeans. She says, 'Hi.'

'I'm Floyd Carter.'

Suzie places the third plate on the table and sits down. 'Do you remember Tamsin, Floyd? She must have changed.'

'She won't remember me.'

Tamsin slips across to the table and takes her seat. 'You're Albie's brother, aren't you? I'm sorry that he died.'

They begin to eat.

The last time I saw Tamsin she had ribbons in her hair, bright ones at the back. Now her hair hangs black as wet tar in waves beside her face. Her smooth skin is the colour of wet sand, and her huge brown eyes are sad.

She picks at her scrambled egg, cutting small pieces of toast and chewing them at the front of her mouth, as if instead of eggs she ate caviar. From the way she dissects her food, I would guess she always eats sparingly. She is small. Her body is that of a slim fourteen year old.

Suzie sees me watching her. 'What do you think of my teenage daughter?'

Tamsin immediately looks uncomfortable.

'She's very pretty.'

Tamsin puts down her knife, and sighs. Suzie smiles. 'D'you see any resemblance? Or do you think she is more like Tom?' She holds my gaze to show that it is all right to use her dead husband's name.

'She has a little of both of you, and something of her own.'

Tamsin drops her fork beside the knife on her plate, and looks up angrily. 'Do you have to discuss me as if I was an exhibit in a museum? I am a person, you know.'

'You're certainly not from a museum,' laughs Suzie. 'From a gallery, perhaps. A work of art.'

'Mum!'

If I wasn't here, a guest at their table, Tamsin would be up and out the door. 'Which school do you go to?' I ask quickly.

'I don't go to school.'

'She's eighteen,' Suzie explains.

I look at Tamsin. To tell her that she looks younger will make her angry again. I change the subject. 'This is only the second time I've been in Britain in ten years. I feel a foreigner.'

'In what way?' asks Suzie.

'Things are different to how I remember. When I step on to a bus or go into a bar I can't make contact. I feel I am watching from outside. I don't live here any more.'

'Lucky you,' mutters Tamsin.

Suzie says, 'A lot has changed in these last ten years.'

I slide a piece of egg across my plate. I may have eaten three mouthfuls. 'London doesn't seem to have changed for the better,' I say quietly. 'When I was flying over for the funeral, I half thought about coming home for good. I thought that after ten years, you know, it might be time I came back.'

'Especially with Albie gone,' Suzie agrees.

I glance across at her. She watches me coolly. Again she wants to show that we don't avoid talking about people just because they are dead. I can read the message. Suzie and I have not seen each other for ten years, but we were always close. I was here during the bad times she and Tom had together, when people spat at them in the street, when they pointed to half-caste Tamsin in her pram, whispering that the marriage would not last. And Suzie remembers when *I* was young. She remembers Albie and me as tearaways. She remembers when we grew to adulthood. She remembers why I went, why Albie stayed.

'So you won't be staying?' Tamsin asks.

I pause a moment. 'No.'

Tamsin looks surprised. 'I thought you would be.'

She jabs her fork through the cold scrambled egg into the flabby toast, and she moves it to the side of her plate. Tamsin won't eat any more. Not her. She won't eat cold egg.

Suddenly she asks, 'Do you know a man called Huey Carmichael?'

'Should I?'

'He seems to know *you*. He asked what might happen now that you had come back. He said you weren't the same as Albie.'

'In what way?'

She looks up. 'I didn't ask. He wasn't talking to me.'

'Who is this Huey Carmichael?'

\*

Huey 'the Snake' Carmichael, they call him. Tamsin says he is British-born, of Jamaican origin, about thirty years old. Sharp dresser, apparently. He must have been one of the tough kids on the street when I left, though he made no impression. I don't remember him.

He would have been coming up fast. Around the time I left here, Suzie says, Huey walked away from the usual street gangs and formed a sleek one of his own. The Diners, he called them. They were hard. They made a display of it.

They had to be visual. Around Deptford were a hundred other gangs. Eighty of these you will never have heard of – they were territorial, into small-time thieving, bouncing cars. The other twenty may have been casually mentioned in the *Mercury* or the *South London Press*: blagging, fighting, GBH. Maybe two gangs – just two out of the whole hundred – would have moved up into running crack and serious offending. These were the gangs whose names you might have heard.

To become a top gang they had to be into more than crime: they had to be seen. Noticed. They had to wear the right clothes, pack heat. They needed identity.

After a while, if they kept at it, they might not seem criminal at all. They would purchase property, open a string of straight-seeming businesses, be occasionally photographed in smart public places – restaurants, nightclubs, races, shows. People would relax about using their name. They would learn to be comfortable with it. They wouldn't ask any more how the gang got where it was, or where the money came from.

Because when you have really made it, when you have crawled to the top of the slithery pile, people smile on your name. Oh sure, they say, I met the guy once, he lived real nearby. Remember the time he cracked that joke? He was standing just there. Remember that bar where we all used to drink? I go there still. There's a score of guys who lent the man money – or maybe he lent it them – the tale varies. Everyone claims a share of his villainous glitz.

You think I'm kidding?

Consider the Kray twins. We all remember them. A pair of murderous extortionists who nailed limbs to the floor, who carved faces, who stood fellers' feet in buckets of slow-setting cement, then dropped them weighted into the Thames. The Krays used electric wire as enthusiastically as the South American police. They were known for these things. They were sent down for life.

In their case, it wasn't till they'd been away several years that the warm glow set in. Sure, the Krays were tough, people said, but they were kind to old ladies. The Krays respected their mother. Even though they thieved a load of money, they were generous to the poor. 'We felt safe with them here,' claimed folk in Bethnal Green. 'They protected us.'

I bet they did. The Krays knew about Protection. People forget the limbs the Krays nailed to the floor. 'They never hurt anybody,' people said. 'Not if they didn't deserve it. Those Krays should be set free from jail. They've served long enough.' Artists wrote songs about them. And plays. And books. Then two skinny pop-singers glamorised them in a film. We all watched it. Paid money to do so. We looked up to the Krays.

Well, a few hundred years ago, families we now call aristocracy made fortunes the same way as the Krays: by plundering, killing, seizing land and sitting on it till there was no one left to claim it was theirs. We look up to aristocracy now, as well.

'How do you know the man, Tamsin?'

'He's my boss.'

I lean back on my kitchen chair. 'What do you do for him?'

'I sing.'

The smell of coffee drifts across the room as Suzie starts to pour. 'Tell me more.'

'What's to tell?'

Suzie asks Tamsin if she wants coffee. She says, 'No, I have to go.'

The look on Tamsin's face suggests that she expects me to ask more about this Huey Carmichael, but I don't. If she wants to be enigmatic I'll just wait and ask her ma.

At the kitchen door Tamsin says, 'Huey said he'd like to meet you. Perhaps you should call in.'

I nod. He'd like to meet me. Maybe he asked Tamsin to deliver that message. She isn't saying. Out in the hall she grabs her coat off the wall, she calls goodbye, she slams the door. Suzie places my coffee in front of me.

'What does she mean that she sings?'

'She's a singer. Carmichael owns a club.'

'What's their relationship?'

'They don't have a relationship.' Suzie stirs her coffee. 'Tamsin is eighteen. She just sings there. She was trying to impress you. She's young.'

The coffee is hot and strong. Suzie asks, 'Will you go to see this "Snake" Carmichael?' She mocks the name.

'You think I should?'

Suzie purses her lips. This is an expression I can imagine her using in the hospital when she gets an unexpected reading on her thermometer.

'Might Carmichael have done business with my brother Albie?'

'I've no idea.'

'Tell me, Suzie, tell me straight: do you know how Albie earned his money before he died?'

'No one ever knew with Albie.'

You can say that again. I swallow the coffee, stand up, and take both our cups and saucers to the sink. I run the tap.

'Are you washing up?' she asks.

'I'm domesticated. Ten years on your own, you have to learn your way around a kitchen, or you starve.'

'Ain't life a bitch without servants?' We both smile. 'Shall I give you a hand?'

'No, you sit. Where is this place Tamsin sings?'

'It's a club called the Parrot.'

'Terry Starr's place?'

'Not any more. A lot has happened since you've been away. Terry died. His wife and son took over, then they sold it to the Richardsons. Carmichael took over from them.'

'How much of their business did he take over – just the club?'

'What am I – an authority?'

'This Huey sounds quite a boy.'

I scrub at the crockery in her hot soapy water. I scrub the pieces good and clean.

'You're just the kind of man I need to stand at that sink. Pity you're not staying around.'

The bowl is empty now, except for hot water. I pour it away. 'There's nothing to keep me here.' I dry my hands. 'But before I go, I think I might see this Huey Carmichael.'

'It can't do any harm,' Suzie says.


# 7


Ludo insists that he knows how to operate the machines. I can leave him here with both bags of laundry, and he will watch the clothes through their wash cycle, then put them on to tumble dry. He will dry them twice. He won't burn them. He knows what he is doing, and he likes it here. It is warm. People come in and out. They talk to him.

He likes to watch the clothes float around the drum of the big tumble-drier. It's his favourite time. Sometimes, while he is waiting for the washing machine to finish its full wash cycle, he sits in front of the tumble-driers, watching other people's clothes swirl around in the heat. It makes him smile.

I leave him in the Washeteria and walk up Tanners Hill into New Cross Road. I cross. Opposite is the market at the bottom of Deptford High Street. It is crowded. Between the two lines of stalls the crowd jostles and sways with local people. No tourists come here. On the stands are cheap clothes, fruit and veg, electrical and hardware, music on tape or disc. Most of the traders are black or brown. The clothes on sale include Rasta hats, silk for saris, African jewellery, Polish shoes. Vegetables are yam, okra, chilli and beans. You can buy salt fish, plantain and paw-paw, natural bracelets and beads.

I squeeze among the people between the stalls in the crowded road. I could have cut behind the stalls and walked more easily beside little shop windows along the empty pavement, but I prefer to walk through the crowd in the street. It may help me get in touch with this area again.

Within a minute, a stall-holder calls out to me. Joe somebody. We used to train together at the Repton Boxing Club, but we weren't the same weight. I'd remember him better if we were. I wave back, and he calls, 'Cut yourself shaving, did you, Floyd?' I move on.

It makes a difference, when someone calls you by name. You feel warmer. You start to smile. I think I detect recognition in other people's eyes, but no one says anything. They watch me as I pass.

My head is up as I approach the Deptford Arms. It hasn't changed. The pub stands on a corner in the middle of the market, its big windows making it almost a part of the street outside. I walk in.

The same old counters, low-set, the lowest I know. You stand at the bar here, dangling your hands as if at a nursery wash basin, and you feel tall. Everyone does. This is a bar where even runts can feel big.

I call for a Jameson's.

Sitting behind me at the tables are market traders, customers, folk dropping by. Two men play dominoes. A quartet of West Indians are dismantling a ghetto-blaster on a table. An old lady reads the *Sun*.

Beyond where the counter ends is a space for a pool table. A group of men play. As the barman hands me my change I nod to the pool table. 'The guy with the crew cut – what's his name?'

The barman looks at me. 'Don't I know you?'

'What's his name?'

'Dirkin. Vinnie Dirkin.'

I put down my glass.

Dirkin. This is the guy who two days ago said goodbye by kicking me in the face. Now he is stooped across the green table setting up an easy pot. His cue jabs, the ball connects, and the shiny red object ball spurts for the pocket. It doesn't make it. I have my hand on it.

I keep the ball in my hand as I stroll round the table. Dirkin checks around him, to see which way he should go. He grips his cue.

One of his friends steps in my way. I tell him move. But he has placed himself in a position where he cannot back off, so he stares hard in my face. I know this isn't his fight, but I haven't time to explain. My fist with the ball in it explodes below his chest. He crumples. Dirkin gulps.

'Put the cue down, Vinne.'

He does not.

But he should have. A pool cue is a poor weapon. He is holding it wrong. He tries to stab me with it, as if the cue were a dagger, but I brush it aside. My left hand grabs his collar and my right slams his mouth. He drops the cue. I drop the ball. His mouth bleeds.

Keeping hold of Dirkin by the front of his shirt, I speak to his friends. I tell them to stay out of it.

I push against Dirkin's throat to make him walk backwards. When we reach the door to the Gents, I thump him through. Inside is white and tiled. Easy to clean.

Dirkin has two choices. Either he waits to see what I will do to him, or he takes a chance. He takes a chance. Unfortunately for him, the fact that I am holding him out to one side means he cannot deliver a good kick. He must use his fist. Naturally, he aims it low, and naturally, I swing my left thigh to block it. Then I drive my right fist into his nose, just above where I have already mashed his lips at the pool table. He yells in pain. I keep my grip on his dirty shirt collar and smash another blow into his face.

Then I let go.

Dirkin folds to his knees, clutching at my trousers as he goes. If someone comes in, they could think he was giving me a blow job. So I put my knee in his face. He falls back. They won't make that mistake now.

While Dirkin writhes on the floor, I rinse my hands at a sink. The public health notice warns me of all the ways I could catch AIDS. If you use drugs, it says, you must never share your works. That's the message of the last decade: you share nothing any more.

I tell Vinnie to get up.

He ignores me. Any moment now I expect the main door to burst open. Those so-called friends of his will have been standing at the pool table, staring at a closed Gents' door and wondering what is happening behind it. Eventually they'll come to find out.

'Who sent you?' I demand of him.

Vinnie groans.

'Answer the question or I stamp on your head.'

He groans again. Then he rolls over and starts to crawl away. I move swiftly towards him, reach down, grab the back of his shirt. As I pull on it, Vinnie whimpers. Buttons burst all down the front and his shirt falls loose.

The main door crashes open.

Finally his three friends stumble in, looking as big as they can manage. 'Out,' I snarl. But they stay and shut the door.

I take a step towards them. I have to be clear of Dirkin in case he joins in from the floor. He doesn't try. Even as his friends take up position, I hear him slither into a cubicle and bolt the door from inside. He'll feel safe there.

In the middle of the cold floor I wait for the first to make a move. They can start it. When it is three against one you always wait. You rush, and they will smash you. You wait, they'll come one by one. The first won't put his guts into it. Somehow, knowing he has two friends behind him, he'll hold a little back. Unlike you.

So we wait.

Then the door opens a second time, and the barman appears. He is not alone.

'Right, everybody out. I want you out of my pub.'

When Vinnie's friends turn towards him they look more relieved than I do. They only came because they ought.

'Your friend is in the cubicle,' I tell them. 'You'd better help the guy clean up.'

'Out!' the barman tells me.

I indicate Vinnie's friends hovering uncertainly to block my way. I raise an innocent eyebrow.

'Let him through,' the barman says.

They move aside.

\*

I smile at myself in my bedroom mirror and decide I don't look so bad after all. I wear the soft navy blazer that I bought in Dusseldorf, beige slacks, and a cream linen shirt. I have taken off the striped tie and thrown it on the bed. It looked too formal.

Earlier, I pulled the sticking plaster off my face to inspect the gash. It was healing well. I replaced the hospital dressing with a smaller piece.

Now, as I come down from my bedroom, I whistle to myself. For some reason, from the moment I stepped out of the Deptford Arms into the Deptford daylight I have felt cheerful. Uplifted. The old vigour has started pumping through my veins as if I was back in my gymnasium. I am like a boy come downstairs from his first successful date.

Ludo looks envious. 'Oh hello, Floyd. Going out again?'

'I have to see someone.'

'Can I come?'

'This is business. But tonight we'll go out together. Maybe eat somewhere.'

Ludo looks down at the kitchen table. 'I'll stay in then.'

I rest my hand on his arm. 'I'm sorry, Ludo. We can't do everything together.'

'I suppose I could watch the telly.'

'Is there nothing else you'd like to do?'

He maintains his sorrowful look. 'No, I don't think so.'

'Nowhere to go?'

'I could walk about a bit. When I come home I could do the ironing.'

'That's right. Fresh air is good for you.'

Leaving him moping in the kitchen makes me feel guilty, but I switch on a smile. As I move into the hall Ludo asks, 'Will you pay them the money?'

I stop. 'What money?'

'That ten thousand pounds. Isn't that where you're going?'

'No.'

'You said you were going out on business. I thought . . . What other business have you got?'

I pause, then step back inside the kitchen. 'Have you ever heard the name Vinnie Dirkin?' I ask.

Ludo frowns. 'Is he a footballer?'

'No. Did Albie ever mention him?'

'I don't think so. Is he a boxer?'

'He was one of those in the street. The one who kicked me.'

'Oh,' Ludo's face clears. 'Are you going to pay him back?'

'I already did. But you never heard the name?'

He shakes his head.

'Do you remember *any* names to do with Albie's business?'

'Like I said, Floyd, he never talked about it. Not to me.'

I turn to go. Ludo asks, 'What about that money then?'

'What about it?'

'They said we had to pay it back.'

'We're paying no one.'

'They might come round again.'

'Don't worry. They won't do that.'

There are two sets of doors. The heavy outer wooden ones act like shutters, protecting a set of pretty glass panels on the main door inside. When the club is closed, these wooden doors are bolted into place, blocking the entrance so firmly that if you tried to ram a truck through you'd more likely crunch the truck. Maybe that's the kind of thing they expect might happen here. You never know.

The Parrot's bleak frontage butts on to an empty concrete carpark. It will be empty till nightfall. During the day, they switch off the neon Parrot sign and the string of rusting fairy lights. The place looks dead.

I have rapped at the wooden door three times, but no one answers. Behind me, the breeze blows empty beer cans and sheets of newspaper across the concrete. In front of me, beside this battered door, posters advertise attractions to come, attractions gone. Reggae Superstars, Soul Soul Soul. Big Bamboo and Vagabond Joy. Dennis Brown. Heats for the Steelband Music Festival.

Backing on to the carpark are tall scruffy houses converted into flats. Metal fire-escapes zigzag down their walls. As I walk to the rear of the building my shoes crunch on broken glass.

The first sign of life is at the corner. From inside the club I can hear the muffled whine of an amplifier, feeding back. A guitar begins, picking random notes and runs. Someone kicks at a drum.

Here at the end of the side wall is a single door. It is open. Above its frame, where you might expect to see a Stage Door sign, is a shabby notice that reads 'Private – Keep Out'. I step in.

Huey 'the Snake' Carmichael greets me warmly, but he does not stand up. He is a lean, useful-looking guy with bright eyes. His skin is swampy brown, and to make it look darker he wears white: white T-shirt, white linen suit, white shoes. He sits staring at me from behind his white desk. On its white leather top he rests his white leather shoes. He lolls in a high-backed soft leather chair, brown, not white, the colour of pale milk toffee. The carpet is cream, the office walls maroon.

Behind him, a rectangular window reveals the clubroom below. On stage down there a black quartet argues among its instruments. I can see them but can't hear them. The room is soundproof. I bet the window is one-way glass.

'I am glad you dropped by,' Carmichael says. His teeth shine whiter than his T-shirt. His thin moustache looks painted above his lip. His eyes are wet. They are a dog's eyes: always moving.

He shifts his gaze from my face and tells the hood behind my shoulder to disappear. We wait. The office door opens, then glides softly into place.

Carmichael swings his feet from the top of his desk and stands up. He offers me a drink. 'What would you like, hey? We are always well stocked.'

'I'll take a whisky.'

His drinks cabinet is low and white and matches the desk. When Carmichael stoops to reach inside, he moves gracefully, like an athlete. His white jacket floats aside to reveal his lean T-shirted frame. It also reveals the pistol stuck in his waistband: a cowboy gun – silver-barrelled, white pearl inlay on the handle.

He pours a generous shot of whisky and hands it to me. For himself he makes a tumbler of Lucozade. He takes ice. I don't.

Carmichael raises his glass in a toast. We could be in the Old Colonial Club, not the Parrot. 'To survival,' he says. I take a sip.

'What d'you think of my place, hey?'

He leads me to the window so we can watch the floor below. By now the group has started: two guitars, a synthesiser, a set of drums. For us they perform in dumbshow, like TV with the volume off.

Carmichael flicks a switch, and his office fills with sudden noise. He turns it down, using a silver knurled knob.

'Too loud, hey?' He nods, agreeing with himself. 'I had the sound up high before they started, so I could hear what they were saying.'

'You learn anything?'

'Not this time. You like this music?'

'No.'

'You're right – it's tame.' He flicks off the switch and cuts the sound.

'We met once, you know?'

'Who did?'

'You and I.' He looks at me quizzically. 'But you don't remember.' He puts on a disappointed look. 'All black kids look alike, hey?'

'When did we meet?'

'You were with your brother Albie. I remember I sold you two palletloads of audio gear – cassette to cassette. I was selling it cheap.'

'You've come a long way.'

'Ten years, hey?' He grins. 'Seems like another world.' He stands nodding, but all the time he is looking me carefully up and down. I stand quietly, waiting for what he has to say. 'And now you're back. I was sorry about your brother, but . . .' He shrugs.

'Were you a friend of Albie's?'

'I knew him. He always said you'd come back.'

'If something happened to him, for instance?' I ask quietly.

Carmichael grins. 'I didn't kill him, Floyd. Not me.' He gives me an open, innocent look.

I ask, 'D'you know who did?'

He pauses before answering. 'No. Are you trying to find out?'

'I am not a detective.' Though if you have something to tell me, Mister, perhaps you'll do it, now I'm here.

Carmichael says, 'Because Albie's dead, I suppose you've come to sort things out?'

'What was he doing before he died?'

Carmichael sips at his Lucozade, then smiles briefly. 'You know better than I do, Floyd.'

'Everyone seems to think that.'

He turns away to gaze through his window. The quartet have worked themselves into a soundless frenzy. 'You need another drink,' Carmichael decides.

His own glass is also empty. He seems thirstier than I am. He refills his tumbler to the brim with Lucozade, then he places a small shot of whisky in the bottom of mine.

'Yes, I remember the old days,' he muses. 'I thought you and I might meet.'

'So I heard.'

'I even thought of offering you a job, but of course you don't need one.'

'Of course?'

'You'll have something stashed away, hey?'

'I do all right.'

'You want Albie's territory?'

He says this so casually that I guess it is the reason he asked me here. This could be what our conversation is about.

37

'What territory?'

Carmichael studies me. It is not an unfriendly stare, just inquisitive. But this time he doesn't mask it with a glinting white-toothed smile.

'Albie was difficult to deal with, wasn't he, hey? Did you find that?' He strolls behind his large white desk and flops into his leather chair. 'Perhaps you're a more amenable kind of guy.'

I don't say anything. Neither does he. We just watch each other. But before the tension builds too far, Carmichael leans back in his chair, places his feet on the desk, and clasps his brown hands behind his immaculate head. The movement lifts his white jacket and exposes the gun for a second time in his waistband. He seems unaware of it. 'How about you make an investment?' he suggests.

I pause a second. 'In what?'

He stretches his arms lazily, forming a neat V of white linen above his sleek head. 'You could invest either money or time.'

'In what?' I ask again.

'Oh, one of my businesses.'

'Which one?'

'Nowadays, the most lucrative enterprises are property and drugs. You agree?'

I don't reply, but I do sit down. This is the point where I'd better show that I'm listening.

Carmichael grins at me across the desk. 'Of course, the deal is I prefer you working on my side. Not in opposition. I wouldn't like that.' He watches me. 'But you weren't thinking of setting up against me, were you, Floyd?'

'It hadn't entered my mind.'

'Do you want to come in?'

I hold back for a moment. Coming into business with Carmichael is the last thing I'd want to do. But he knows something about Albie's death – more than he has so far revealed. I play along with him. 'Why me?'

Carmichael opens his arms in an expansive gesture. I can see that he is given to these. 'A man with your connections, Floyd? All you have to do is push them out.'

'Running crack on street corners?'

Carmichael brushes the idea away. 'No, no. I can find a hundred hustlers. I need your kind of brains close at hand.'

'Again, why me?'

'Your reputation.'

'I've been away ten years. What reputation?'

'Folks have long memories here, Floyd. And Albie kept the family name alive.'

'In what way?'

Carmichael's dog eyes slide across my face. 'Don't be modest, Floyd.' Suddenly he leans across the bare white desk. 'Are you in or not?'

He has faced me with the question, but I back away. 'Neither. I'm just a neutral here.'

'Neutral?' He snorts in disbelief, leaning back again into his soft brown chair, the fingers of one hand straying to that pretty little pistol tucked inside his trousers. 'What do I make of that?'

'What it says.'

'You have something of your own?'

'Drugs are not my business.'

'I divide the world into two classes,' Carmichael says, stooping forward again. 'Those for me, those against. Are you saying you're not for me?'

'Nor against.'

'Well, I tell you this.' Back he leans again, this time with the pistol popped out in his hand. He doesn't point it – he just caresses it lovingly in his palm, like a set of worry beads. 'In the drugs business, you know, you grant no mercy, you take no prisoners.' He underlines these preposterous words by nonchalantly raising his little silver gun and pointing it at my face. His finger stays outside the trigger-guard. 'Bang, bang,' he says, and he smiles.

'Maybe you don't need to earn money,' he suggests, lowering the gun. 'You've returned well stacked, hey?'

'As I said, I'll get by.'

'Let's hope so. But if you do decide you have money to invest . . .'

'I won't. Anyway, I'm not staying.'

'No? Well . . .' Carmichael grins again, though his eyes don't. 'I'm always here, Floyd, if you want to talk.'

'I'll bear it in mind.'

I stand up. Carmichael remains in his soft leather chair, cradling his pistol against the white of his crotch.

He says, 'Till the next time we meet, hey?'

# 8

Next morning, Ludo and I step off the bus at the Brockley Jack and cut away from the busy main road.

'You should buy a car,' Ludo says.

One side of the street is washed with weak morning sunshine, the other side stays in the shade. These lines of little houses were built for Victorian dockers and labourers. Their low skylines saw generations of stunted cockneys – chirpy, wisecracking, uncomplaining at their meagre lot. In streets like these, wives stood with arms folded, chatting on doorsteps. Barefoot kids scuffled in the dirt. Tallymen came knocking at the door.

As we approach Suzie's house a rag and bone man overtakes us on his cart. He has little on board: an old fridge, two boxes, a bundle of old clothes. 'Ennyallarn!' he calls from the cart. He rings his bell. The brown horse maintains its plodding pace. It doesn't slow. No one calls out to the rag and bone man, though a child waits at the kerb to watch the horse trundle by.

At Suzie's door Ludo tries again to dissuade me. There is no need for this, he says. He can fend for himself.

'Everything's arranged, Ludo. Just a couple of days.'

He slaps the soft travel-bag against his leg, and he chews on his lip. 'I'm not a baby,' he says.

When Suzie opens the door he gives a brief, shamefaced grin, then hangs his head down. He knows it is too late to argue now. We go in.

Suzie leads us straight through the hall into the kitchen, and she tells us sit down. She fills the kettle and lights the gas. 'I'll show you up to your room,' she tells Ludo. 'Watch the kettle for me, Floyd.'

In half a minute she is back. 'He's unpacking,' she says.

'Thanks again, Suzie.'

'Yes.'

As she spoons tea leaves into the pot, I watch her face. Her mind is elsewhere. I begin to think she has had second thoughts about having Ludo stay here, and I ask if I am right.

'No, of course he can stay.'

'What's the problem?'

She flashes a tired grin across the kitchen table. 'How many problems do you want to hear?'

'Just the main ones. But if you'd rather not have Ludo . . .'

'It isn't Ludo. It's Tamsin.'

I nod my head. 'Ludo won't be any trouble to her. He doesn't think about girls.'

'She hasn't come home. She's been out all night.'

Tamsin went out last night to sing at the Parrot, and she hasn't returned. She always comes late – the place keeps late hours. But it's mid-morning now.

'When would she normally get back?'

'Oh, one in the morning, sometimes two. I don't always see her. I could be asleep, or working nights at the hospital. But she's always in her bed by the morning.'

'Got a boyfriend, maybe?'

'It isn't that.' Suzie attempts another smile as she pours out the tea. We hear Ludo clumping his way downstairs. 'Not much of a mother, am I? Let her stay out late at night. I'm often out all night myself.'

'You're both working. Not everyone works nine to five.'

'It doesn't make me feel better.'

Ludo hovers in the doorway. He can sense strain in the air. I tell him to come in and sit down. 'Suzie's worried about Tamsin. She's been out all night.'

His eyes widen. 'Is she lost, do you think? It was raining last night.'

'She isn't lost.'

'If ever I'm going to get home late,' Ludo declares, 'I have to ring Albie to say where I am.'

He remembers about Albie, and stops. Then he asks, 'Didn't she ring?'

'No,' I say. 'She may have stayed with a friend.'

'Well, I would have phoned – someone,' Ludo says. He grabs his cup hastily and sips at the tea.

Suzie is standing in the middle of the kitchen with a cloth in her hands. She flings it on the draining board. 'I should have phoned the police,' she says. Her eyes begin to shine.

I jump up and put an arm round her. 'She'll be all right. Kids don't think at eighteen.'

Suzie hides her head in my shoulder, and I know there are tears leaking down her cheeks. 'Where *is* the stupid girl?'

'Did you phone the Parrot?'

'There was no one there.' Suzie's voice sounds choked and dry.

I try reasoning with her. 'Nightclubs in the morning, staff don't arrive for a while. What time did you ring?'

'About nine.'

'Nine? You've been fretting here since nine?'

'I rang again about ten.'

'Someone will open the place soon.'

'They'll have nothing to tell me,' Suzie sobs. 'She isn't going to be in the Parrot, is she, sleeping at a table?'

'Is there nowhere backstage?'

'It isn't that sort of club.'

I pull Suzie in close against me, and as I pat her shoulder I think, not for the first time, that maybe I was lucky to have no kids of my own.

Ludo stands up. He thumps his fist gently on the table. 'I vote we go out and look for her.'

'Sit down, Ludo,' I tell him. 'Where would we start?'

'At the Parrot,' he says firmly. Then he sits down.

'How well does Tamsin know Huey Carmichael?' I ask. Suzie mumbles into my neck. I continue, 'She said he was looking for me. Perhaps she wasn't meant to tell me that.'

Suzie starts to break away. 'She isn't close to Carmichael. She just sings there. What has that to do with anything?'

'It may have something. Is Carmichael on the phone?'

'How do I know?'

I draw Suzie back for another cuddle, then sit her down to sip some tea. Ludo starts a meandering tale of how he was lost once at Drakes Funfair, and I slide into the hall to find the phonebook. When I come back, Ludo has reached the part where they announced his name across the tannoy and Albie had to claim him like a lost child. 'He was ever so cross,' Ludo recalls.

'Where does Carmichael live?'

No one knows. There are hundreds of Carmichaels in the book. 'Do you think he lives local?' I ask.

'He's rich. He can afford somewhere decent.'

I close the phonebook. 'I'll try the Parrot again.'

When I leave them, Ludo has found the hoover and begun demonstrating his skills at housework. Suzie has phoned the police. No, they hadn't any corpses that could have been Tamsin. No, they couldn't suggest where she might be. Eighteen? She'll turn up.

With the hoover in his hand and dusting still to do, Ludo has resigned himself to his new abode. It will be better for him than sitting around all day in our empty house, waiting. It will be safer.

The threat giving us three days to find the money is something I can't dismiss. I can't assume that because I thumped Dirkin, the gang will now call the whole thing off. Those four lumps won't be running the show in any case. Whoever is behind them wants his ten grand paid back. Meanwhile, I can't sit in the house waiting for their next visit, and I certainly can't leave Ludo there while I am out. He is strong, but not clever. Against four of them he would have no chance.

So he stays with Suzie.

No one links her to me, so her house is sanctuary. A haven. Or it was until little Tamsin did her disappearing act. The silly bitch. She must have shacked up with some slob who praised her singing last night. Probably said he could push her career into the big-time. And she believed him. Eighteen years old.

The result? Suzie is sick with worrying, Ludo has been foisted on her, and I'll have to try to find the girl.

I know where to start.

The doorman at the Parrot says he cannot let me in. I explain my reason.

'Tamsin Peters – the half-caste one?'

'I want to find her.'

'Yeah, she's pretty, ain't she? There's no point going in, though. She ain't there.'

'How d'you know?'

'My job, ain't it?'

'Did you see her leave last night?'

'I ain't here *all* the time, you know'

'Huey Carmichael in?'

'No.'

'Then fetch the guy in charge.'

We walk between the tables to the bar. I am with a pale lean guy who has black curly hair. He could be Latin, or maybe an eighth Caribbean. I don't ask. He is the sort of man you don't ask personal questions.

Daytime lights are on – harsh, unflattering. The smell of ashtrays and last night's beer mingles with perfumed disinfectant. Two black cleaning ladies clank buckets across the floor. The man who has walked beside me tells the barman he can talk. 'Man's looking for Tamsin. Know anything?'

The barman shakes his head. He is a mangey looking white feller, wearing yesterday's shirt with the collar open, and he is drying glasses. The minder taps my arm. 'Feel free.'

'Did Tamsin sing here last night?'

'Does usually.'

'But did she last night?'

'You a cop?'

'A friend.'

He sniffs. The minder has not left us. The barman says, 'You're a bit old to be a friend of hers, aren't you?'

'So what?'

'Got an interest?'

'The girl didn't come home last night. Her mother's worried.'

'Oh dear.' He pulls a long face and thinks himself droll. 'Mummy's worried? You better tell Mummy that her little girl is a big girl now – in case she hasn't noticed.'

'Was she here?'

'Who – the mother?'

I sigh. 'Just answer the bloody question.'

'And what was that question again?'

I spell out every word. 'Did Tamsin sing here last night?'

'You know something? I think she did. You *are* the Bill, aren't you?'

The minder cuts in. 'He's Floyd Carter. Albie's brother.'

The barman raises both eyebrows, pulling a face again. 'Well, well. So you're not a cop.'

'That's right,' I say patiently. 'I just want to know what happened to the girl. Who did she leave with?'

'How much is it worth?'

'Cut it out,' snaps the minder. 'We haven't got all day.'

The barman looks at him, then looks back at me. 'I think my memory's gone,' he says.

'Listen, prat,' the minder says, leaning across the bar, 'just tell him who she left with.'

The man resumes his droll face and picks up his cloth and glass. 'I don't remember.' He walks away.

We watch him go. 'I'll have his bollocks later,' the minder says. 'Come on.'

As he leads me round the central bar towards the rear of the hall I ask again if Carmichael is in. The minder says not. I glance up to locate the one-way glass window, and I wonder if Carmichael is standing behind it even now, watching us. I wonder if his microphone is switched on. I wonder a lot of things.

The minder pushes open a narrow door and leads me into the

backstage corridor. 'Only two dressing rooms,' he says. They are both empty. 'There's her gear.'

On hangers on a rail are several dresses. I ask if they are all hers.

'No. That and that.' He indicates a pair of stiffened party frocks, one white and one cream. They look incongruous here – the kind of costumes a kid might wear. I turn away.

'Make-up's still here.'

A clutter of jars and tubes lies across the top of the shared dressing table. 'Looks like she means to come back.'

'I hope you're right. Is there anyone else I can ask – musicians maybe?'

As he checks his reflection in the greasy mirror he pulls a steel comb from an inside pocket. He runs it through his black curly hair. 'Too early in the day. You'll want the night staff.'

We return to the main clubroom and pick our way between the tables. The barman watches us with a grin on his face. We ignore him. I ask the minder if Tamsin is popular.

'With staff or customers?'

'Both.'

'She gets along. Moody kid. Unpredictable.'

'She's close to Carmichael, isn't she?'

'Not that I know of.'

His face shows nothing. We leave the clubroom and make our way along the corridor back toward the rear exterior door. 'Sorry we couldn't help you,' the minder says.

'Thanks anyway.'

'She's bound to turn up, Kids, you know.' He grins sympathetically. He is about thirty, lean as a tiger, and doesn't need to act tough.

As I pause in the doorway, the old doorman squints at me across his glasses. 'Any luck?' he asks.

'Not a thing.'

'Except that she was here last night,' the minder points out. 'You learnt that much. If you want to try the band, they're called Pepys Dairy Crunch. Pepys as in Samuel. Dairy as in Crunch.'

'D'you have an address?'

The doorman picks up a scruffy notebook and rifles through the pages. 'Could be rehearsing,' he says. 'This time of day.'

'They weren't inside.'

'They wouldn't be. Try down the Albany Empire. They're often there.'

'Thanks.'

Just as I am about to leave I add, 'That book of yours: you got an address for Vinnie Dirkin?'

'Dirkin,' the doorman says. 'Yeah. Not that *he* can sing.' He thumbs through his book while I lean casually against the doorpost. I avoid the minder's eye. This is a longshot I didn't think would come off. 'He lives near the Laurie Grove swimming baths. You know it?'

'In New Cross, yes.'

The doorman scribbles Dirkin's address on a scrap of paper and hands it to me.

'What d'you want with Dirkin?' the minder asks. 'She wouldn't go out with a dickhead like him.'

'This is another matter. Does he work here?'

'Used to.'

'What happened?'

'He got the push.'

They watch me as I stroll away beside the side wall of the building towards the carpark at the front. So Vinnie Dirkin used to work for the Snake Carmichael. That's interesting.

'I'll tell Mr Carmichael you came,' the minder calls. 'Take care now.'

You bet.


'Hello, Ludo. Is Tamsin back?'

'Floyd, is that you?' He sounds nervous. He had let the phone ring seven times.

'Yeah, it's me. Is she back?'

Ludo clears his throat. 'Hello, Floyd. How are you?' His tongue stumbles around the words.

'I'm fine, Ludo.' I drum my fingers. 'Is Tamsin back?'

'Well, no. Not yet. I've got her lunch ready.'

'Have we heard from her?'

'I don't think so.'

'Is Suzie there?'

'She's gone to work. I'm on my own here. Are you in a phonebox, Floyd? Suzie said I should answer the phone if it rang.'

'And has it?'

'Has it what?'

'Has it rung?'

Ludo hesitates. 'Well, only this time. But that was you.'

I breathe out slowly. 'If Suzie calls, tell her that I haven't found Tamsin yet, but she was at the club last night.'

'I hope Suzie will be all right, Floyd. She didn't look very well.'

'She's worried about Tamsin. Are *you* all right?'

'Well, not really, Floyd. I'm bored. I want to go home.'

'We both have to stay out of sight for a couple of days. You know what they said.'

'Who?'

'The guys who want the money. They'll be looking for us.'

'Oh, them. Yes. They'll be looking for you.' He sounds aggrieved.

'I can take care of myself.'

In the Albany Empire I am the only white face. Daytime is rehearsal time. Pepys Dairy Crunch are burning a hole in the sound system, dancers are limbering up against chair backs, and scattered around drinking soft drinks is something called the Black Comedy Club. They don't look funny to me.

When the Crunch crashes to the end of its number the drummer continues bashing at his cymbals as if trying to hammer them into silence. The two guitar players pluck whining notes at each other to bring their tortured instruments back in tune. The saxophonist shakes spit on to the floor. I walk up to him.

'Little Tamsin? Yeah, she sang with us last night.'

'But she never made it home. Did you see who she left with?'

'No, man. I had things on my mind, right?'

'Has she got a boyfriend?'

'No one special. – Hey!' He calls across to the others. 'The singer Tamsin: who she leave with last night?'

They don't know.

'Did she leave alone?' I ask.

They don't know that either.

'Any idea where she could be at this moment?'

They look dumb.

'You Floyd Carter, right?' the saxophonist asks.

'Right.'

He nods, as if that settled the matter, and shakes another blob of spittle out of his sax.

'How d'you know me?'

'I don't know you, man.'

I give him a look.

'I knew your brother Albie. That was a bad scene, right? I'm sorry, you know?'

'Yeah, I know. I am also looking for the guys who ran him down. Any suggestions?'

'Not me, man.' He places the sax in his mouth and blows a trial riff.

'Why d'you think Albie got himself killed?'

The man takes the reed from his mouth and flexes his lips. He shrugs. 'I keep out of things like that, right?' He replaces the saxophone, and blows again. Then he licks his lips.

'You keep out of what things?'

He plays another short sequence, keeping his eyes on my face. I stare back. When he comes to the end of the phrase, I say, 'Help me, will you? I have a brother someone ran over. I have a friend's daughter disappeared. I don't want to put this on you in any way, but I need help.'

He nods several times. 'I don't know who killed your brother, and I don't rightly know who's out with Tamsin. She's a wild kid, you know?'

'Meaning?'

'She could be anywhere. I wouldn't worry about it.'

'She hasn't disappeared like this before.'

'Is that right?' He sniffs. 'Well, she ain't so very reliable neither.'

'You mean she sometimes lets the band down?'

He shrugs again. 'If she's with us, she sings. If she ain't, we play.'

'You don't work as a unit?'

'Hell, no, man, we not good enough for her. She like all these young singers: too much ambition, right? She want to be a big star. Big. She want it now. But she don't put the work in. You understanding me?'

'I understand. Isn't she a friend of Carmichael?'

He snorts. 'I hope not, man, for her sake. I don't think so.'

I guess I am looking pretty glum. 'Look,' he says. 'I'll put the word out. I don't promise nothing.'

'I'd appreciate that.'

'She'll turn up, man. Don't you worry.'

I grab a beer and sandwich in the Marquis of Granby, then continue past the Laurie Grove baths. I turn down a scruffy street built too close to the railway. Twenty times a day these dirty little houses are shaken by trains rumbling past the ends of their cramped backyards. Nobody lives here from choice.

Vinnie Dirkin has the shabbiest door on the block. It's the kind of place I wouldn't house a dog in. I rap at the knocker.

It echoes. Behind the door, the house sounds empty. I check if I have the right address, and knock again. Nothing.

I stroll back to the Marquis of Granby, and settle down with a second glass of beer. I take my time drinking it. Here inside the pub, the air is smoky. Wispy grey light filters through frosted windows on to dusty furniture. Traffic throbs outside. I close my eyes.

Dirkin's front door reminded me how shabby London looks. After ten years in Europe, everything here seems dirty and poor. Clothes are grubby and shapeless. People in the streets look browbeaten, defeated at war.

I drain the dregs of my beer and stand up. Suddenly I miss my local café. I miss the smell of strong coffee and sharp cigarettes. I miss my friends. Deptford is sucking me into a world I thought I'd left behind. That bloody Albie. He never was anything but grief.

New Cross Station. I try the phones. The second one works.

'Hallo, Ludo. Any news?'

'Oh hallo, Floyd.' His voice brightens, as if he had expected to hear a stranger on the line.

'Is she home yet?'

'Tamsin? No, she's not. Suzie phoned.'

'What did she say?'

'She asked about her. Then she swore.'

I nod, though he can't see me. 'I still think the kid's kipping with her boyfriend.'

'I was shocked a bit, Floyd.'

'Shocked?'

'The swearing. I didn't think Suzie was like that.'

'She's under strain, Ludo. Worried. It makes you swear.'

'She seems a nice woman.'

'She is. Women do swear, Ludo.'

'Can I go out, Floyd?'

'Out where?'

'Well, anywhere. I don't like staying in.'

'Listen, Ludo, you don't have to stay in. But it's useful to have you there by the phone. You're in charge of the office.'

'Oh. I hadn't thought of it like that.'

'You're doing an important job.'

'Right. I'm in charge of the office.'

'Goodbye, Ludo.'

'I'll be here, Floyd. In the office.'

Dirkin, like Tamsin, seems to have disappeared. Several times I rap on his door but nothing happens. No neighbours come out to take a look. They keep their heads down.

I cut back up past the baths, down Lewisham Way into Malpas Road. The sky has turned that London grey colour, a lack of colour:

no sunlight, no blue sky, no clouds, no threat of rain. Just a grey toneless ceiling across the town.

I reach Jamie's house and ring the bell. He had better be in. Trudging around Deptford after people I can't find has made my feet sore.

He is in.

Though it is halfway through the afternoon he looks like he has just crawled out of bed. He wears a striped pyjama jacket roughly tucked into dark crumpled slacks. He hasn't shaved. His hair is a mess. His skin is the colour of today's sky.

He mumbles hallo.

I follow him up the narrow staircase to the tip he calls his flat. The main room is strewn with newspapers and clothes. His settee has rolled over on its back and died. I ask if he has been burgled.

Jamie groans. 'I had a party, few friends round. Give us a hand, will ya?'

We heave the settee back on its feet, and I pat it, like I'd pat a dog. Dust rises. I suggest we open the window.

'Not yet, it's bloody freezing. Lemme get my clothes on.'

Nowhere can be freezing if it smells like this. I open the window and take a look along the street. This time I have not been followed. Malpas Road is dead.

'Christ, it's cold,' Jamie moans. And he means it. He sits huddled on the settee, shivering like a bush in a hailstorm.

'I'll put the kettle on,' I say. 'Have you eaten yet?'

'No.' He shudders. 'Couldn't face it.'

'Are you sickening for something?'

'Maybe. A touch of flu.'

'Or a hangover.'

'Could be that.'

I drift into his kitchenette and fill the kettle. The draining board and sink are cluttered with unwashed crockery.

'You need the loving hand of a good woman. Starting here.'

He grunts. I stroll back. 'The way you're shivering, you should be in bed.'

'*You* got me up, didn't ya? Anyway, I gotta go out.'

'Believe in fresh air, do you?'

'I need some shopping.'

'Want me to do it?'

'I don't need a nursemaid.'

'That's what you think.'

The kettle boils. I walk through to deal with it. 'Coffee or tea?'

'Neither.'

'What *do* you want?'

'Nothing.'

But I pour two cups of strong black coffee and bring them through. I place one cup in his hands and sit beside him. 'Drink your medicine. There's a good boy.'

He doesn't. After half a minute of staring at it he puts the cup on the floor and stands up. 'Gotta go out.'

'Don't stand on your cup.'

'Listen, I don't want to be rude, Floyd son, but what have you come for, anyway?'

I hesitate, and place my empty coffee cup carefully beside his full one on the floor. ' I *was* going to ask you to put me up for a couple of nights, but it doesn't matter. I'll go somewhere else.'

Jamie blinks at me. He brushes the lock of lank hair from his eye. 'What's wrong with your place?'

I tell him about the threat to me and Ludo, and I keep it simple. 'I only need a couple of nights, before I fly back.'

'Well, you're welcome to stay here, sunshine.'

I glance briefly around the room. 'Maybe not.'

'Come on, Floyd, you need a friend.'

'Don't worry, I'll find a boarding house. There's no shortage of bed and breakfast places.'

Jamie looks uncomfortable. 'There is round here. Listen, I'll be all right when I've had some air. Come back in a couple of hours.'

'Two hours? You couldn't stay on your feet for two minutes.'

'Don't you believe it. Don't go to no boarding house. Come back later. You can help me clear up.'

I grin. 'You drive a hard bargain.'

Jamie sways on his feet, blinking around the room. 'Jesus,' he says

I reach out a hand to steady him. 'Are you all right?'

'Yeah.' He wipes his forehead. 'Just need a bit of time.'

As Jamie staggers to the door, I hover behind like a nurse when the patient takes his first trembling steps. 'You're not fit to be let out.'

He opens the door from the flat on to the landing. 'See you about five, shall I? I'll be right as rain by then.'

We creep slowly down the stairs to the front door. Before he opens it, he slips on a pair of dark shades. Out in the street he winces at the bright grey light.

I approach our house from the other end of the road. It isn't dark yet, so I don't expect Vinnie Dirkin's boys to be waiting in the street. Though if they are, they'll be in the same place where they waited last time. It's quieter there.

Our house looks empty and untouched. So they haven't called yet. I am sure of that. Three days they gave me, and it runs out tonight. If they don't get paid this time they'll do some damage. They'll enjoy that. Whoever sent them would rather have his money, but the boys won't mind some pleasure first.

I walk up to my front door and slip the key in the lock.

I turn the key, push the door open. Silence.

I step inside and close the door.

Two minutes it takes me to check the rooms. No one is here and no one has been. Tonight is when they'll call.

You know how it is when you've been away? You come back to that silent empty house, it feels cold. Warmth has drained from the air like body heat from a corpse. That's how it feels here.

Must be my imagination. Ludo and I walked out of here only this morning. I've returned no later than a normal man might come home from work. Yet there is that chill. As if the house knows.

I stand in the kitchen, waiting for the electric kettle to boil. Splinters of warmth reach out through the air. In the bottom of my cup, dark brown coffee granules lie waiting, like the first handful of soil on the lid of a coffin. I think of Albie. I think of the way everyone expects me to avenge him. I think of the guys he owes money to. I wonder how deep he was in.

When the phone rings I think I know who it is.

While it rings in the empty hall I pour hot water into my cup. I stir my coffee thoughtfully as I carry it through to the hall. I pick up the receiver.

'Yeah?'

'Is that Floyd Carter?'

'It is.'

'Your time is up, Carter. You got the money?'

'What d'you think? Every time some punk tells me my brother owes him money, I pay him off?'

'You'll pay us.'

'Yeah?'

'Ten thousand quid. Tonight.'

'Get stuffed.'

'You'll be the one to get stuffed, Carter.'

I put down the phone and walk up the stairs. As I throw clothing into a bag, I muse on what I must do next. I will need a few days to sort out about the house and Ludo, during which time we cannot stay permanently out of sight. The debt-collectors will wait till we reappear. If I meet them without the money, they will kick my face in again and give me one last day to pay up.

I could tell the police.

I did think about this. I did wonder what the reaction of the Deptford police would be to a cry for help from the Carter boys. Don't bring your gangland squabbles to us, they would say. We are not here to protect villains. The more you slobs take each other out, the more we will like it.

Which is a shame, really. It means I'll have to deal with this nuisance on my own.

# 9

I have hardly put my finger on Jamie's bell when he pulls the door open. He looks excited. His lips draw back in a strange kind of grin and his eyes blaze. He flicks a hank of hair from his face and says, 'Hey, Floyd. I thought you'd never get here.'

He pulls me inside and shuts the door. In the dim hallway he holds his head close to my face. The brightness of his smile lights up the darkness. 'You brought your things?'

'In this bag.'

He nods at me. His face is sweating. 'Great to see you.'

'Are you running a fever?'

'I'm happy. Come upstairs.' He slaps me on the arm and turns away.

'Is someone up there?'

He replies across his shoulder as he strides up the stairs. 'No. I'm just glad to see you. We can have some fun.'

Halfway up I grab his elbow. 'Who's in there, Jamie?'

'Ain't nobody here but us chickens! Come on, for Christ's sake.'

He pulls away from me, and clatters up the remaining stairs. When I ease through the door I take a peek inside each of his cluttered hidey-holes – the kitchenette, the bedroom, the lavatory. Then I come back to him. 'Why so excited?'

'Ah Christ, Floyd son, I feel better. Can't I laugh when I'm happy?'

I put down my bag. 'Happy?'

'Jesus, Floyd!' He stares at me in disgust, as if I'd just confessed

I'd seduced his sister. 'Can't I be happy in my own flat? Is there a law against that?'

'I thought you were ill?'

'I'd just woken up. Have a beer.'

On the table is a six-pack with two empty. Jamie's fingers claw at the cardboard outer. We each take a can. He shakes his up, pulls the tab, and watches beer foam spurt into the air. He hoots at the spray. 'Come on, Floyd, drink some. Miserable git.'

I pull the tab and raise the can to my mouth.

'That's better,' he shouts. 'We're having a party. Right?'

'You have a head start.'

'So catch up.' He stares at me. Then he grins. 'Forget it. Wanna help me make your bed? It's this settee.'

I continue talking in a casual tone, ignoring the way that Jamie keeps shouting. 'Does the bed shake out or does it stay like that?'

'Do me a favour. This is a double bed. See this lever here?'

We each stoop over an end, open the settee, and watch it spring forward into a flimsy bed. Anyone sleeping in this tiny double bed had better like his partner.

'Good enough for ya, is it, you fussy bastard?'

'Yeah.'

Jamie paces around the room like an expectant father in Maternity. 'Listen,' he says, and stops. He licks his lips. 'You only just got here, right? I don't want you to think I'm hustling you, but . . .'

He grins. I wait for him.

'Ah Christ, it's all coming out wrong.'

'What are you trying to say?'

'Agh . . .' He waves his hand through the air as if smacking a moth away. 'I have to ask you something.'

'Then ask it.' I speak in a flat voice, because I know what he will ask.

He licks his lips some more, decides they are wet enough, then carries on. 'Have you got some money with you, Floyd? Did you bring some cash?'

'How much d'you want?'

He sets off around the room again. 'I mean, it's just temporary, like a loan, you know?'

'How much?'

He stops, giving me his old familiar little-boy-lost look from beneath a curl of hair. 'Have you got a hundred?'

'A hundred quid?'

'Yeah. Have you got it with you?'

'A hundred. Not in my pocket, no. Why d'you need a hundred?'

'I just need it. I gotta have it.'

'Today?'

'Yeah, now. Right this minute, point of fact. I was waiting for you, wasn't I?'

Jamie has stopped pacing around the room, and quivers like a dog. I ask, 'You charging me rent?'

'No, no.' He shakes his head. Like a dog again. 'Just a loan. But I need it. Christ, it's only a hundred.'

'I don't carry that much loose in my pocket.'

'Didn't you bring travellers' cheques from Germany?'

'You think I'm a tourist?' He is desperate, all right.

'Oh shit, you must have money, Floyd. Look at the flash clothes you wear.'

All the excitement ebbs from Jamie's face, as if the electricity that powers him is running out. His shaky smile looks as if it is about to crumble into tears. 'I need the money, Floyd.'

These are the first quiet words that he has uttered. I come forward now, and place my hand upon his arm. There is a moment's awkward silence. I feel restrained by English customs: I should take him in my arms, but I don't.

'You need a hundred, right now?'

'That's right.' He looks up with sudden hope. 'Have you got the money, Floyd? Can you let me have it?'

'Not this minute. I told you.'

'You don't have travellers' cheques?'

'Of course not.'

'How about a cash card – you know, for banks?'

'A cash card?'

'Like you stick in a machine on the wall to get money out.'

'I don't have one.'

'Ah Christ, Floyd, everybody has one of those.'

'Not me. I don't live here. I don't have an English bank account.'

He looks at me in the way he'd look at the girl who shattered his dreams. It takes him three attempts to wrap his tongue around his next question: 'Where do you get your money from, Floyd?'

'Banks, like most people. But they're shut now.'

'That's why they have machines,' he mutters. 'Twenty-four hours a day.'

'Why do you need a hundred pounds?' Come on Jamie, spit it out.

He pulls away from me, and sinks on to the edge of the unmade bed. It almost tips over. Again I feel I should sit beside him and put my arm along his shoulders. But I don't. Not in England. Not on a bed.

Jamie shivers and says, 'It's the rent, Floyd. I got behind. I gotta pay it today.'

'That's pathetic.'

A last surge of dying electricity charges his desperate words: 'If I don't pay it immediately, you and me will both be on the streets tonight. Can't you sell something?'

'Don't be stupid.'

'I gotta have the money.'

'I know you have. What drugs are you on, Jamie?'

At first he denies it: he spins me the old hangover tale again. Then he says he might have flu – it being damp for the time of year. I wait.

'I gotta have the money,' he whimpers. 'It's only a hundred, for Christ's sake.'

'And how much tomorrow?'

He glares at me. 'Some fuckin' friend. And you want a *bed* for the night.'

'I told you. I can find somewhere else.'

'Yeah, walk out on me.'

I pick up my bag. 'Sorry, Jamie, you're on your own.'

Before I reach the door, he is across the room and grabbing my arm. He pulls me round to face him. 'You give me some money!' he shouts. I stare into his eyes. He lets go of my arm and fumbles in his pockets. I put down my bag. His hand reappears with a flick-knife in it, and the blade springs from its sheath. Down cracks my left fist on the base of his thumb. In smacks my right fist to the pit of his stomach.

As he folds to the floor I reach out and take the knife from his hand. 'You're right,' I say. 'Some fuckin' friend.'

I close his knife and slip it into my pocket. Jamie crawls away from me across the dirty carpet. He starts to cry.

Looking at the guy who used to be my best friend, huddled on the carpet blubbering like a kid who took a beating, ought to move me. But it doesn't. I stand detached from him. His tears don't flow because I hurt him. They flow from self-pity. They leave me cold.

'I only need one hit,' he sobs, 'to build up my strength. If I can just get my strength back, you know. You can help me kick it, if you're still my friend.'

'The way you kick it is you stop.'

He shakes his head. His face is wet with snot and tears. 'It ain't that easy.'

'I never said it was.'

'You don't understand. I can't break it on my own.' Jamie drags himself into a sitting position against the shakedown settee, and sniffs back his tears.

'D'you want me to help?' I ask.

He looks up at me suspiciously. His eyes are brown and wet. They are the eyes of a baby seal floundering on the snow, before the hunter's club thumps into its skull.

'There are two ways I can help you,' I tell him. 'One way is I fetch a doctor. The other is I lock you in here for a week and keep the key.'

'Those ways don't work.'

He begins to shiver again. He remains sitting on the floor with his knees drawn up. He wraps his arms round them to pull them into his chest. 'Stake me just this once, Floyd.'

'I'm going out. I'll be back late.'

# 10

'I phoned the police from the hospital,' Suzie says. We are sitting in her tiny front room: Suzi and I in Habitat loungers, Ludo plumb centre of her two-seater settee. Suzie looks tired. The shadows around her eyes are like smudges of soot.

Ludo says, 'The police said they'd look for her.'

'When Tamsin hadn't showed up by this afternoon,' Suzie explains, 'I couldn't wait any longer. I was too worried. I was doing everything wrong. There was a man I was supposed to give an oil-rub for his bedsores, but I poured it into a tablespoon and gave it him to drink.'

'Did he like it?'

'Then I forgot an old lady who was sitting on a bedpan. She didn't dare lean over to call me on the buzzer in case she fell off the pan. When I finally got back to her, her bum was welded to the rim. Her pee was cold.'

I grin. Then I ask what happened when Suzie phoned the police.

'Men. They suggested she was out losing her virginity. Thought she might be so grateful that she forgot to look at her watch.'

'*Is* she a virgin?'

Suzie scowls. 'Are you interested, Floyd?'

'She's half my age.'

'So when did that stop people? She attracts older men.'

I change the subject. 'Did the police come round to see you?'

'What do you think? They said if she hadn't turned up by the time I finished work I should stop by my local police station on my way home. They didn't care that she could be dead by then.'

'If she wasn't dead already,' says Ludo.

He notices the pause. 'Oh, sorry,' he says. 'I bet she's not.'

I turn back to Suzie. 'Did you go to the station. How were they?'

'Not openly unsympathetic. They managed to find a policewoman – from the kitchen, I suppose, or wherever they keep their ladies occupied – and they left us in a room together. The policewoman wrote Tamsin's details on a clean piece of paper. She didn't want it on the same sheet as burglaries and missing cats. She needed it on a fresh sheet so she could file it later under Miscellaneous.'

'You don't think they care?'

'They go through the motions. I recognise the way admin systems work, from the hospital.'

'Now what happens?'

Suzie glares at me. Her blonde head is thrown back, her defiant green eyes are moist. 'What *can* happen now? They've made out a record, they'll check reports coming in. They won't send patrol cars scouring the streets of Deptford for a half-caste girl who's looking lost.'

'Is that what they called her – half-caste?'

She nods. 'When I told the policewoman that Tom was black, it made her glance up from her clipboard. It never fails. White women always do look up at you, wondering what it's like, wondering if they'll ever find out.'

'You're imagining that.'

'White people have called me a black man's harlot for nineteen years. I know what they think.'

Ludo sits leaning forward attentively in the two-seater settee. 'I think they're rude,' he says.

I ask if Tamsin has any friends we could call.

'I don't know her friends.'

I stare glumly at my hands. 'Should she be working tonight?'

'Yes. Perhaps she will, who knows? Maybe work will come first. Oh, I know, I'm a rotten parent. I let her out late at night. I don't know her friends. Maybe she *has* cut loose.'

'You're not a rotten parent, Suzie.'

58

'While she was growing up, Tom was always here. When I worked nights it didn't matter.'

'And when he died, I guess she seemed old enough that it still didn't matter?'

'I thought so. We talked about it. Tamsin said a woman shouldn't put her home before her job. At fourteen she said that.' Suzie smiles.

Ludo coughs, then says, 'I liked Tom. He was nice.'

Suzie holds on to the breath she has just taken in. She looks at Ludo. Then in a sudden gasp she lets out the breath and bursts into tears.

# 11

At the main entrance to the Parrot the wooden boarding has been removed. Through the glass doors glow orange lights. Above the doors a purple neon parrot throbs in the darkness.

The two bouncers inside the foyer seem amiable. This may be because Ludo is bigger than either of them, or it may be because they are amiable fellers. They like respectable folk with respectable money in their pockets. They like trouble to stay away.

We pay admission and step inside. Beyond the small foyer is a large anteroom decorated in soft peach colours broken up with mirrors. Padded doors lead to the main clubroom and the cloaks. A flight of stairs curves up to the executive offices, to Snake Carmichael, to the strongroom, and to whatever other discreet parlours the Parrot may provide.

'Place has changed since the old days, Ludo.'

'I like the mirrors. I can see myself three times.'

'The club's gone upmarket since the Starr family.'

'The Starrs kept it cosier, but this is nice.'

We push through the dark swing doors into the main club area. This morning's smell of old beer and disinfectant has gone. Instead is a smell of charred steak, new cigars and fresh perfume. On stage a young band plays an old number, repackaged for dancing – one of those watered down R&B ballads about lonely roads and pretty women. This is not Tamsin's band. Pepys Dairy Crunch would not descend to dance numbers: they play to be listened to. But for the early evening audience, this band mixing old standards with current chartbusters is right on key.

Ludo and I lean against the central bar and survey the room. Women aged twenty to thirty-five, men somewhat older. White outnumbering black by three to one. No jeans allowed.

'Still looking for your girlfriend?' the barman asks. I turn slowly. He is the mangey little stick who tried to be funny this morning. Now he wears a bow tie.

I ask if she is in.

'We *are* still looking then? Nobody seen her?'

'It seems not. What time is she due on?'

'I couldn't say. When you're working, everything merges into the background din. She *has* been a naughty girl, hasn't she?'

Ludo takes him up. 'How has she been naughty. What d'you mean?'

'Are you two together – or are you just listening in?'

Ludo frowns at him.

'Don't get huffy,' the barman says. 'What's your pleasure, gentlemen, if I may ask?'

'A Saint Clements,' Ludo says.

'Saint Clements?'

'Yes, you know, oranges and lemons.'

'This is not a fruit market, dear.'

'I want orange juice and bitter lemon.'

'Oh, we *are* going wild. Who's drinking which?'

'Together,' Ludo says.

'I can see that, dear.' He turns away to fetch the drinks.

'The barman didn't ask what *you* wanted,' Ludo says.

The barman reappears with two glasses. 'Don't nurse your drinks too long,' he sniggers. 'It makes the glasses cloudy.'

Ludo says, 'I asked for them together, in one glass.'

The barman pulls a face and pretends to recoil from the drinks as if he has seen them for the first time. From the shelf above his head he reaches down a long glass. He tips the two juices into it.

'You've trebled my washing up, but never mind. Keep the customers happy. I suppose you'd like a cherry in it, and a little paper parasol?' He turns to me. 'And for madam?'

'Just a parasol,' says Ludo.

As the barman's eyes meet mine they flicker. He wonders if he has gone too far. He twirls back to Ludo: 'Pardon?'

'Just a parasol, please, not the cherry.'

'You want a parasol?'

'I like parasols. You can take them home.'

The barman giggles. 'I suppose you can. Parasols are for cocktails, dear. Or for ice-creams at the table.' He turns back to me. My face is wooden. His sneer dies.

'Then why did you offer?' Ludo asks. He looks offended. He is a big man to offend.

The barman registers the expression on Ludo's face, and buries his sneer with a simpering smile. 'You can have a parasol, if you'd like.'

'Yes, please,' says Ludo.

'And I want a whisky.'

'Yes, sir.'

We don't pay for them. He doesn't ask.

We sit at the bar through a couple of drinks. Behind us on the dance floor, people do an early evening shimmy. I think the band is trying to sound like Dire Straits, which is some ambition. Ludo shreds his parasol.

After ten slow minutes, Carmichael's pale minder appears silently at my elbow, and he smiles. 'Have one on the house,' he suggests.

'On you or Carmichael?'

'He'd like a word. There's no hurry.'

'We'll skip the drinks.'

I do not wish to stand here another five minutes nursing a drink while Carmichael gazes at us through his window as if we were two dirty beer glasses to be cleared off the bar.

'Upstairs,' the minder says.

'I don't believe you came for dancing, so this is business, hey?'

Carmichael has changed out of his white linen suit into a silky black evening number which he wears above a white rollneck shirt. His shoes have gold medallions on them. They are propped on his white leather-top desk. His left arm rests nonchalantly along the arm of his toffee-brown chair, and the skin of his brown hand is wrinkled, like a tobacco leaf drying in the sun. In his other hand he holds a glass of Lucozade.

'I am looking for a girl who sings here.'

He cocks an eyebrow. It makes such an elegant crescent above his eye you could believe he plucks it. He stares at me and Ludo, seated in front of his desk on comfortable squab chairs covered in the same milk toffee leather as on his. We both have drinks in our hands. So does the minder. He leans against a side wall and seeps into the maroon wallpaper.

'A girl singer?' Carmichael asks.

'Her name is Tamsin,' Ludo says. 'Miss Tamsin Peters.'

Carmichael nods. He doesn't say anything. He wants to hear the story, to see where it leads.

I continue. 'The girl is just eighteen and lives with her mother. When she finishes singing here she always goes home. Last night she didn't.'

Carmichael studies his desk. There is a pause.

'I know,' he says.

'You know she didn't go home?'

'This afternoon we had a visit from the Bill, asking where she was.'

'That surprises me.'

'It surprises *me*, you asking the Bill to help, Floyd. It doesn't sound like you.'

'Her mother asked them. She's worried sick.'

'I don't like the Bill sniffing round my club, you know?'

'Could you tell them anything? Have you any idea where she has gone?'

Carmichael shrugs. 'What's your interest?'

'I'm a friend of the family.'

'Floyd, you've been away ten years. The last time you saw that girl she must have been – what? – eight years old. How well d'you know this girl, hey?'

'I know her mother.'

'Ah.' He throws his head back. 'Is she pretty, like her daughter?'

'Then you know the girl I mean?'

'Of course I know her. What do you think I have here – a harem? I have three girl singers. I know each of them very well.'

'Does she have a boyfriend?'

'A few. None that lasted.'

'Any reason?'

'Who knows? Eighteen year old girls play the field, don't they. Besides . . .'

'Yeah?'

'She has too much mouth, you know? Thinks a lot of herself.'

A silence falls again. We sip our drinks. 'So that's why you've come this evening, hey?'

I nod.

'And I hoped you'd come to talk more business.'

I shake my head.

'Let me tell you something, Floyd. Things have changed since you went away.'

'I've noticed.'

'Maybe you thought this club was still run by the Richardsons. I kicked them out. I didn't just kick them out of this club; I kicked them out of deals all over Deptford.'

'I heard about that.'

'So if you're wondering who is on top here, you are talking to him, right?'

I nod appreciatively.

'And if you're looking to get into some action, Floyd, you talk to me. No one is independent any more. Those days are gone.'

Ludo clears his throat. 'What sort of job could you give us, Mr Carmichael? We can both work hard.'

Carmichael smiles at him. 'If you worked for me, Ludo, you could call me Huey, not Mr Carmichael. What sort of work d'you do?'

'Well . . .' Ludo looks uncomfortable.

I cut in. 'He works with me.'

'I thought he did,' Carmichael says. He leans across his desk towards Ludo. 'But what exactly is it that you do, Ludo?'

Ludo looks like an overgrown retriever puppy, anxious to please. 'I help out,' he says.

'You're a big man,' Carmichael purrs. 'Do you fight?'

Ludo avoids his eye. I suggest that we leave Ludo out of this.

'But I'm interested,' Carmichael says. He has the smile of someone spoiling for a scrap. I begin to see why they call him the Snake. 'What sort of jobs did you used to do for Albie?'

'For Albie?'

'Yes, your brother, remember him?'

'Did you know Albie, Mr Carmichael?'

'I met him. Did you help him in his work?'

I stand up. 'It's time we were leaving.'

Carmichael gives me a bland look. His minder unpeels himself from the wallpaper. 'Don't get excited,' Carmichael says.

The minder drifts closer to us, to loiter at the corner of the desk. He stands a yard away from me.

'Are we going, Floyd?' Ludo asks.

The minder looks as pale as ivory. His black curly hair glistens. All the man's weight is thrown forward on to the balls of his feet. He is like a cobra, and he shakes his head.

'No, we're not,' I tell Ludo, and sit down.

Carmichael has been hunched across his white desk, watching what was happening. Now he leans back in his soft office chair and grins. 'I'm glad you said that, Floyd.'

He lets his hand casually brush open the front of his dark jacket to reveal the pistol in the band of his trousers. It is a different gun

63

to the one he had this morning: a black, ugly little piece, starkly silhouetted against the white of his rollneck shirt. Carmichael's eyes glitter.

'Tell me, Ludo, are you any good with one of these?'

With his left hand Carmichael removes the gun and drops it on the desk. Then he withdraws his hand and lets it droop from the arm of his chair. The gun lies unattended between us. Three feet closer to him.

'Is that a real one?' Ludo asks.

'Browning thirty-eight. Recognise it?'

Ludo shakes his head.

'What sort do *you* use, Ludo?'

Ludo grins nervously. He assumes that there is a joke being played which he has not yet understood. He is used to that. 'Oh,' he says, 'I never had a gun.'

'Not even when you worked for Albie?'

'Go on!' exclaims Ludo, blushing red. 'No.' He giggles. He doesn't need me to speak for him. His innocence is inescapable.

Carmichael turns to me. 'How about you, Floyd?'

'I didn't work for Albie.'

Ludo interrupts him. He has decided that the Snake is a nice man who is playing games with us. 'Did Albie work for *you*, Mr Carmichael? Did he owe you money?'

'Money?'

'Did Albie owe you money before he died?'

Carmichael's eyes flicker between us. 'What makes you think Albie might have owed me money?'

'He owed somebody . . .' Ludo sees the expression on my face. 'A lot of money,' he finishes lamely.

'How much?' Carmichael asks.

Ludo presses his lips together and hangs his head.

I say, 'Some guys have been pressurising us for a debt they say Albie owed them. One of these guys is Vinnie Dirkin.'

'I remember him.'

'He used to work for you.'

'In a small way. He was never on my payroll. How much is this so-called debt?'

'Ten thousand.'

Carmichael nods, as if ten thousand is a reasonable amount to owe. 'Hey, Floyd, did you think I had something to do with this?'

'Are you telling me you haven't?'

'I am.'

'Do you know who has?'

Carmichael pauses, then turns to his minder. 'Any ideas, Dixie?'

Dixie had kept his eyes on me, but now he turns towards his boss. 'Someone who would trust Albie with ten thousand quid?'

'That's right.'

'Who could that be?' Dixie asks.

Carmichael looks me full in the eye and throws up his hands. 'We can't help you, Floyd. Tell me, are you going to pay these people?'

'It's not my debt.'

'What do they say will happen if you don't pay them back?'

'No one spelt it out.'

'You want some help against them?'

I look at him. He grins at me. Then he picks up his pistol from the desk, strokes it, and replaces it in his waistband.

'If you were working for me, Floyd, I'd have to help you, hey? To protect my investment.'

# 12

You can visit a lot of pubs in an hour, if you put your mind to it. And we had to. By the time we left the Parrot there was only an hour left to closing time. In the first two places, we didn't pause to drink. Ludo and I just took one side each and approached every table with snapshots of Tamsin. Had anybody seen her? No.

The third pub was the Harp of Erin, where it is not advisable to interrupt a drinking man without a Jameson's or a Guinness in your hand. Preferably both. The sign outside may say *Céad Míle Fáite*, but inside you watch your step.

Then we blitzed through the Noah's Ark, the Windsor Castle, and the Mechanic's Arms. I let Ludo do the Deptford Arms, since I am banned there on account of Vinnie Dirkin. Then together we tried the Royal Albert and the Star and Garter.

Funny the way territories persist. The Harp of Erin is Irish, the Windsor a dive. The Deptford Arms is white, both the Albert and the Garter are black. Tamsin, being half and half, could have been in any of them.

Pushing between the tables among drinkers I don't recognise brings home how long I've been away. The territories are new to me. In the white pubs are mainly young kids, with a few old men and just one or two middle-aged. Black pubs are full and loud.

Ludo and I shuffle from pub to pub, table to table, like the Salvation Army rattling tins. We show Tamsin's photo. People shake their heads.

Some think we are plainclothes cops. Some think we want Tamsin's dues. Either way they shake their heads. Back in the Harp, Irishmen stared eagerly at her photo. 'Now there's a pretty one,' they'd say. 'Will you look at that? I wish to my heart that I *had* seen her, and that's the truth.' In the Noah's Ark was a guy who recognised me, but he didn't know Tamsin. In the Mechanic's they knew Ludo.

But in the Royal Albert we meet with hassle. Six black heavies hem us in, want to know why we are snooping. They don't like whities asking questions while they drink. Then from behind the bar a hunk the size of Ludo and with a nose like a squashed pear tells them to cool it: we aren't police, he says. He knows the face of every cop.

When we try the Star and Garter next door it is crammed tighter than a coal bucket, and it belts rap at a thousand watts. We can't ask if they've seen Tamsin because nobody can hear. I try yelling in a Rasta's earhole while waving her snap in front of his eyes. He grins and shakes his head. He thinks that I am selling her for the night.

Outside, it is closing time and we have drawn a blank. Inside they are drinking up: two hundred and fifty black fellers nursing their last long drinks. The music switches off. The street stops quivering. The night is no longer young.

Ludo and I turn our collars up against the chill April evening, and ram our hands in our coat pockets. He looks disappointed. He was sure that if we checked enough pubs we were bound to find her. He thought that if we really tried, we would be rewarded. He has faith. Besides, he was with his older brother. Ludo also has faith in me.

'There's a bus stop along the road,' he says sadly. 'The 141.'

To catch a 141 at this time of night will take all the faith Ludo has. But we start to walk. Two black guys block our way. There is a tall one with seven days of stubble, who wears a navy tracksuit and white polo. There is his friend in a loose wool suit.

'Why you looking for Tamsin Peters?'

'D'you know where she is?'

'I asked why you want to know.'

This being our first promising response, I explain briefly our reasons once again. As I speak they watch my face.

'You a cop, right?'

'No, we live here. My name's Carter. He's my brother.'

They both nod. Then the wool suit asks, 'You're Floyd Carter, right?'

'Yeah. You know me?'

'Your brother just got killed.'

'That's something else I am interested in.'

He shrugs. 'Can't help you, man, you know?'

The four of us stand watching each other in the dark street while the laughing crowd drifts past us from the pub's side door. I decide that these two are worth another try. 'Listen,' I say. 'I need a lead on this. Can you give me a little help? Please.'

'We don't know who killed your brother.'

'D'you know where we can find Tamsin?'

'Sorry.'

I take a breath. 'I told you, her mother's worried. This is the first time the kid's been out so long. Now, if Tamsin is all right, whatever she may be doing, she only has to phone her mother. OK?'

The tall one with the stubble nods at me. 'If she is not all right?'

'I need to know.'

He nods again. A dozen other blacks from the Star and Garter hang off from us, listening to what goes down. From the wide-open pub doors, heat and liquor-smells flow into the street. The black beard smiles.

'We know this girl, right? But we don't know where she is. I tell you something: maybe we get some of the brothers to keep an eye out. You understand me?'

'I'd appreciate it.'

'Where you living, man?'

I hesitate, then give them Jamie's address.

'Well, that's handy. Not far at all.'

The onlookers part to let us through. As we leave, I glance around to see if anyone shows more than idle curiosity. Those two white guys might. Thirty yards back along the street they sit in a murky Cavalier. They might be talking to each other. They might not.

As we walk away from the Broadway the pavements become empty. Ludo whistles to himself. I stay quiet. When we reach the bus stop we read the timetable to see how late the 141 is supposed to run. We can either hang around here hopefully in the cold or start walking. If we walk, I can deliver Ludo to Suzie in twenty minutes. If we wait, we could freeze on the pavement inside five. We think about it.

The Cavalier has stopped twenty yards behind us on the road.

I tell Ludo not to look at it. But he looks at it. I say I'll have a word with them and he shouldn't follow me. But he follows me.

The two men watch us come towards them. Their car is parked on our side of the road with its engine running. I watch the driver's hands. Pavement or no pavement, if he kicks the car forward now I could die the way that Albie did. Albie was on the pavement when he died.

They don't do anything.

When I reach the passenger window I knock on it. The guy sitting inside is thin, looks tall, and has neat dark hair. He wears a beige topcoat and gunge tie. It tells me something.

After a moment, he winds the window down. 'Yes?'

'You have something to say to me?'

'Why don't you come in, out of the cold?'

'Why don't you step out on to the pavement?'

He continues to study me. He has pale amber eyes. 'Mind the door,' he says mildly, and he opens it. I step back.

Now he is outside the car I see that he is a little over six feet tall and carries no more spare flesh than does an iron poker. He looks soft as a poker, too.

'Your bus may not come for ages. You should have brought your car.'

I am about to retort that I have no car, when it occurs to me that it might be something he wanted to find out. This is not the kind of guy who makes polite conversation. Every word has a purpose. He speaks quietly, pleasantly, with an even delivery that would sound the same even if he was threatening your life. He has Policeman written all through his body. He would look a cop if he was soaking in his bath.

I ask why he is following me.

'Following you? Why would we do that?'

'You tell me.'

His pale amber eyes register no expression. The pause hangs in the cool night air. 'I'm sorry,' he says. 'I didn't catch your name.'

'What's yours?'

'Kellard,' he says. 'Frank Kellard.'

'Rank?'

He hesitates only one moment. 'Detective Sergeant.'

'A sergeant on motor patrol duty? Bit of a comedown, isn't it?'

'And what's your name, sir?'

So we go through the identification rigmarole and I don't hide anything. There's no point.

'Carter,' says Kellard slowly. 'I knew an Albert Carter, but he's dead.'

'We're his brothers. You knew that.'

'Why should I know that, sir?'

'D'you normally follow people for no reason?'

'Why were you at the Star and Garter, sir?'

'It's a pub.'

'So it is. Not your regular, is it?'

'Why d'you ask? What's special about it?'

'I didn't say it was special, sir. Did you stay there long?'

'If you were watching, you'd have seen when we went in.'

'Did you stay there long?'

I decide that I don't like answering questions in the street. 'Don't let me keep you from your work,' I say, and turn to go.

'One moment, sir. If you wouldn't mind.'

His face hardens. 'We have reason to believe you may be carrying controlled drugs about your person.' He delivers a few more sentences of standard cop-speak. Then they search us.

The driver does it. He turns off the engine, comes out of his car, walks round it on to the pavement, then tells us to turn and face the wall.

'Put your hands flat against the brickwork. You know what to do.'

Ludo and I lean against the wall side by side as if we were doing press-ups standing up. A cold breeze numbs the back of my neck. While the driver runs his hands along our limbs looking for suspicious objects, Sergeant Kellard stands aside. The driver, of course, doesn't find anything, so he begins to work his way through our pockets. The only thing he finds of interest is that Ludo and I both carry photographs of the same girl.

'And who might she be, sir?'

'It isn't your business.'

'Would you be looking for this girl, by any chance?'

We both stay stumm.

Kellard turns to Ludo. 'Mr Carter, would you care to tell me what you were doing in that public house?'

Ludo shuffles his feet.

'Did you have any particular business to conduct – or just the usual?'

When I try to say something, Kellard stops me. 'Nearly finished, sir, if you don't mind. Now, come on, Ludo, I've heard about you. You're not the sort of man who likes to get into trouble, are you?'

'I try not to,' mumbles Ludo.

'Not like your brothers, for example?'

'That's enough,' I snap. 'We're off. If you want any more, copper, you put us on dab.'

'Have you done something wrong, then, sir?'

We start walking away.

'Ludo,' the sergeant calls. Ludo stops. 'I knew your brother.' Ludo turns to face him. 'And do you know what? I always believed that though Albie was unquestionably a villain, you were not. Was I wrong?'

Ludo mutters something. 'Let's go, Ludo,' I say, drawing away.

'Innocent people,' the sergeant says, 'don't mind talking to police officers. So why are you both running away?'

'Here comes my bus,' says Ludo.

He is right. The long-lost 141 is grinding downwards through its gears as it approaches the bus stop. 'That's my bus,' Ludo says again.

'We can drive you home, sir. We know where you Carters live.'

'I'm not going home,' Ludo admits.

'Really, sir? Where are you going instead?'

'You run for the bus,' I tell Ludo. 'And I'll talk to these guys. You just catch that bus.'

Kellard looks me briefly in the eye. 'Run along, then, Ludo,' he says. 'You don't want to miss it.'

I have not sat in the back of a British police car, marked or unmarked, for twelve years. They haven't changed.

'Cold out there, wasn't it?' says Kellard. 'But now that you're tucked up in here, none of your mates will notice that you're talking to us. It's better that way, isn't it?'

I stare at the back of the driver's head.

'You're a villain, like your brother,' continues Kellard evenly. I don't reply.

'Now, Mr Carter, sir, the Star and Garter – not the obvious pub for a man like you, is it?'

'I like the music.'

'Very loud, I'll say that for it. Were you meeting someone there?'

'No.'

Kellard doesn't say anything. He doesn't do anything. He just settles himself into the cushion of the rear seat and waits for me to speak. If he had a pipe, he might light it. From the untroubled expression on his face, you'd think he was remembering the taste of its tobacco.

I realise that I have little I need to hide. I had wanted to keep

Tamsin's name out of it, but it's too late now. He has seen the photographs. So I tell him about the search for her, and he sits and listens. When I have finished, he says, 'Bit of a long shot, wasn't it, trying the pubs?'

'Where else could I look?'

'Her friends. The people she goes around with.'

'I tried the only ones I knew.'

'Did you try the police?'

'Her mother did.'

'Did she really?' He seems surprised. 'Your brother Ludo – you say he's staying with them? Any chance there was something going on between them?'

'Going on?'

'You know – hanky panky.'

'Tamsin and Ludo? Do me a favour.'

'How about her mother – anything there?' He sees what I am thinking. 'It's a bit unlikely, I suppose. But most disappearances of teenage girls are due to domestic difficulties. They seldom get abducted. You say the police are looking into this already?'

'I doubt it's top of the list.'

'Someone will be dealing with it. And I hope that when that officer has to interview someone he gets more co-operation than I had from you.'

'I'm sitting here in your car answering questions.'

'But you're not co-operating.' There is an edge to Kellard's voice. 'What d'you think police work is, Carter? Petty crooks like you and Albie – you turn everyone against us. You call us the filth, the enemy, bogies, fuzz. You have a hundred poisonous names. But when your Mrs Peters finds that her little girl has stayed out late, what does she do? Calls the police. And when our constable makes the rounds, interviewing her daughter's friends, what do *they* do? Act clever, play dumb, be as unhelpful as they can. Yet we're all part of the same community, Carter. We're supposed to be on the same side.'

He breaks off. I sneak a look at what I can see of the driver's face, to check how he likes his boss's sermon, but his face is wooden. So I look at Kellard. His face shows nothing either. I say, 'We treat you guys like that because of the way you act. Hassling people. Stopping guys in the street for no reason and then searching them.'

'But you're a villain, Carter.'

'I'm here for a funeral. I have not lived in this country for ten long years.'

'I've worked this manor for twenty-two. You may not know me,

71

Carter, but I remember you. And I knew your brother. He didn't move away.'

'So you've got us labelled, have you?'

'Like you've got me.'

We sit in silence for half a minute. Then I ask, 'Were you staking that pub or watching me?'

He hesitates. 'We were watching the pub. We had reason to believe . . .' He changes tack. 'When you and your brother came out from it, things began to fit.'

'Made a mistake, didn't you?'

'We may have done. You had nothing on you, and a reasonable story. But your brother Albie used to use that pub.'

'The Garter?'

'You could be picking up where he left off. Am I right?'

'Picking up what?'

'Are you involved in it too?'

'Involved in what?'

Kellard's pale amber eyes look tired. 'Innocent as a new-born baby, aren't you, Carter?'

'I don't know what you're talking about.'

'They all say that.' He sniffs. 'You can go now, Carter. We won't offer you a lift.'

'I've missed my bus.'

'The 141 doesn't go where you are going. Unless *you're* spending the night with Mrs Peters too?'

'I'm not.'

'No. But it's odd that your brother is. What's the reason for that again? I forget.'

'I can go then, can I?'

'You can go. I'm sure you can walk home from here, a big boy like you.'

'Yeah. If the neighbours saw you and me together, Kellard, they might talk. Think you were leading me astray.'

'We're in plain clothes. This is an unmarked car.'

'Not around here, it isn't.'

I get out. I take a glance at the outside of his Cavalier so I'll remember it. Then I slide off in the direction of New Cross Station. I hear them turn the engine on. Then they pass me.

I continue along the dark pavement with my hands thrust deep inside my pockets. Enough came out of that conversation to keep me brooding half the night. The cops saw me where they thought I shouldn't be, so they got curious. And once the cops get curious, there's no stopping them. From now on, they could keep plodding behind me, dogging at my heels, convinced I have a bone to throw to them. They are not alone. Huey Carmichael wants to offer me a job. He employs a singer who slips the word to me, and she disappears. I have a bunch of hoods lurking around some corner wanting ten thousand pounds that I have not got. I have taken Ludo out of our house into hiding. Well. Whatever Albie got himself into seems to have caught the attention of a lot of people. And whatever I try to tell them, they seem convinced I am a part of it. Wherever I go in Deptford, I have people watching me. Watching and waiting. But no one will tell me what it is they're waiting for.

That's for me to find out.

# 13

Jamie's light is on.

I linger across the street, looking up at it. It is perfectly reasonable he should still be up. Jamie is not the type to tuck himself in bed early. Back in our early twenties we could be up all night. Remember I told you he had that job checking street-lamps? Sometimes when I wasn't in training, he and I would spend the evening round the pubs, carry bottles home, listen to music and talk till four. Then, to sober up, we'd spill out on to the streets and do the street-lamps until dawn.

But he's older now. And I have stopped taking things for granted. Someone thinks I should pay them ten thousand pounds. Someone killed my brother with a car.

Behind the curtains a shadow moves.

It could have been Jamie. Why should it be someone else? He has his light on, and he crossed the room. Nothing wrong with that.

But I wait. I stand another long minute on the cold pavement opposite his terraced house, and I watch. Nothing happens. I cross the street.

Quietly, I slide his key into the lock and turn it. I push the door slowly forwards so it hardly creaks. I step inside.

The hall is dark. No lights are on. When I close the front door behind me, the hall is lit only by the streetlight, glowing faintly through frosted glass. I creep toward the stairs.

When I was a kid I used to practise stalking up the stairs. According to what it says in books, you have to tread carefully right out on the edges of each step, where they are fixed against the wall. They creak less there.

But it never worked for me. Either I am too heavy or I just don't do it right. As a kid I used to wonder how burglars could creep round your house at night without waking you. No one could do it in our house – not even Albie. I decided not to be a burglar.

Jamie's stairs creak every one in three. Anyone straining their ears up there will hear me coming. I reach the landing and stand outside the door, key poised, listening. I hear someone move across the floor. Then something clunks. It could have been a glass put down upon a table. It could have been Jamie, padding softly around his flat so as not to disturb the neighbours. He could be waiting up for me.

So I slip his key into the lock, turn it, and step inside. The hall is empty. There are lights in the other rooms. I close the door.

When I move into the living room, someone is waiting. It isn't Jamie. It is a girl.

# 14

She stands small and thin by the curtained window, wearing a black sweatshirt, black wool leggings and pointed black suede shoes. Her hair is red, cut with a machete, and her face is china white.

We watch each other.

'Jamie in?' I ask.

She tilts her head. 'You a friend of his, or what?'

'A friend. And you?'

She nods, a short movement of her head, once up, once down. 'You usually call this late?'

'I'm expected.'

She nods again. 'Who are you, feller?'

'I came in with a key. Who are *you*?'

'I look after things.'

The state of this flat, that is not a proud claim to make. We hold eye-contact a few more seconds. I decide that whoever this hobgoblin is, her business is with Jamie and not with me.

'OK,' I say. 'Let's start again. My name is Floyd Carter. I'm a friend of his. I'm sleeping here tonight in that bed.' I point to the sofa. 'And where do *you* sleep?'

'You look like a cop to me.'

'I don't care what I look like.'

For another two seconds she studies me. Then she switches on a dumb schoolgirl smile that wouldn't fool a grandma and she says, 'Hey, you dealing, man? You got some bags?'

'Bags?'

'You know, man. I can pay.'

'You got the wrong man.'

She sighs. 'You really a friend of Jamie's?'

'I told you who I was,' I say quietly. 'Now it's your turn.'

She draws a breath. 'Look,' she says, 'it's a bad scene here. OK? Jamie is sick. Asked me to help.'

'What kind of sick?'

She points a finger to the bedroom door. She wears red nail varnish. 'Take a look.'

I start towards it and then stop. 'You first.'

A tired smile flickers across her face. 'You think I have a boyfriend in there, armed with a razor? Come on.'

She opens the door and strolls into Jamie's bedroom. I follow. His room looks as if the contents were emptied into it from ceiling height. Sprawled across the unmade bed is Jamie, a blanket over him. He lies on his side with his eyes shut and his mouth open.

The pale stringy redhead hovers over him, defiant but anxious. We stand on opposite sides of the bed. Jamie's head lies motionless between us on the dirty sheets. When I rest my hand on his forehead the skin feels cold and damp. He is hardly breathing.

I lift the blanket and peep underneath. Jamie is half dressed, one knee bent up towards his stomach. I let the blanket fall. 'Has he had an overdose?'

'How close a friend are you, feller?'

'Will you try *answering* questions instead of asking them?'

'OK. D'you want your coffee black or white?'

The girl's name is Eva. She sits me down in Jamie's heap of a living room while she clatters in the kitchenette. She doesn't take long. The kettle was already warm.

Eva ambles in with two mugs of steaming coffee. 'Can't offer you alcohol,' she says with a smile. 'It's all used up.'

'What exactly is wrong with Jamie?'

'You know he uses heroin?' Eva begins.

I blow on my coffee. I am sitting on the edge of the shakedown bed I had hoped to sleep in. Eva perches on the side of the mangey armchair.

'Well, what is wrong with him,' she tells me, 'is that because he couldn't find heroin he used a substitute. One he was not familiar with.'

I ask which one.

Eva goes back to the kitchenette, opens a cupboard, and returns holding a small white supermarket tub. According to the label, it contains bicarbonate of soda. Eva opens the lid and I glance inside. Down in the bottom of the tub lies a pinch of pink powder.

'Jamie thought he'd bought Diconal – dikes, you know? Pink tablets. He crushed them up. But this powder turns out to be Soneryl.'

'He used this instead of heroin?'

'Sure. He just didn't know that these tablets were barbies. He thought they were dikes. Maybe whoever sold them to him said that they were. Listen, dikes are an opioid, right, from opium? Like heroin. They have a similar effect. But Soneryl is a butobarbitone.'

'That's a big word.'

'Don't patronise me, feller.'

'Sorry.' I pause to sip some coffee. 'Where do you fit in this, Eva? Are you supplying, or what?'

'I'm just a friend.'

I can't blame her for not admitting anything: we have only just met. 'I'd better take a look at my patient,' she says.

I follow her back into Jamie's bedroom. The way she stoops over Jamie's body, I could believe he *is* her patient. First she opens one of his eyelids to check the pupil, then she puts her finger inside his mouth to make sure his tongue does not block the airway. Then she times his pulse.

'His skin is still clammy,' she tells me. 'But he's breathing better. Not so shallow now. The pulse is stronger too.'

'You a doctor?'

She ignores the question – a habit of hers, as I've learned already. 'He's pulling through, you know? That's good.'

'No chance of a coma?'

'Not now. There could have been. Barbies are strong sedatives, right? They come in tablets because you are meant to swallow them, not inject them in your vein.'

I wander around his untidy bedroom, wondering what I can do.

Eva says, 'The trouble with barbies is you have to be precise. If you inject the right amount you could feel like you had six glasses of your favourite tipple. You'd be so merry you could cry. But you get the dose wrong, slip in a pinch too much, and you're unconscious, just like that.'

She rearranges the way that Jamie lies on the bed, and she tidies the blanket over him. 'He'll survive,' she says. 'Now comes the boring part. I sit around here all night to make sure he doesn't have a relapse. It's still a risk, you know?'

I nod.

'He should be in the A and E,' Eva says. 'But that spells trouble, right? Registration, a load of questions, forms to fill. He'd be a marked man after that.'

She walks past me into the living room, and I follow like her student nurse.

Eva points to the sofabed. 'You said you were sleeping the night. There's your bed. There won't be any more excitement from here on.'

'Will you be in there with Jamie?'

She nods.

'I'll take a turn. You can't stay up all night.'

'Yes I can. No disrespect, feller, but if something happens, you gotta know what to do.'

'I'll wake you.'

'This is my job.'

She stands before me solid as a rivet. I ask, 'What *is* your job, Eva?'

She closes her eyes. 'It's late, man. We'll talk tomorrow, OK? You get some sleep.'

'I couldn't sleep now.'

She grins at me. 'You can have some Soneryl, if you want. That'll help you sleep.'

I don't take the Soneryl, of course, so I don't sleep. I can't drift off to dreamland on a shakedown settee while Eva paces round the flat, watching that Jamie does not slip into coma.

I take a walk.

Out in the damp night air I consider my position. You have to admit that so far I have played Honest Joe. I came back for my brother's funeral, and I wore my collar and tie. They told me someone killed him, and I didn't say a word. I have been done over in the street. I have been searched by the police. Throughout all of this have I reacted? Apart from losing my cool with Vinnie Dirkin in the Deptford Arms – which I think you'll agree is excusable – I have not hit back. I have been soft. I have been quiet. And you know what? It doesn't work.

When I reach the end of Jamie's street I pause at the corner. I turn to take a long look down. There are no people. On the empty pavements, street-lamps burn glumly. Cars sleep at the kerbsides. A cat prowls. One of the houses has a light on, because someone else can't sleep.

I turn up my collar, cross Lewisham Way, and head up the road towards Broadway. Twenty yards along, someone says my name.


# 15


There are two of them. Tucked into the shadows ahead of me along the pavement the two blacks had melted out of sight. Now they stand swaying in front of me, easy and relaxed in the dark. I listen for anyone else behind me, but hear nothing. These two are alone.

'We just coming to get you,' one of them says.

'You want something?'

'We found her for you.'

It takes my tired brain another second to realise that these are the two I met outside the Star and Garter. I relax. A little.

'You mean Tamsin Peters?'

'Who else – you lost more than one?'

'Where is she?'

The guy with the stubbly beard says, 'She around Woolwich somewhere by now. But we find her easy enough.'

'No address?'

'Who need an address, man? She on the river.'

They tell me that Tamsin is out on a boat at an all-night party with two or three hundred other people and a stack of booze.

'People buy a ticket, you know? Like a club. You coming, or what?'

I pause only a moment. 'I'm coming.'

'We drive you to the river. Then this man got a boat.'

'Where's your car?'

The way I look at it is this: I asked for help, and they gave it. Some things you can't do on your own. You have to join with people and work on it together. So now that these two have offered to help me, I should not be suspicious. Helping other people is not unnatural, is it?

Is it? It is a question I ask myself twice more: once inside their car, once when we stop. We are out in the Greenwich Marshes now, in those river wastelands behind the South Metropolitan Gasworks. The breeze is wet. Out here is dark and lonely, and as convenient a place as they could wish for to stick a knife in and leave me cold.

We walk along a footpath beside the river. It is muddy. Beside us, dark Thames water laps against the stonework. Across the river on the northern side it looks no brighter than over here. A few dim street-lamps in industrial estates. No cars. No pretty lights.

After about two hundred yards we stop. Tethered to a bollard is an outboard wooden dinghy. It rocks on the water.

'Let's go hunt ourselves a party,' says the one who owns the boat.

Chugging across the dark river with these two fellers in the outboard, I relax with them. The bearded guy gives his name as Rufus, and the boat-owner is called Des. They laugh at fetching Tamsin. What the girl needs, they say, is a firm father. Or a firm something. Then they watch how I react. Will I laugh with them or not? What do I really want with the girl?

They offer to come on board the party boat to help me find Tamsin, but I say no: they might scare her. 'You think *you* won't?' asks Des. They laugh again.

'What's the joke – something I should know?'

'No, man,' says Des soothingly. 'It's just she eighteen, you know what I mean? She at a party with her friends. What she going to think you've come to do?'

Des cuts the engine and we bob to a standstill. The big pleasure-boat looms over us, dark and noisy in the choppy water. It is moored here in the middle of the Thames about a hundred yards inside the Barrier. Little can be seen in the darkness. Either side of the river the banks are dead: dockyard slums and wasteland, waiting for the pendulum to swing back. Only the Barrier is new: a long row of big silver bathtubs upended in the water, waiting for that one freak high tide when it must stop London sinking beneath the rushing sea.

I suppose the party could have been louder. It could have been a lot more brightly lit. It could not have been more crowded. Music throbs and surges like an ocean swell: synthesisers and unyielding rhythm. Plastic bluebeat. Synthetic soul. Under strobe lights flickering like a tropical storm across the deck, the kids dance close-packed, sweating, eyes glazed against the lights. Around the dancers swills a crowd of onlookers, some watching, some drifting into corners. The air is damp, but it isn't raining. Smells of hot-dogs taint the air.

I lean my back against the side rail and look for Tamsin. Most of the kids seem about her age. There are a few older fellers trying to keep up. I don't envy them. Just watching it all is tiring. Kids are jumping, twitching, jerking their arms. You don't need a dance mistress to learn these steps – you need a gym.

There may be a dozen of the older fellers – early thirties, dressed younger, staring hungrily at the girls. They hang around the edges of the dance floor, drinking, jostled by gangs of teenagers milling around.

I ease away from the crowd along the railing, wondering where she will be. Des and Rufus have agreed to stay down in the outboard and wait. I have come on board alone.

Round the far side of the cabin-house, away from the dance deck, the lights are dimmer. Most parties when I was young, this is where you'd want to bring your girl – quiet, secluded, romantic view across the water. But I haven't got a girl, and I push my way among the couples along the narrow gangway like a wandering voyeur. I feel my age.

I complete the circuit around the deck area. Tamsin is not there. She must be downstairs.

The doorway leading down is narrow and jammed with kids. Some push their way in, some squeeze themselves out, some wait hoping that a tide may carry them through. I am bigger than any of them, but I think the reason they let me through is because I am older: they assume I am crew.

Stairs lead down to the bar area. It is as crowded as the dance deck, but more garishly lit. Down here are more of the older fellers, seeking comfort at the bar. I peer at the kids' faces, and feel like a teacher at an end-of-term disco. No Tamsin.

I edge round to the side corridor and watch the queues for the His and Hers. I get that teacher feeling again: the one where he walks unexpectedly into class, and after a sudden flurry the kids settle down and look innocent.

It's because I didn't join the queue. It's because I leant against the wall at the end of the corridor and watched them. Hallo, teacher.

At the front of the queue, but not part of it, is a lanky white guy about thirty years of age. He nudges the boy standing next to him. The boy strolls up. 'You want something?'

'I'm waiting.'

The boy looks into my face, wondering what to say next. 'I smell a cop,' he says.

'Get your nose fixed.'

80

'You're snooping, man. Get out of here.'

'Tell your friend I am standing here another five minutes. He can deal or walk. It's up to him.'

The boy goes back to deliver the message, and the lanky feller looks at me. So do the kids in the queue. One of them curses and walks away. Another follows. As the queue starts to break up, the lanky guy sends his runner back to me. 'If you don't get outa here, mister, we're gonna take you apart.'

'I look forward to it.'

But the lanky one will not come over. A man carrying merchandise will not walk into trouble. Whether I am police or not, he has too much to lose. He and the boy disappear deeper inside the boat. Half the kids stay to wait in line.

Suddenly, two girls fall laughing out of the Ladies into the narrow corridor. I push myself off from the wall and walk across.

'Was there a girl in there with you – half-caste – not black not white?' Half-caste. Forgive me, Tamsin.

The girls both look at me, and the giggler slows her giggling. 'There is a black girl,' she says.

'How black?'

She laughs outright. 'How black d'you want?'

Both of them find this funny. I ask if they think the black girl will come out soon.

'Why don't you go look?'

'We'll hold your hand,' splutters the giggler. They both hold their sides and laugh till tears run down their cheeks. Everyone begins to smile. Tension begins to melt.

'You lead the way,' I tell them.

The two girls totter to the lavatory door, laughing at the funniest thing they've seen since Grandma sat on her chihuahua. It's just as well they are going back inside the lavatory.

Until I come right inside, I am hidden from the wash basins. So the two white girls standing in front of the mirrors are caught by surprise. In the tiny room they both have their backs towards us. They freeze in mid-action. We watch their reflection and they watch ours. Each girl holds a little handbag mirror in the palm of one hand, and a coiled cylinder of paper in the other. One end of each paper cylinder hovers below their nostrils, the other hangs above the mirrors. On each shiny mirror is a thin line of white powder. Slowly, in unison, the two girls lower their hands. Their reflections stare at me.

'Don't laugh,' the giggler warns them. 'You'll blow your stuff away!'

My two start laughing again. The two by the mirror do not. As I take a step forward I say not to worry, I am not police. They keep their backs to me. My eyes are on the black girl sitting on the floor, slumped against the wall, her eyes closed. I reach out to her.

She feels cold. When I touch her cheek her head sways. Her mouth opens and she groans. It is a deep groan. 'What are you girls snorting?' I ask.

They giggle into the mirrors. I snap, 'Come on!'

One of the girls at the basin takes her finger out of her mouth, and simpers, 'Volatil. It's a kind of speed.'

She watches me in the mirror with big brown eyes. Slowly she turns towards me and raises her little hand-mirror so it is level with her chin. She places the end of her paper cylinder at the end of the line of powder. She pokes the other end inside her nostril. She keeps watching me. Daring me to stop her.

I don't try. I notice that her paper cylinder is a rolled-up five pound note. The girl inhales steadily through her nose. She takes several seconds to sniff up the whole of the line. Then she lowers the paper cylinder and stands watching me again. Nothing happens. She does not freak out. She doesn't stagger. She simply looks satisfied, as if she had just bitten into the most delicious slab of chocolate she ever tasted. She licks her lips. 'You know what it tastes like?' she asks dreamily.

'What?'

'Like ground-up brick dust, peed on by a cat.'

They burst out laughing. But then the second girl wails that she has laughed away her whizz powder. All four swarm like seagulls round the tiny sink.

The outside door opens. A new girl asks, 'You still got that man in there?'

I point to the black girl on the floor. 'We need some help. Get one of the stewards down here.'

Don't worry, the others say, they can deal with her. 'Is she the black girl you were looking for?' I shake my head.

'Then you can leave now,' the new girl says.

'She needs a doctor. Whatever it was that hit her, it wasn't speed.' I remember Jamie. 'Maybe barbiturates.'

'We can deal with her. Listen, you've had your peep inside the Ladies. So now scram, mister, OK?'

I hesitate, but against half a dozen girls in a tiny lavatory there is no contest. I slink out. In the corridor the youngsters give a sarcastic cheer.

*

The barman sighs and nods his head. 'No one hit her?'

'She overdosed on some kind of speed.'

'I'll get the medic.'

He slides towards his phone. I pull away through the crowd to the narrow flight of stairs. That girl will have a mother like Suzie. She'll want someone to help her little girl.

Waiting for me on deck is the black guy with the beard, the one called Rufus. 'We thought we lost you, man. Thought you staying here the night.'

'I ran into trouble.'

'You bringing her home?'

'If I find her.'

'Why, she only dancing. She right here all the time.'

The man is right. Out in the middle of the crowded dance floor, Tamsin Peters bounces with the rest. She wears a white childlike party frock, edged with lace, stiffened with gauze, decorated with flounces and bows. It should look ridiculous, and yet somehow, on her slim little body, that laughable, crushable, rub-your-face-in-it white dress makes Tamsin look frail, in need of protection, as sexy as a sprite.

She does not look tired. Three o'clock in the morning, bopping through a weird limb-jerking dance routine, and she looks like a child at playschool. Half these kids do. They could be at a skipping game in the playground. Other kids look exhausted. Sweat pours off them, their faces crease, their dancing slips out of step. They slow down. I see a boy's shoulders sag as they lose their strength. His arms flop loosely. His feet wearily repeat the old pattern, dragging him round the dance floor in a last slow spin. He is like an insect caught in fly spray, whirling crazily, while the poison spreads paralysis slowly through his veins.

As I push through the dancers towards Tamsin, the boy sinks helpless to the deck. Two men from the side come in to drag him away. I hope they're friends.

Now that I am closer to Tamsin I can see that she is more tired than I had thought. She smiles but her face is strained, and she is not smiling at me. She is smiling into space. She looks as if she hasn't slept these two whole days. I doubt she has.

When I position myself in front of her, she barely notices. Her face bobs up and down. I say, 'Hallo, Tamsin, remember me? It's Floyd Carter.'

She says, 'I know.'

'I came to fetch you.'

'Come on, dance, you Floyd. You Floyd.'

'We're going home.'

Her face tilts to look up into the sky where there ought to be stars. Exasperation gnaws at the edges of her gaze. 'Just move, Floyd. Feel it talking.'

She keeps her head up. She keeps the smile on her lips. She won't let me intrude on what she feels. I accept that. At this time of night, after two days away, I don't have to drag her immediately off the floor.

'Dance with me, Floyd.'

I make a stab at it. I am the sort of man who enjoys dancing, but these steps are outside my ken. I don't know the rules.

'That's Boogie you're doing, you Floyd.'

'It's what I know.'

She giggles. 'Then I'll have to take you in hand, won't I?'

Look at this kid: eighteen years old, three in the morning, hasn't slept for two nights. Pooped on pep pills, has a mother worried sick, and she is going to take me in hand!

'We're leaving now.'

'You Floyd.' She laughs to the inky sky.

'Come on.'

'One dance. It hasn't finished.'

This is the kind of music that never does finish. There hasn't been a break since I came on board.

'We are going home.'

Tamsin glowers up at me. She has wide brown eyes.

Then she opens her pretty red lips and smiles with pretty white teeth. In that crushable taffeta ballet dress she has no right to look so cute. Not at this time of night.

'I'm not coming, you know, Floyd. We'll have fun here.'

'We are leaving now.'

'We are not.' When a girl smiles this beautifully, she is about to throw a fit.

'Please, Tamsin.' I try it gently.

'I'll scream.'

'I thought you would.'

Swiftly I bend forward and grab her by the waist. I lift her soft and easy as a male ballet dancer would lift Giselle. I drop her across my shoulder and walk away.

She starts kicking.

I smile at the watching people and say she is always this way at bedtime. Tamsin screams.

'I'll smack your bottom. In front of all these people.'

The kids laugh at us. Because I am grinning, they think we're

84

fooling. I continue making light of it. Tamsin kicks and splutters. She wriggles in my grasp.

When we reach the hand-rail where the ladder is, I pat her lace backside.

'Hold tight now, Tamsin honey. We're going down.'

Trudging along the footpath through the Greenwich Marshes, Tamsin slows with every step. Inside the jacket that I lent her, she shivers. Without it, I shiver too. The four of us plod silently through the darkness: Rufus and Des camouflaged in the night, me in my shirt sleeves, Tamsin in that white taffeta frock beneath my jacket. Her legs look thin and cold. Her little frou-frou skirt bobbles like an ostrich's rump.

Halfway along the path, I lift her up a second time. This time I do not fold her across my shoulder. I carry her like a baby in my arms.

In the car she falls asleep.

Suzie comes into the room with a mug of hot chocolate. She puts it in my hands. 'Don't get up,' she says.

I am sitting in an armchair in her tiny front room. I have my shoes off. Suzie has lit the fire, and has set one small light to glow in the corner of the room. My eyes droop.

She sits for a moment on the arm of the chair, and rests her hand on my neck. It feels cool. 'You look exhausted,' Suzie says.

'Mm.'

'You'd better sleep here.'

'Mm.'

'You can use my bed. Both the other beds are occupied.'

Tamsin never really awoke. I carried her in her crumpled dress up the short flight of stairs, and laid her on her bed. When I left the room, Suzie went in and closed the door. Ludo was hovering on the landing in his size forty-six pyjamas, looking for ways that he could help. I said we should leave Tamsin and her mother to themselves. He came downstairs with me. When Suzie finally emerged she sent him back to bed.

Now she and I sit in her little front room like middle-aged parents. The kids are tucked beneath their duvets, and I have a mug of chocolate.

Suzie leans down to brush her lips against my cheek. 'Thanks again,' she says.

Then she stands up and crosses to the other armchair. She sits in it and drinks from a china cup.

'What's that?' I ask lazily. 'Chocolate?'

'Coffee. I won't sleep now.'

Outside it is still dark. The low light here in the room seems to draw the walls in closer. I feel cosy in my armchair.

'If you'd made me a cup of coffee,' I say, 'I could have walked home.'

'Aren't my sheets clean enough for you?'

I grunt.

'What are you trying to prove, Carter? You're not going to walk off now into the rising dawn. Even Clint Eastwood waits till sunset.'

'I don't want to be a nuisance.'

She laughs. 'You're so damned independent, aren't you? You spend all night looking for my daughter. You drag her off a boat in the middle of the river. But you don't want to be a nuisance? Get upstairs and go to bed.'

I grin at her. 'I'll drink my chocolate first. It'll give me the energy to get up there.'

'And who was going to walk all the way home? I thought you said your house wasn't safe? That's why Ludo's here.'

'No one will be at my place at this time of night.'

'Nor will you. What happened to this friend you were supposed to be sleeping with – she throw you out?'

'I didn't say it was a she.'

'Just checking, Carter.' She smiles at me. 'Do you want to go up to bed now?'

'Is that an invitation?'

'The state you're in? You won't make it up the stairs.'

Her room is the colour of russet apples. Her bed is soft and smells of her body. I lie naked beneath her duvet, sliding my legs slowly across her undersheet, imagining they trace the patterns that she made.

Through the curtains a soft grey light is creeping. Two cars drive past. Occasionally I hear Suzie downstairs clink a piece of crockery. She runs a tap. A door closes.

I lie dozing, unable to fall asleep. I wonder whether later she might slip back up the stairs and come to me.

I fall asleep.

# 16

Eva's black cat-suit looks as if she slept in it. Her face is crumpled too.

'Our man's all right, considering.' Her red hair stands erect as bristles on a scrubbing brush. She leads me through to Jamie's bedroom, which she has tidied. Jamie is propped up in a neatly made bed on which lie two discarded magazines of which he might have read the covers. He looks pale. His black hair needs a wash.

He welcomes me with a weak grin and a feeble cough. When I quip that he sounds as if he has just come round from anaesthetic, Eva says, 'He has.'

'I brought you these flowers.'

I don't need to tell him this because I am clutching them upright in my hand. I hold the bunch stiff as a tennis racket waiting for a serve.

'A man with flowers,' laughs Eva. 'Now that's something.'

'Thanks, mate,' Jamie says.

Eva whisks them away from me. 'Don't often see a guy bring another man flowers. It's kinda nice.' She leaves the room.

Jamie grins his tired grin. His teeth look green. 'Flowers, eh?'

'This place could use them. How d'you feel?'

He shrugs. 'I got the shakes, my throat's sore, my head's busting apart. What else d'you wanna know?'

'You were worse last night.'

He nods and looks away. 'It's bloody freezing in here. Eva's all right, isn't she?'

'She saved your life.'

'I'd have slept it off.' He grins defiantly as Eva sweeps in through the door.

'You'd have slept right through your funeral service,' she says. She has my flowers in a vase. 'Barbies are a bad scene, Jimbo.'

'Pinkies,' mutters Jamie.

'Pink Soneryl. There's a barrowload on the streets right now. Someone must have bust a factory. The things are turning up all over.'

'He said they were Diconal.'

'You're a prat then, aren't you, Jimbo? You believe everything you hear on the street? What was the feller's name?'

'I got a headache, Eva.'

'Surprise, surprise. You asking for a pill already?'

'Yeah.'

'It's kinda early.'

'Just gimme the damn thing.'

Jamie opens his eyes and sticks his hand out. He glares at Eva with something close to hatred. She shrugs. Out of her black handbag she brings a packet of Silk Cut cigarettes. Inside the package are no cigarettes – only little parcels wrapped like toffees in bright coloured paper. She unwraps a blue one, revealing a dozen capsules – orange and turquoise. Four of these capsules Eva shakes out into her hand, and places on his chest of drawers. She rewraps the rest, slips them back inside the cigarette packet, and drops the pack inside her handbag.

Then she hands a capsule to Jamie.

'These have to last till tomorrow lunchtime. If you score anything else, you stop taking them. You hear me?'

'Yeah, yeah.'

'Only one now. Drink lots of water.'

Jamie snaps open the capsule and sprinkles its contents into the palm of his hand. He frowns at the little mound of coarse white powder, then claps his hand to his mouth, and swallows. He grimaces. He grabs the glass of water, and drinks. He grimaces again. He closes his eyes and opens them. Then he licks the residue off his palm, and swallows the rest of the water. 'How long will it take?' he asks.

'About twenty minutes. Less, 'cos you broke the shell.'

'Tastes bloody awful.'

'That's why they wrap it in a shell, Jimbo. You're supposed to swallow the capsule whole.'

'No point waiting for the goo to melt. My head hurts *now*.'

Jamie leans back against his grey pillows, his eyes closed and his face screwed up. I ask Eva what she gave him.

'Tuinal. It's a barbiturate. Not too strong.'

'Wasn't that what he OD'd on?'

'He's come through that now.'

'Why give him another?'

Jamie snarls at us from the pillow. 'Will you go talk about me somewhere else? My head's thumping.'

'Come on,' Eva says, and we leave the room. I follow her to the kitchenette.

'We have to ease him down gently,' Eva says. 'If we made him do cold turkey straight after the barbs, he'd get the DTs, you know? Could throw a fit. Choke on his own vomit. You wouldn't want that to happen to your friend.'

'Is he on barbies too?'

'No man. He takes four pills today, two tomorrow, then he stops. Understand me? I hate barbs.'

'But you carry them.'

'I bought a few, just in case. They will wind down the pain. Only cost him a couple of quid.'

'You sell these pills?'

'What d'you think – I'm a charity? This is an emergency supply, you know? Like the flying doctor.'

'Private medicine.'

'I ain't National Health. Jimbo has to pay.' She hands me a cup of coffee. She did not make one for Jamie. 'Caffeine is a drug, feller. The man has enough in his body as it is.'

'A cup of coffee won't hurt him.'

'You ever drink expresso? It gives you a lift, right? Straight away. You put caffeine behind some other drug you've got inside you, and it gives that drug a kick. It's a catalyst. Shoots the other drug round your body all the faster.'

I sip from the cup that she made for me. I decide that coffee tastes good, whatever she says. 'What you're doing, Eva, is handing me the old "everyone's a junkie" line, right? We're all hooked on something: coffee, tea, cigarettes, alcohol.'

'Or the drugs your doctor prescribes. You know – the "safe" ones? People get a script from the doctor, right? They like what the drug does, they get repeats. They are hooked. Except they don't realise they are hooked.'

'What drugs are *you* on, Eva?'

'Everyone's a junkie, feller. You just said so yourself.'

# 17

I sit in the back of the white Mercedes with Huey Carmichael. Beneath his white linen suit he wears a turquoise woollen rollneck. It clashes with his skin colour, making it more dunglike than usual. I can't shake that comparison: the way his skin glistens, the soft-packed oozing quality that he exudes. When I breathe in beside him I expect to recoil from the smell.

But he smells of citrus.

Dixie the minder is in the front seat, driving. He wears a pale grey striped suit, white shirt and silk floral tie. His black hair lies in a hundred casual curls. Some guys would spend an hour teasing each curl into place. Not Dixie. I bet he just runs a comb through.

These are a couple of expensive lookers, all right. When we step out of the white Merc, people will wonder which one is boss. But I am sure Carmichael knows who killed my brother. I have only to get in close and I'll find out.

There are two possibilities: either Carmichael himself had Albie killed, or he knows who ordered it. He sent for me to meet him. He pressed me to join his gang. Would he have done these things if he'd killed Albie?

I think Carmichael wants to test me. If I pass his little test, he may talk. I have no interest in Carmichael's enterprises, but keeping in seems to be the only way to find what happened. And why. Until I know why Albie died, I won't know whether Ludo and I are also in danger. Until I know why Albie died, I can't wrap this business up. So I have to pass Carmichael's test. He holds the key.

He is the only lead I've got.

We have come north through the Blackwall Tunnel beneath the river, along East India Dock Road and into the Isle of Dogs. On my right through the car window I see what money has done here. Flattened out the docks with a giant's bulldozer. Laid two square miles of building site. Brought in cranes and preformed building blocks. Built a plague of offices.

Look at them. Brightly coloured, futuristic; made of metal, gaudy plastic and glass. When they do use bricks here, they paint them brick red so you will know they are bricks, then they stick them on to the front outside walls as an ornamental display. Every building seems designed to house desks and computers. But I remember when people lived here.

We stop the car below the Blackwall Basin, in front of one of the few remaining terraces. These friendly brown houses won't last much longer: three are boarded up, the others prepared for siege. Two tall cranes loom above their roofs. Across the fronts of the tired houses drapes a long banner: 'LDC And The Council: The Blighters Of This Terrace'.

Carmichael glances up at the grubby banner, and he shrugs. He is not affected. These are not his customers. These are not who we've come to see.

'Time to introduce yourself,' he says. I step from the car. Dixie climbs out to join me, but Carmichael stays inside. He nods at us through the car window, then snaps shut the central-locking, making himself secure. The sound of the four doors clunking is like rifle-bolts slamming home.

Dixie says to follow him.

We stroll back along the main road, across the drawbridge, towards the first spot on the strip – a small expensive development where rich people live. At the entrance, a smart blue and white placard announces its name: 'Cotton's Landing – A New World'. I guess it is.

These immaculate little new houses are like modern fortresses. They remind me of tiny wooden houses on a Monopoly board. Over-simplified. Pretend. Across the choppy water from them stands Billingsgate Fish Market, smartened up to tone with the neighbourhood. Its bright-painted metal girders hang like an awning above its roof. The market hall looks like a trade marquee. But it isn't. It is real. Every day, the porters work there from five till noon. Yuppies won't like living across from all that noise. They won't appreciate the five a.m. early call.

'You see him there?' asks Dixie.

The guy is a businessman. He is in his late twenties, very smart, with beautifully polished hair. He is dressed like Dixie, because around here suit and tie is the uniform.

The three of us drift together, as if we met quite by chance near the water's edge. The man keeps his eye on me. Dixie tells him I'm OK.

The man asks my name.

'John Burns,' I say quickly. 'I'll be your touch from now on.'

All this is said so nonchalantly, with so much gazing across the water and into the cloudy sky, that a spectator might be convinced we really did bump into each other in our lunch break. We admire the view. Flocks of pale grey gulls skim low above the brown water.

'You brought the stuff?' the businessman asks Dixie.

I say that I am the one who brought it. The man nods. 'Does the deal stay the same?' he asks.

'Only the face has changed.'

The man licks his lips uncertainly. He asks Dixie, 'This is kosher, yes?'

'Straight up,' says Dixie.

'I don't know.'

'This is me standing here,' Dixie says patiently. 'You know me. I introduce you to my friend—'

'John Burns,' I supply.

'There, you see,' babbles the businessman. 'You don't even know his name. What kind of friend is that?'

'A business friend,' says Dixie. 'We don't need names. I don't even know *your* name, do I?'

'I told you my name.' The guy glances at me again.

'I don't know it's your real name,' says Dixie.

I watch this played out before me and I keep my own mouth shut. I just want to pass Carmichael's test.

Dixie says, 'If you don't want the stuff, we leave. We have a busy day.' He means it. The man can see he does. He reaches out his hand to touch Dixie on the sleeve.

'I'll take a sample,' he says.

'What's the matter – don't you trust me?'

I can sense when a scene is about to turn ugly, so I interrupt. 'Are you dealing or not? The minimum's an ounce.'

The neat young businessman stares at me. He tries to peer right through my eyeballs to read what is written on my retina. 'Same price as before?'

'Same price, same quality. Thousand an ounce.'

He tries to look as if he is considering the fairness of the price, but while he hesitates his head has started nodding. 'OK. I'll take it.'

'Just one ounce?'

He nods again. I pull the *Daily Telegraph* out of my coat pocket and as Dixie explained to me I point to an article on the front page. The man leans forward, grasps the paper as if to take a closer look at it, and removes the small white packet of cocaine from behind my thumb. Then I take back the paper. While I flick through to the centre pages, the businessman puts his hands in his pockets and waits. I give him back the open paper. When he brings his hands out of his pockets, the newspaper masks the brown envelope that he is holding. He pretends to read an article. I watch the seagulls. Then I take back my *Daily Telegraph*, fold it to hide his envelope, and return the paper to my pocket.

'You see,' I say. 'Nothing has changed.'

He nods his head. 'I'll see you again, then, will I?'

'Don't be so nervous next time. You sure one ounce is enough?'

Now that he has the cocaine in his pocket, his confidence has returned. It's as if he'd just had a snort of it. 'No problem,' he says. 'This'll keep them happy for a while.'

He steps back, one hand rammed in his trouser pocket, the other punching in the air. 'We'll go for it, right?'

'Right.'

'Right,' says Dixie.

The man blows.

Carmichael pushes the button to make his rear window glide down.

'How did you get on?' His eyes are on Dixie, standing behind me.

'The man was nervous,' I say. 'Only bought one ounce.'

'Little and often,' says Carmichael. 'Now for the gun.'

He says it real casual. I glance out of the corner of my eye towards Dixie. He says, 'OK.'

Neither of them seems to find it in any way remarkable. I make sure that my face shows nothing too. Though this is the first time they have mentioned a gun.

'Come on,' says Dixie.

We leave Carmichael snug in the back of his Mercedes, reading *Daltons Weekly*. We cut through Managers Street into Coldharbour – a narrow street, hard on the riverside, one of those enclosed lanes you find around docks. Half of its houses are boarded up. Caravans stand on muddy plots of waste land. Round here used to be where working men lived. See it now before it's pulled down.

Hidden on the bottom corner stands an old black and white pub, backing on to the river. It is called The Gun.

I see.

We buy two pints of Taylor Walker and take them out on to the rear balcony. There would be a fine view across the Thames, except that all there is to see opposite is the gasworks and Delta Wharf, a place that has not been prettified. Heaps of sand lie scattered about it like soft pyramids. Cranes tower above. A dozen old boats dry out on its sloping river shore.

Around the other side of that point of land, round where the river bends back on itself and we cannot see, lie the Greenwich Marshes. As the crow flies, they are half a mile away. The Thames Barrier is half a mile further towards the sea. But from over here on the island, those south-of-the-river places are in another world. Inhabited by another people – my people. I have been back in London long enough to know my place.

In The Gun, whatever lunchtime crush there was is thinning out. Dixie and I are alone at the south end of the balcony, breathing in the strong Thames air.

'That dealer seemed worried,' I say.

Dixie sips at his beer. 'You trade around here, you trust nobody. And never trust a straight. They don't trust each other.'

'You think that schmoe is in the nearest lavatory, checking out his stuff?'

Dixie shrugs. 'Would he know what to look for? It's eighty per cent talc anyway. Lemon fragrance.'

All cocaine is diluted for the street, usually one to five. It can be cut with many things – baby powder, glucose, icing sugar, flour. For snorting up your nose you want cocaine about twenty per cent. At that bulk it is also easier to divide into little bags.

Sipping at his Taylor Walker's, Dixie nods at the view. 'That bend in the old river ought to keep this pub nice and sheltered. But it doesn't. When the wind comes up, you smell the gasworks.' He sips beer again.

'D'you live around here, Dixie?'

'Across the way.'

A man materialises beside us so unobtrusively I don't realise he is there until he speaks. He is the next breadhead – about my age, with grizzled hair. He is loose-limbed, smart casual in his dress. He might work in advertising, if he is not too old.

'Two, if you've got them,' he requests.

Dixie introduces me.

'John Burns?' the man queries. 'That's a famous name on the Isle of Dogs. Union leader in the last century.'

'My dad was a docker.'

'I bet he wasn't called John Burns.' The man grins. 'Have a read of my newspaper. Nineteen hundred in the envelope.'

He hands me a folded *Guardian* so we can work the indoor drop. Dixie is proud of these handover tricks. He invented them himself. There are just the two.

The Indoor is where the man hands me his newspaper at the table and I unfold it sitting down. The envelope which he has placed inside slips beneath the table to my lap. I uncrease the paper and open it across the table as if to read. The bottom half hangs down, allowing me to transfer the envelope to inside my coat. I exchange this particular envelope for two one-ounce packets and hide them in my hand. Then I refold the newspaper and return it. In a perfect world, he would simply stuff the paper straight into his pocket. He would know I had placed two packets there inside. But this is not a perfect world. Those two tiny packages represent nearly two thousand pounds. They are so small it is quite possible a guy could drop one. But if the breadhead was to walk away and tell me later that he found only one packet, what would I say? You must

94

have dropped one. So the procedure is that when I return his folded newspaper, I place the packages in his palm. Then he knows that he has got them. I know it too.

'How about a bigger discount?' he suggests. 'I buy two ounces and I save only a hundred pounds. That's not a lot. What's the discount if I buy four?'

'I'll talk to my supplier.'

'Appreciate that.' He stands up, and he smiles. 'Because I'd prefer to continue buying from your company – Mr Burns. But I have to keep an eye on prices. Understand?'

'Found another source?'

He shows me the clean pink palms of his hands, and he raises his bushy eyebrows. 'London is a big city, isn't it? See what you can do.' Another smile, then he walks off along the balcony and back inside The Gun.

'What d'you think?' I ask.

'I think he's testing out the new man. But he's a regular. Carmichael wouldn't want to lose him.'

I try probing about Carmichael. 'How come Huey doesn't carry drugs, yet he wears a gun?'

Dixie smiles. He says, 'Everyone has a weakness.'

Sitting beside Carmichael in the back of his white Mercedes, I pretend that I am comfortable. Dixie is driving. Carmichael seems in an expansive mood and talks philosophy.

'We run a business, you understand me? Several products, several markets. They overlap. The market on the Island takes a single product – cocaine. No heroin, speed or MCD. People here don't want downers, they want kicks. And they don't like speed because they think it is not a pleasant stuff to sniff. Like ground-up razor blades, hey? People don't like the smell. Coke is cleaner, they say, more subtle, less demanding. It costs more, but money doesn't worry people here. They *expect* pleasure to cost money. They know the Lady is an aristocrat.'

He is talking to me as if I could be a partner in his business: he is drawing me in. So I try to sound interested. I say, 'Cocaine is sophisticated.'

'Customers think so. That's what matters. That's why they pay six times as much for it. These are the people who buy an exclusive wine when others buy Spanish red. They still get drunk on it. It's the same with drugs: coke is refined, speed is effective. Speed keeps you up there longer – five hours, maybe more. Take a snort of cocaine and you're down inside one.

'But for these people in their high-pressure offices, that's an advantage. Coke gives them a quick high and a safe return. It gets them up through a business meeting and brings them back down to earth when the crisis is passed. Christ, if they took speed they could be high six hours. They'd go home, not get to sleep. Come in to work next morning looking shit. Cocaine is right for these people. That's why they buy it.

'Cocaine is a fashionable product, right? Listen, d'you know anything about modern marketing? Every product has what they call a life cycle, like a curve on a graph, rising up from development on to a plateau of maturity, until finally the product curve declines. Most products have that life cycle. Very few exceptions. Occasionally a product may be reborn. You know: it had declined, it looked dead, but really it was sleeping. Cocaine was reborn that way.

'What you also have to realise, Floyd, is that *markets* have a life cycle too. They have to be sought out, developed, milked in their maturity, then kept fertile as long as we can. Here on the Island we have a mature market. It needs a particular strategy. If you're going to work it, Floyd, you need to know what our strategy is.'

I nod wisely. I don't say anything. I don't want to stop his flow.

'A new market initially needs three things: investment, faith and vision. Then, to help it develop, we spread the word. Get publicity. Convert the trendsetters, hey? When our market becomes mature, it needs firm management. Finally, as our market dies – and all markets die eventually – we cut our costs and squeeze out our last profits. Squeeze out every drop.

'As I say, we need different strategies. I need different people to control those strategies. I need visionaries to see opportunities, I need trailblazers for when an area takes off, I need a firm hand when it matures.

'You, Floyd, will be my firm hand. Dixie can set trends. Dixie will move north into the city to bring new markets on, while *you* run the Isle of Dogs. The yuppies on this island have already been converted. The networks are all laid down. But the customers need to remain impressed. They need to see a tough manager – someone like you, hey? – so they never think that the organisation has gone soft. People must believe that you're such a tough shit you would snap them in half if they sneezed. And you know what? The yuppies will like it. They like dealing with professionals. They want to be part of where it's at. You see why I want you in my team?'

We are emerging from the south end of the Blackwall Tunnel, back on our side of the river. Dixie concentrates on his driving. But

I can see his eyes in the little mirror. He is grinning. He has heard it all before, and he has his own opinion. I turn to Carmichael.

'Why me? Tough guys are ten a penny.'

'Sure they are. But you're not from the ten-a-penny tray, Floyd. I remember you from when I was a kid, back in the days when you don't remember me.' Carmichael smiles at the extraordinariness of that idea. 'And I have heard people keeping your name alive all the years you've been away. I know what people think of you. You have an image. You have brand identity. You are the sort of manager that I need.'

# 18

If I want to break a lock on someone's front door, I can think of three ways. One is I pick it – for which I need the right jiggler. Two is I break a pane of glass, reach through and turn the knob. The third is I use a Lloyd. I have to try this method because I don't have a jiggler and a smashed glass is hard to hide. My Lloyd comes from Deptford market. It is a six by four-inch rectangle of white celluloid, for display on a fruit and veg stall. It says 'Don't squeeze me till I'm yours'.

I slide it through the crack at the edge of Vinne Dirkin's front door and work it round to the bolt of the Yale. Celluloid is good for this. It is flexible enough to bend around the channel in the woodwork, and hard enough to push back the steel Yale bolt. You know how the bolt sits, with the curved edge towards you and the flat one faced away? Your Lloyd pushes against that curved edge and eases it back into its slot. The Lloyd is firm enough to hold the bolt there when you push open the door. Then you're in.

I close his door quietly and creep gently along the hall. I don't think he is home. Ten minutes ago I knocked at the front door, waited in the street. Nothing happened. It never does. Three times I've come round here, and three times no one answered. Either no one lives here, or they don't want visitors.

Ten minutes ago I walked to the end of the street and waited. No one showed. So I came back and let myself in. It is towards eleven o'clock at night. He must come home sometime.

Someone lives here: it is almost furnished. Downstairs I find a through room, a kitchen and a john. The through room is where

Dirkin lolls around, watches TV and takes exercise at the dartboard. The place looks like an empty public bar.

I creep upstairs.

Two bedrooms, a bathroom and unoccupied. The bathroom is sparse and may occasionally get used. Say once a week. The bedrooms get used more often. Both hold an unmade double bed.

Vinnie Dirkin does not look married. I guess this place is shared by two men, both with a double bed. Both optimistic.

I start opening their drawers. The contents don't tell me much, except both men have a feeble taste in clothes. There *are* two guys living here, but I don't know whose clothes are whose.

I come downstairs.

The problem with two men living here is I don't know who will come home first. It could be Vinnie or the other guy or both of them together. I sit and think.

Suppose it is the other guy – what do I do? Do I tell him I'm waiting for my friend Vinnie? Suppose they come together?

If we're going to have a fight, I'd better get in first. But I haven't come to crunch the guy, I want to hear him talk. Can I persuade him to talk without crunching him?

I guess not.

I have been sitting in this armchair for about an hour. It smells of damp clothes. I remember we used to have an old Labrador cross that used to sleep under the kitchen table, till it finally gave up and died. The dog smelt like this chair.

Albie used to like that dog. He would drag it out for exercise every day. Their favourite walk was down across the waste ground along Deptford Creek. The dog always ended up in the water. Maybe that was why it died, rubbish leaching into that creek. On fine days they would walk the length of the creek, down past where it trickled under Deptford Bridge into the sports field at Saint Johns. They'd look at the waterworks and come back.

He was my big brother and now he's dead. Somebody singled him out and smacked him with a car. Why did they do that?

He wasn't carrying anything. Those guys didn't stop the car, jump out and pick up a parcel. Ludo said that they just left him there. Like an accident. Like it was meant to look an accident. Hit and run. The police would go through the motions, but they wouldn't make a meal of it. It wasn't murder, the police would say, just an accident. A misdemeanour has been committed but the offender has not been caught.

What had Albie done?

And why did they ignore Ludo?

I guess that part is not hard to answer. They thought Ludo was too stupid to be a threat to them. A big idiot is what they'd say. And it wasn't Ludo they had a quarrel with. He was just a bystander. They could leave him gawping from the pavement while they accelerated away.

I sit here wondering how much Vinnie Dirkin knows about the murder. He and his friends claim Albie owed them ten thousand pounds. That doesn't give them a motive. If a guy owes you that sort of money, you do not squash him with your car. Not if you want to be paid.

So the question I am wondering is this: does the person Albie owed money to – the man behind Vinnie Dirkin – know who it was that killed him? Because it seems that Albie got himself into trouble two times over – once for the money, once for something else. The two things ought to be connected. Maybe he got ten thousand from one place so he could pay off someone else. But if he paid off that someone else, why would they kill him?

It does not make sense. The only thing that is certain is that Albie died in debt. Dirkin says that the debt has passed to me.

I'll feel a whole lot easier when I hear the name of Dirkin's boss. One look at the fleapit that Dirkin dosses in convinces me that if Albie owed ten grand to anyone, it was not to him. Dirkin would be lucky if he was owed a ten-pound note.

Someone opens the front door.

I am into the kitchen like a mouse slips in its hole. I stand out of sight. The man closes the front door, passes through the hall, and enters the room that I just left. He sounds like he lives here. He doesn't talk.

The man crosses the through room, comes into the kitchen and turns on the light. It is Vinnie Dirkin. We look at each other.

Dirkin glances quickly around the kitchen. Maybe he is looking for a knife he can grab. But there isn't one. So I wait.

'What d'ya want?' he asks. His eyes still dart around the room looking for a weapon. Or for an exit.

'How d'ya get in here?' A time-wasting question while he thinks what to do. There is nothing he can do. I continue watching him, knowing that my silence is more effective than anything I could say. I am like a spectre in his house, come to claim his soul. All we need is a clock somewhere to chime the midnight hour.

'You get outa here. You hear me?'

I nod, and start towards him.

'Get out!' He is shouting now.

'Sit down, Dirkin.'

He hesitates. He wants to defy me, but he thinks better of it. He might feel safer sitting down.

I walk round behind his chair, place my hands on his shoulders, and squeeze them gently. They are thin and bony. I don't touch his neck, just his shoulders. He twists around. I tell him to face front. He does so. I stand behind him and feel him shivering. 'Start talking,' I say.

'What about?'

I stay silent.

'What d'ya want me to say?'

Instead of replying, I massage the base of his neck.

'I dunno nothing. We just delivered a message.'

'Whose message?'

'I dunno—'

My hands close around his neck. His own hands involuntarily rise to clasp at my fingers. I tighten my grip. 'Put your hands down, Dirkin.' But of course he won't. He tries to loosen my fingers.

'Who was it from?'

We are struggling now. Suddenly I let go. I jerk my arms wide, break his grip.

'Don't get up!' I warn, but he does. He dives from the chair and hurtles to the door. We reach it together.

I slam a blow into his cheek, and it knocks his head against the wall. With my other hand, I grab his throat.

'Don't let me get angry, Vinnie.'

I keep my hand upon his throat and haul him stumbling to the centre of the room. I stand facing him, one foot away, my fingers on his larynx.

'You tell me who sent the message, or I hurt you till you do. Who was it?'

He shakes his head. I increase my grip. Again his hands rise to pull at mine. I raise my other fist nine inches from his face and he shrieks, crossing both arms before his face to ward off the blow. He is terrified.

'Tell me, you stupid bastard.' I pull one of his arms away and I glare at him. His eyes bulge. His head nods. When he tries to say something I relax my grip. He backs off a pace from me and stands sobbing.

'It ain't worth it, Vinnie. Just tell me who it was.'

'All right. I'll tell you.' His breath keeps catching in his throat. He is still shivering. 'His name is Richardson.'

*

Tod Richardson. The man is Neanderthal. His whole family is evil. Theirs is the sort of dynasty that in some small corners of the world forms dictatorships of terror. Tod has a brother in Gartree Maximum Security, and another drowned in the Thames. He had been dropped there in a sack.

Time was when the Richardson clan could scare this area witless. People pale at the name even now. But the clan is broken – they belonged to a primitive dark age. Brute strength and viciousness aren't the powers that they were.

Though you don't ignore them.

Discovering that the man who has been passing threats to me is the mighty Tod Richardson will not help me sleep peacefully in my bed. Runners like Vinnie Dirkin I can handle. Tod Richardson I cannot. He is not the sort of man you wait to see what he will do to you. Nor do you try to run away. You listen carefully to what he wants. And you do it.

'Tod Richardson,' I repeat, speaking flatly, nodding to Vinnie Dirkin as if I'd guessed it all the while. Richardson. He is the one to see. I explain to Vinnie Dirkin that we are going round there. He does not seem pleased.

He is not eager at all.


The Richardsons have a long, single-storey ranch of a place in Blackheath. They would do. It has a wrought-iron garden gate flanked by two brick pillars and an entry phone, the whole thing set out as for a country house. Except their garden drive is only thirty yards long.

The gate is locked.

'Gimme a leg-up over the wall.'

'I ain't coming in there,' says Vinnie. 'Bastards will kill me.'

'Clasp your fingers together.'

I put my toe into his cupped hands and hoist myself up on to the wall. I sit astride it and reach down for him.

'Not bloody likely,' he declares, and he runs. He just takes off. This being the first moment that I have not had my hand on him, he seizes the opportunity. He gambles that I will not leap down and pursue him along the pavement. And he's right. A big reason for bringing him was so he would not call Tod Richardson on the telephone and inform him I was coming. It's too late to do that now.

I jump softly down into Richardson's front garden. The house is in darkness, unlike the garden. Halfway up the little tarmac driveway I trip a sensor. Lights come on. From beneath the low rain gutters two floodlights blaze down and blind my eyes. Who would have guessed it? Tod Richardson protects himself from burglars.

No burglar would be that foolish.

I ring at the door. It makes a two-note chime, like in the Avon commercial. Dogs start screaming from around the back. I step away from the front door into the floodlight and realise that the dogs aren't round the back. They are close at hand. They have loped around the side of the house to see who has come. Two large Rottweilers, black and slavering. Two yards away.

They growl and show their fangs. Oh Grandma, what big teeth!

I glance at the front door: no one showing yet. I glance at the wrought-iron gate: it's a long way off. So I back away from them.

Whichever way you react to Rottweilers, you will lose. If you run, they'll chase and catch you. If you stare them down, they'll take the challenge. Your best bet is to act unconcerned.

Which is easily said.

I try to drift away from them, keeping a hopeful eye on that front door. Is no one in there?

The dogs start stalking.

In the flick of a tail, it all happens. Their growls change to a panting whine. I step back. They hurtle forwards. I leap sideways. I dive to the only place I can go: shoulder first through Richardson's window. Amid a shower of broken glass I crash sprawling on his carpet.

The dogs' heads appear above the windowsill, howling through the rift left in the glass. An alarm bell rings. One of the Rottweilers nudges at shards of glass in the bottom of the windowpane. The other tenses its shoulders ready to spring.

I am on my feet. I scuttle to the door. As I whip through, the dogs land lightly on the carpet. I slam the door on them.

Here in the hall the lights are on. But no people come. I peep through another door, open across the hall: no one. I peep along the corridor: no one again. This is a single-storey building. There are no stairs, just a hundred yards of corridor. I take the left.

The alarm stops ringing. The air hums. The only sound now is of the dogs, howling from the closed front room.

On the right-hand wall of the corridor ahead of me, a door opens. A man in a dressing-gown steps out, carrying a shotgun. He points it at me. I show my palms and turn on my sweetest Bugs Bunny grin.

Then I hear another voice behind me. I squint across my shoulder. A second slab of beef has crawled out of bed and found his doorknob. He wears pyjamas. No dressing-gown. But like his friend he holds a shotgun. For one mad moment I consider diving to the floor. Would both the pillocks blast off along the corridor and shoot each other? It happens in the movies. But Bugs Bunny is not real life.

'What the fuck are you doin'?' asks the first one.

'Good evening,' I reply. 'Is Tod Richardson in?'

The dressing-gown stomps up to me and jabs his shotgun against my chest. 'How d'ya get in here?'

I reproduce that wide open smile. 'Through the door, of course.'

The one behind asks what the dogs are yelling at, but I don't turn round. I smile encouragingly at the hulk who has his twelve-bore pressed against my breast.

'You grinning at?' he shouts at me. 'I'll tear you apart.'

'Can I see Tod Richardson?'

'Too right you'll see him.' He laughs at me. 'What're those dogs goin' on about?'

'Must've heard this fucker coming in,' deduces the striped pyjamas. 'How'd they get indoors?'

Dressing-gown jabs my chest again. 'You let them fuckers in?'

'The dogs?'

'Of course the fuckin' dogs. You leave the window open when you climbed in?'

'I came in through the door.'

'What fuckin' door?'

'The front.'

'The fuckin' front?' He draws spittle for his next question, then makes eye-contact with the man behind, and says nothing more. The dogs stop barking. They have done their duty. We can hear the two dogs whining behind the lounge door. I ask for Richardson again.

'Why d'yer wanna see him?' says a new voice from behind.

I lift my head and I take a breath. But I keep my eyes to the front. I grin at Dressing-gown and I sing out nice and loud: 'Hallo, Tod, how are you? Been a long time, hasn't it, my friend?'

Then I turn round.

He gawps at me. Like his buddies, he is fresh from bed. He wears a black and red kimono over blue striped pyjamas. He has lost half his hair, and that which is left could use a comb. His face is puffy. Either he has just woken up or he has been grinding his face into his pillow. 'Who the fuck are you?' he wants to know.

'What d'you mean "Who am I"? You send your boys round with

a message, tell them to be sure they deliver it, then you ask who I am? I'm offended.'

'You fucking bust in here, or what?'

'You've aged some, Tod. D'you know that?'

He clumps forward and squints at me. 'You're Carter's brother.'

'He was mine.'

'Think you're fucking clever, do yer?'

'I don't walk out in front of cars.'

'What yer mean?'

'Who wrote the contract on my brother Albie?'

Richardson stares at this blond stranger throwing him questions in his corridor. He says, 'Fuck knows,' and waits for me to speak. So I do.

'Thought you and I should have a talk, Tod.'

'Did yer?'

He studies me, his brain creaking behind his eyes. Dressing-gown sniggers. Richardson freezes him with a glare. We all wait.

'What about?' he asks at last.

'Money.'

He sniffs. 'Fucking late, you know that?'

'I wanted to be sure you were in. Is there somewhere we can talk?'

From his front room, one of the Rottweilers moans. Richardson frowns. 'Those fucking dogs inside?' he asks. No one answers. He turns away. 'Bring him in the lounge.'

The bozo in pyjamas gets there first. He opens the door for Richardson and the two dogs burst out. They hurtle around the hallway and try to bark it down. The noise is deafening. Richardson shouts at them. They shout at him back. He demands that his minders sort them out.

Pyjamas seems afraid of them: he stays close to the wall. But Dressing-gown knows his stuff. He wades in among the pair of them, grabs their studded leather collars and starts yanking them away. So he's the dog-handler. He and the two Rottweilers slither down the corridor. Peace returns.

I let Pyjamas and Richardson enter the lounge ahead of me. Then we all stand gazing at it. The room looks as if it was hit by a howitzer. Curtains billow in the breeze. Broken glass lies across the carpet like sprinkled water. An armchair lies on its back. Two small tables lie on their sides. Cushions have been pulled from the settee and torn apart.

'If they were mine,' I say, 'I'd have those dogs put down.'

\*

He is not bright at the best of times. And for Richardson, the best of times is not at one in the morning when he has suddenly awoken and jumped out of bed. He listens to me explaining that the front door was unlocked. That I pushed it and walked in. That I peeped into his lounge. That the two dogs saw me through the window, and jumped clean through the glass. Because they thought I was an intruder.

It is too incredible a story to disbelieve. He stands in the hall, shaking his head, as if he himself is a Rottweiler that crashed through some glass. He shouts at everybody. He shouts down the corridor at the dogs. He shouts especially at Pyjamas, who skulks off for a broom. Then Tod leads me to his den.

It is a small room, cosily lit, though the study walls are not lined with books. The only bookcase he has is stacked with video tapes whose titles I do not read. There is TV and audio and a heap of magazines.

'So you wanna talk money?' I nod.

'Middle of the fucking night?' I nod again.

'Sit down,' he says.

They are big comfortable armchairs – the sort you should sink into with a glass of whisky. He doesn't offer. He sticks a cigarette in his mouth and lights it. I begin.

'You sent your boys round, Tod. Some debt Albie owed you.'

'Ten thousand fucking quid.'

'Albie's dead.'

'I fucking know that.'

'Then so is the debt.'

'Like fuck. You're his brother.'

'Would you pay *your* brother's debts?'

His eyes blaze at me. 'Leave my fucking brothers out of this.'

I shrug. 'We both lost a brother.'

'Too fucking right. Now what?'

'A man dies, his debts die with him.'

He considers this. 'No. Being dead don't kill your debts.'

'Dig Albie's body up and explain it to him.'

Richardson breathes in. He doesn't like arguments, not verbal ones. 'I'm fucking telling you, right?'

'Albie's debts are not my business.'

'Fuck they're not your fucking business. You inherited.'

'You have a receipt?'

I could have asked had he got a book of Chinese poetry. Receipts do not exist in Richardson's world. 'Your brother owed me. That's what counts.'

I don't ask why I should believe him. I don't suggest I might doubt his word. 'Why did Albie borrow this ten grand?'

'That's my business.' He blows cigarette smoke irritably across the room.

I throw my hands up. 'I have to know the reason. You've got to tell me that.'

'Why?'

'You want me to pick up the tab.'

'Fucking Albie didn't tell yer?'

'No.'

'Then it's private, innit?'

I lean back in his comfortable armchair and I sigh. 'I can't help you, Tod, can I? You're demanding money without a reason. *You* wouldn't pay a man on that.'

'It's not me that fucking owes it.' Richardson leans forward to stub his cigarette out in a dirty ashtray.

'Nor is it me.' I stand up. Richardson won't manage a longer chat. 'You understand my position, Tod? I can't pay for something I don't know about. It's the principle.'

He stands too. 'Same thing with me. Fucking principle. I want the money.'

'You'll have to write it off. Due to an unfortunate decease. A bad debt.' I look round his room. 'You can afford it.'

'What the fuck do *you* know?' He takes a threatening step towards me. 'You ain't fucking walking out on it, Carter. I want my money or all the fucking stuff back.'

'What stuff?'

He hesitates, his angry head two foot from mine. 'The stuff. You know.'

'I *don't* know.'

'The fucking heroin, that's what.'

Richardson would be into it. If it pays and it's illegal, he wants in. Remember, the Richardsons have run gangs in Deptford since the war. That's what they do. Thieving, extortion, gambling and sex. All of which activities are declining around here. Thieving needs to be done outside of Deptford – somewhere there are decent things to steal. Gambling and sex take place up west, north of the river, where punters play. Even extortion has gone off the boil. There isn't the money left in Deptford to extort.

The Richardsons ran forays into other parts of London, muddying other people's water, but it was not appreciated. It could be why his brother went swimming in a sack.

Here in Deptford, the Richardsons moved inevitably into drugs. Amphetamines, at first. Then heroin. In the last few years, drugs are a business that has grown. Plenty of customers, close at hand. Plenty of profit.

Nowadays, it's the most profitable thing Tod does.

And it gives him power. Selling drugs involves a lot of little dealers, a lot of networks, a lot of outlets. Many people are involved. And all those working folk rely on Richardson. Heroin is a currency: control its supply and you control the economy.

'Albie was a dealer,' Tod tells me. 'But you knew that.'

Everybody thinks I know things that I don't.

For Albie, apparently, dealing was just a sideline at first. Richardson supplied, Albie sold it on. Then Richardson suggested Albie work for them on salary – in much the same way, I think to myself, that I am supposedly working for Carmichael. But I don't mention this to Richardson.

'Your brother knew his fucking way around.'

'Well, he lived here all his life.'

He also understood what was what. If Richardson said he wanted to employ him, Albie would not resist. Albie would know that this was not a matter he had a choice in. He would also look to make things work his way. From the way Richardson talks about him, Albie did it well. Tod found him reliable. As he says, Albie knew his way around. And Albie was not a user. Among the thick-headed rhinoceroses that Tod employs, Albie would shine like the evening star.

But Richardson's own light was fading. These last ten years have not been kind to him. His family had declined in power before I left. Now, ten years later, he has one brother recently dead, the other two years' inside, the whole of his south London empire in decay. It isn't even *his* empire any more. He has competition.

'That fucking wog Carmichael got my club.'

We stand facing each other, Tod and I. Occasionally from along the corridor comes the sound of banging, as his minders hammer temporary repairs to his front room window. Richardson ignores the noise. He slumps back into his chair like an embittered tramp, drawing deeply on his cigarettes, sinking into an early morning reverie. He broods on how he lost the Parrot.

It was the year he lost Sam, the first of his brothers. Sam Richardson is still early in his term at Gartree Maximum Security. Tod says Sam should not have gone soft on a blab who squealed. Going soft, in their terms, means Sam did not kill him. He just nailed the feller's hands to a door.

107

'Should have nailed his tongue,' Tod says.

In what remained of the once-great Richardson clan, Sam was the closest that they had to brains. Losing him meant that they lost a lot of revenue. Business grew worse. They had to raise money. The Parrot was one of their more recent acquisitions, and when Huey made them an offer, they took it. The best deal they could strike.

A mistake. Owning the Parrot had given them status. Selling it said they were no longer top of the heap. They realised that people were sneering at them. The Richardsons couldn't have that. So Tod and his brother Frank scraped some money together: asked Carmichael to sell the Parrot back. He wouldn't.

'So we fucking did the bastard.'

But not in the usual Richardson way. The old-style brothers would have called on Carmichael uninvited: smashed him, smashed his property, or smashed both. That's how the Richardsons got the Parrot in the first place. But this time, what Frank and Tod did was to fight Carmichael out in the territory. Huey the Snake had a grip on the local drugs network, so the Richardsons moved in to break his hold. Commercially. Sam told them what to do from Gartree. He told them to put their pushers out to undercut Huey's prices. Carmichael cut back. They cut again. During all this, the Richardsons didn't abandon their old techniques. Whenever they caught one of Huey's candymen, they gave him a kicking, broke some bones.

I ask if Albie was involved in that.

Not in the violence, Tod tells me. Albie stuck to dealing. Having lived in Deptford all his life, Albie knew every jabber, snorter, speed-freak and pot-head in sixteen square miles. He ran round them all like an angel down from heaven, dropping packets of heroin at a bargain forty quid a gram. Smackheads said prayers for Albie. He could move stuff faster than ice-cream in July. Tod pumped more stuff out to him and increased his float.

'Where was it all coming from?' I ask.

Tod looks up from his memories. A cigarette dangles slackly in his mouth. 'Plenty around,' he says. 'Always is. Even at measly forty quid I made a fucking profit.'

'So did it work?'

'Did what work?'

'Did you manage to stuff Carmichael?'

'Oh yeah, he don't touch scag now. Sticks to fucking cocaine, north of the fucking river. He's out of things down here.'

'Carmichael would not have been pleased.'

'He's off my fucking manor. That's what matters.'

'He would not have liked Albie stealing away his trade.'

'He fucking didn't.'

'Someone killed Albie.'

'Carmichael ain't got the fucking balls for that.'

'No?'

'Fucking wog.'

We sit in the deep armchairs, both brooding on private thoughts. Richardson has admitted Albie owed him ten thousand pounds. What he doesn't seem to know is that Albie had been talking to Carmichael. But Albie was not *working* for Carmichael. He was 'difficult to deal with', Carmichael said. Now, since somebody killed Albie, the smart money has to be on Richardson or Carmichael. But which? Both men are prepared to talk to me: Carmichael went out of his way to, and now he even employs me. Would he have killed my brother? But equally, would Richardson kill one of his best employees – especially while he was holding ten grand's worth of his heroin? It's hardly logical. So who *did* kill Albie? And more to the point, what am I going to do about it?

The house is silent. The dogs have been kennelled, and the bodyguards have either gone back to bed or have fallen asleep in the hall. Eventually I get up to leave. When I stretch I hear my bones creak.

'I still want that fucking money,' Richardson says.

'What money?'

'Ten thousand fucking pounds.'

'What did Albie owe it for?'

'Fucking told yer. Didn't you listen? Albie carried a fucking float. Ten fucking ounces. That's ten thousand fucking quid. Right? And I'll tell yer something else: you're his fucking brother – you're gonna fucking pay it back.'

# 19

Ludo grins and bobs up and down as if he has just unwrapped a toy train set. Morning sunlight catches in his red hair. He has come out into the road wearing slippers. The buttons of his shirt are done up wrong. He paces around the car at the kerbside, and pokes at it.

'A Fiesta,' he exclaims. 'They're really good. They keep their value secondhand.'

'It isn't mine.'

'Nought to sixty in less than ten seconds. That's a lot of car.'

'You want a ride in it?'

'Wow, thanks, Floyd. Where shall we go?'

'I'm taking you home.'

'Oh good, that's really great. Two lots of really good news.'

'Just one thing.'

'What's that, Floyd?'

'It's a small car. Can you fit inside?'

'Can I fit?' He pauses. Then his face clears. 'Oh, you're joking, aren't you? A Fiesta's not that small, Floyd. Quite roomy, really. I've seen the advertisements.'

'We'll get your bag.'

In the house, he thanks Suzie and tells her that he is grateful. Just because he is happy to go home doesn't mean Suzie should think—

'Of course not. We enjoyed having you. You were our guest.'

'That's right.' He beams. 'A guest.'

'Careful with that coffee, Ludo.'

He had forgotten that he held it in his hand. Now he gapes at the cup and saucer, tottering at the end of his extended arm. It's as if he has just noticed an extra thumb.

Suzie smiles at me. 'There is a man next door who's been looking for a job at least five years. You come home and find one inside five days.'

'I have a lucky face.'

'Maybe, now the bruise has gone. I hope this job is one you can talk about.'

'I'll bring you any gossip from the canteen.'

'Do I know the company you'll be working for?'

'Not this one.'

'Oh-oh. You're not going back in the family business, are you, Floyd?'

'Meaning?'

'The furtive kind of life that Albie led.'

'Furtive?'

'Lay off the one-word questions, will you? Is this car legit?'

'Taxed and insured. Legally owned.'

'And is the job legit?'

I begin a flip answer, and with anyone else I would complete it.

But I stop. Suzie waits, her green eyes watching me. I drink some coffee.

'Albie never had a car,' Ludo says.

'He reckoned that in London you didn't need one,' I say, glad of the change of subject. 'By the time he was in his mid-twenties and he still hadn't learnt to drive, he was afraid he'd fail the test. How's Tamsin?'

'In bed,' Suzie says. 'I woke her about ten. Cup of tea, lots of smiles, sympathetic hand on the shoulder. I was nice to her all day yesterday. Thought it might make her feel guilty and ashamed. D'you think I should stop her singing in that club?'

'She's eighteen.'

'And I'm her mother.'

'She's too old to be kept in, Suzie. She's making her own life now.'

'She's still my kid, and she needs my help.'

'She needs the sort of help you're giving her – cups of tea, smiles, warm hand on the shoulder.'

'Don't we all? And she's had eighteen years of that.'

'Which is why she came home. Kids have to break out. She didn't do this to hurt you.'

'She could hurt herself.'

'Even if you keep her in another day or two, you'll have to let her out sometime. Singing is her career.'

Suzie glares at me. 'Easy for you to talk, big boy. You're not a parent.' She looks away. Then she picks up her cup and blows on it. 'I'm sorry, Floyd. I shouldn't have said that.'

'Yes, you should. I understand.'

There is a pause. Ludo frowns and says, 'Floyd nearly was a daddy once. Weren't you, Floyd?'

'Yeah, that's right.' Now it is my turn to pick up my cup.

'That wretched Albie,' Suzie says.

After I have settled Ludo back into the house, after I have rebuttoned his shirt, after I have bought some groceries with him, after all of that, I drive back to the Isle of Dogs. This time I work alone. Dixie has shown me the circuit, today I start the routine. Today is easy. Three of yesterday's heads hadn't enough money so were not supplied.

Much of their business is run on credit. Their newest users pay cash up front, and for a while they stick to that. But then a user will get stuck: no money for the next fix. It's just temporary, they will plead: give me a little on account. They'll be persuasive. They'll be plaintive. Anything, they'll say, that's what they'll do.

Which is how the breadhead likes it.

The usual thing is the breadhead smiles. No problem, he says, here's what you do. But the first time the breadhead says it, you expect the worst: he'll ask you to thieve, to sell your body, to start a life of crime. But not at all. Nothing like that. Nothing difficult at all.

It could even help you.

What he will do is lend you one gram on account. Let's say that's sixty quid you owe him. But here's your out. You take your gram and divide it into twenty-five standard hits. Put each hit in a bag. Sell each bag at the usual going rate – five pounds – and you make a hundred per cent profit. You can repay that sixty pounds and still have change.

Except you're a user. You won't sell it all. But that's still no problem, the breadhead says. Just keep half the gram he lent you for your own use, and sell the rest. The money you earn from twelve bags will pay the whole of what you owe. Simple, right?

Except you want some more. You have none left. You used half the hits yourself, earned sixty for the rest. That sixty will pay off what you owe. But to buy some more you need more cash. Which you haven't got. So you'd better borrow another gram and start again.

That one gram's credit will keep you locked in to your dealer. And you've become part of the supply line now: selling on to finance your need. You had better be careful. If, from every gram, you are selling a dozen bags, that's a lot of trading. The breadhead sells once while you sell twelve times. And you sell to amateurs, to anybody. You're the kind of dealer who gets caught.

Possession with intent to supply. First offence. Six months inside.

There is another problem. Selling twelve bags to every gram means a lot of footwork. Keeping only half of every gram is an act of will. Footwork and willpower you could run out of. Especially if you're using.

The time comes when you sell less than half, and use the rest. You haven't made the sixty pounds you owe. But you still have that craving. So you start shouting at your breadhead: come on, supply me. Come on, tell me, what the hell do I have to do?

He makes suggestions. You're out of options. You decide that maybe what he suggests wouldn't be so terrible. Not unbearable. Not if you only had to do it once.

So I wouldn't be a breadhead. They're the ones who really turn the screw. Me, I am temporarily in the wholesale business. Selling to little traders on the street.

Funny how the rich don't carry cash. Two of the three I have to see today wear suits on their backs could buy ten grams apiece. Yesterday all three told Dixie they were out of money, so he should return today. Maybe it was because he had me with him. They listened politely to his introduction, but they hesitated. I could have been a set-up. Maybe they said Not Today Thank You to see how Dixie reacted. In business it never hurts to be cautious.

But today they'll have to make a choice because I'm on my own.

I have already made *my* choice: for a little longer I play along with Carmichael's test. I have few qualms about it. Cocaine is the kind of drug that does not have to do you harm – unless you're stupid with it. You use it for a high, like a shot of whisky. There's no reason you should be hooked. But if you do get hooked – and if you are the kind of smart-suited city type who has driven ordinary folk off this island – well, that is your affair. Don't expect *me* to wipe your tears.

Both the men in expensive suits meet me on big-suited territory. The first man chooses a pub along Marsh Wall on the Millwall Dock, which in my day was the kind of place no one ever wore a suit. Now the dock is unrecognisable. Bullet-proof glass-windowed offices that scream of money. Marble walls. Revolving doors. The pub is like a five-star hotel lounge: huge windows and modern chairs. It is called the Spinnaker, for a nautical touch.

We exchange newspapers.

The second suit waits up Westferry Road in the City Pride. It ought to be familiar. There always was a pub here but it has been transformed. In my day it even *faced* the other way. Now it is green and white, has a trendy garden, and plays music big and loud.

'You can skip the newspaper,' the striped suit says. He is the kind of man who grins and touches your arm. 'No one reads a paper in the City Pride.'

I guess he's right. They just shout at each other. They pretend they're at a party in their lunch break. They shake off the office, freak out, go back to work.

We do the business plain as Peter among the punters. He hands me a white envelope. A minute later I give him a smaller brown one back. 'No one watches anyone in here,' he says. It seems to me that everyone watches everyone all the time. That is, when they're not watching themselves in the mirrors, making sure that they are still up to the mark.

I leave the car where I have parked it and walk to my last appointment. The way those clouds are building in the sky, I ought to drive. But I like fresh air. I want to take in the scenery. There is plenty to see, because they have certainly spent money here. Just half a mile away is the crowded, run-down Poplar High Street. Yet here am I on a road that instead of tarmac looks like a patio laid in bricks – every one hand-placed in herringbone pattern.

Looking at the road makes me notice that old white van. The one crawling like a milk float. Most vans around here scoot straight through. This one doesn't. It creeps along. Behind me.

I turn to stare at it, and the driver stares at me. So does the man beside him. Then the van rolls forward, gathers speed, and drifts on by.

I watch it go.

Probably it was nothing. Doing a job like this, you get imaginative. I continue walking down to the north section of West India Docks, to the Sugar Warehouses. It must be because they are historic that they have been left standing. Huge six-storey hulks, brick built nearly two hundred years ago. Always gloomy, and now empty. The windows are guarded with iron bars, those on the lower floors viciously spiked to keep out thieves. In the shadow of these oppressive brick carcasses I sense the power of the original sugar barons. As their men humped coarse sacks down this narrow lane, the gritty sugar inside would wear through the hessian and rub raw against their shoulders. Men dripped blood from flayed skin here. That's why they named the place Blood Alley.

My man waits at the end of it. He wears a smart grey fisherman's jumper and blue slacks.

'I'm your touch now,' I remind him. 'What d'you need?'

'Three ounces.' Despite the jumper he looks cold.

'I only brought two. That's your usual supply.'

'OK. Two.'

'That'll be two grand.'

'Don't I get a discount?'

'Not on two ounces. You want the other one tomorrow?'

'I suppose so.' He shivers.

'You using?'

'I caught a cold. Here's your money.'

He pulls a wad of notes from his trouser pocket and starts to count them.

'You should have had this money ready and wrapped up.'

'Thought I might buy three.' He doesn't look at me.

'When we deal again,' I tell him, 'you have the money pre-bagged, in thousands. Anyone could be watching this.'

'Sorry. I thought you'd want to count it.'

'I'll count it afterwards. Like you will check the weight.'

'I'm still new to this, Mr Burns.'

'The rules are simple: no one cheats. Don't ever try.'

He finishes counting. I take the two thousand and he stuffs the rest of his money back in his trouser pocket. He handles the wad carelessly, like a handkerchief. The money seems valueless to him.

'Same time tomorrow?' I ask.

'If you like. I can wait a few days.'

'It's up to you. I'm coming anyway.'

'OK. The other ounce.'

We separate. I let him leave first. For a man running a fast-moving high-ticket business, he sure has lost his interest in life. I walk back along Blood Alley. I shiver. Whenever a wind blows anywhere, it always nips through here. In the shadows it is cold. It is about to rain.

When I come out into the light at the end, I look for the white van. I didn't like the slow speed it moved at. I didn't like the way that shortly after I noticed it, I did business with a nervous man. I didn't like the casual way he counted his money.

But there's no sign of the van.


Because the Isle of Dogs is really a peninsula, it gets congested where it joins the land. The worst spots are Poplar High Street and East India Dock Road. To avoid them, I cut back round Marsh Wall and up the eastern side. I am in the Fiesta again, cruising comfortably with the window open, driving home. Halfway along Preston's Road, I see the white van in my mirror.

Who is it? No one knows I'm here except Huey Carmichael. I suppose this could be part of Huey's test. This is the first time I have worked without Dixie. Maybe Carmichael sent some guys to keep an eye on me.

Then I see the police car.

I couldn't miss it. It is parked ahead of me. Two large blue uniforms have leapt into the road and are signalling me down. I pull over. As one of the two cops comes to lean into my window, the white van overtakes and glides on by.

'Excuse me, sir. Just a routine check.'

Like hell it is.

'Are you the owner of this vehicle, sir?'

'The driver, not the owner. It's insured for any driver.'

'You have the papers?'

I reach for the glove compartment.

'Just one moment, sir, if you wouldn't mind. It's very busy out on this road, sir. Would you mind pulling into there?'

He indicates the quieter road to our left, leading back along the top of the Enterprise Zone.

'Is this necessary?'

'If you wouldn't mind, sir. A purely random check.'

Naturally. The police just happened to be checking cars today. They just happened to pick on mine. They just happened to move me off into this quieter road.

I stand in a light mist of rain. Any minute now that dark cloud will open: a short, sharp shower. Here in the quiet side street everything remains polite and formal. Nothing is as it should not be.

As long as you ignore Detective Sergeant Kellard, sitting quietly in the back seat of the police car. As long as you ignore the police dog, sniffing around mine. Sniff, sniff. Sniffer of the Yard. I think I should stroll across and talk to Kellard. Too late copper, I should say. The stuff's delivered.

# 20

April sun improves the look of Malpas Road. It washes over the low roofs of the two-storey terraces and dries the dirt on the pavements. Scraps of paper, previously sodden, begin to stir in the gutters. Cats bask on windowsills, children chase each other screaming round a corner, a man comes out of his house to mend his car.

Jamie walks me down to Brockley Cross, inhaling fresh air through his nostrils like Islanders sniff cocaine. He greets an old woman as she peers through the window of Patel's newsagent shop. She smiles back.

At Brockley Cross five roads meet. There is a garage, the Howarth Timber Yard and a bunch of shops. Apart from Jim's Café and the fish and chip shop (with Chinese takeaway), there is also a locksmith, the Baytree Florist and the double-fronted Birds Dress Agency ('Good As New', established 1830). It makes me think. Mr

Bird (not Mrs – not in 1830) started that secondhand clothing business more than a century and a half ago. Through all the Bird generations it passed down to today. Each generation chose a new youngster to be trained in the family business: buying and selling old clothes. I wonder if those kids welcomed the opportunity, or whether they yearned to escape the smell of unwashed cloth.

'I could murder a bacon sarnie,' Jamie says.

'Good.'

It is why we're out. Jamie was moping around his flat, existing on cups of tea and stale bread toast. I hauled him off to Jim's Café.

'Afternoon, Ida. Breakfast please.'

'Just got up?'

'Don't start,' says Jamie. 'What you got?'

'It's on the board, same as always.'

On Ida's board are all the fried permutations: egg and bacon; egg and sausage; egg, sausage and bacon; hot pies; hot pies with chips and beans; sausage with egg, chips, bacon, beans, tomato. Bread and butter. Coffee or tea. Jim's is an unprepossessing corner caff – shabby furniture, steamy windows, pine tongue-and-groove walls. But whatever food you order will be cooked for you fresh.

Jamie and I sit down at a side table to wait.

'My own fault,' he says suddenly, flicking back that lock of troublesome black hair. He grins at me.

'What was?'

'The barbies. Could have sworn they was dikes. I should've tested them.'

'You a pharmacist?'

'Nah, but I shouldn't have injected them straight off, should I? Always sample a new supply. Don't inject nothing till you have snorted, smoked or sucked it. Find how strong it is.'

'Is that what Eva said?'

He grins. 'She's OK, ain't she?'

'Is she your girl?'

'Eva? Do me a favour!'

'You could do worse.'

'Heart of gold, body of iron.'

'Does she always act that tough?'

Jamie shrugs, picks up a fork, and polishes it on his sleeve. 'She used to be married.'

'Tough girls do get married.'

'Usually to wimps. Reckon I'd be too much of a handful for her.'

'You think so?'

'One tea,' says Ida, appearing beside us at the table, 'with eggs, tomatoes, chips and beans.'

'That's mine,' says Jamie.

'And a bacon, egg and chips,' she says. 'Two slices and a tea.'

'That's mine.'

When she has shuffled back behind her counter I nod at Jamie's pile of food. 'I'm surprised you can face that, sliding around your plate.'

'I'm convalescent, ain't I? Invalids like sloppy food.' He tucks into it, breaking the egg yolk on to the beans, mashing the fried tomato into his chips. 'Anyway, I'm vegetarian now. Meat's bad for you, innit?'

I eat my bacon, hot and salty. Two men in shirt sleeves stroll in through the open door. They fetch cups from behind the counter, and pour some tea. They say hallo to Ida, sit down, and light their cigarettes. Ida continues reading her *Daily Mirror*. When the men have finished their tea, they will leave money on the counter. She need not ask for it. At her café table the two men can sit as they would at home at their kitchen tables. More comfortably perhaps: here in the caff there is no noisy kid, no smelly old dog, no scolding harassed wife. Jim's Café is the cosiest place they know.

'Was Albie supplying you?' I ask.

Jamie looks up from his plate, the fork suspended. A blob of red tomato falls off. 'You know about that?'

'I know he was dealing. Had a lot of customers.'

Jamie sniffs. 'He was beautiful, your brother. Always a fair price. Always there. Man was a marvel.'

'So I hear. And after he died, you ran short?'

'Yeah.' Jamie twirls his fork in his egg and beans. The yolk blends into the red sauce, leaving flakes of egg white among the beans. 'After he got topped, we had a drought. Nowadays there's very little heroin about. And it's gone back to the old prices. I had to switch to Diconal.'

'Just to make do?'

'Nah, I prefer them, tell the truth. Dikes are clean ... They *usually* are. You get smack cut with all kinds of shit. A geezer down in Catford once mixed smack with flour. Imagine cranking up with that! Flour and water's an adhesive, innit? You don't want glue in your veins, do ya? Bloody Catford – they're out of the ark down there.'

Jamie scoops the last of his beans, and forks them into his mouth. 'What the hell? Better than watching telly all day long.'

'Is it?'

He pushes back his chair. 'You haven't lived here these last ten years. Bloody government destroyed the life of ordinary people. You know why? Because politicians hate the working class. They were either born rich, or they're getting their own back on the kids who beat them up at school.' He stands up. 'I think I'll blow a quid on the Eight Ball Deluxe.'

The Deluxe is one of two machines standing just inside the door. Apart from when the weather is really cold, that door will always be open. All through the day, local people will walk through, treating the caff as an extension to their home. They won't always buy things. They may sit down at a table to chat to a friend. They may share a joke with Ida. They may take a toasted sandwich to eat outside. The radio plays continually, and some folk come in just to check the hourly news.

While I finish my mug of tea, Jamie loses his pound on the old-fashioned pinball table. He considers the Tik Tak Cash fruit machine, but shrugs his shoulders. 'No fun in that.'

When we walk back to his flat, the sun has melted the last greyness from the sky. Jamie punches my arm. 'You don't like the way I live, do ya, Floyd?'

'It's your life.'

'Think I'm a hopeless junkie, don't ya? Well, I'm not. I got the whole thing under control. What you saw last night was an accident, wasn't it? I've been doing smack on and off for about five years. What harm has it done? The only problem I get is finding my supply. When it's available I get by on half a gram a day. That's all. I've been doing that amount all the time. It's no different than some blokes smoking fags.'

'You think *they're* not addicted?'

'We're all addicted. So what? Drinking, smoking, shooting drugs. It's what gets us through the day.'

He stops beside the kerb and looks into my face as if he has seen something there he never saw before.

'Why shouldn't we have a little pleasure, some support? Tell me that. Life don't mean doing only what is good for you, Floyd. What sort of life is that? I know the life this country has marked out for me. They want to bend me to their will like a factory machine, so they can scrap me when I wear out. Well, I tell you, if I'm a dumb machine I want my fuel. Regular. Gimme a gram a day and I'll stay numb.'

# 21

Tamsin puts her feet up on the table and asks why not. Come to that, she wants to know, who will stop her?

She wears a large loose-knit white sweater and a pair of tight black pants. Her hair is everywhere.

'I'll stop you,' Suzie says calmly. 'I've taken a day off and I've changed my shift.'

Tamsin glares at her. 'I'd have thought it was a bit late for playing mother.'

'That's who I am.'

'Well, shit,' Tamsin says, her eyes defiant. There is a silence. She turns to me. 'You're staying too, I suppose? Did you bring an overnight bag?'

'No.'

'You could sleep in the spare room like your brother did.' She stares at her mother. 'I suppose you'll be happier with Floyd.'

Suzie's green eyes blaze. 'What is that supposed to mean?'

'Huh!'

'Well?'

'As if you didn't know.'

'Tell me,' Suzie says.

I look at the carpet. I hear the pause.

Tamsin says, 'This is bloody ridiculous, you know? You can't keep me locked in.'

'Try me.' Suzie looks stern. Tamsin pouts. They flash their eyes at each other so much you'd think they were rehearsing a scene from *Carmen*.

'It was only a party,' Tamsin says. 'On an ordinary boat.'

'What time did it start?' I ask.

She frowns at me. 'What does that matter?' Then she stops.

'You were away two nights,' Suzie points out. 'No party runs from one night to the next.'

'This is a damned inquisition. I don't remember where I was.'

'Exactly,' says Suzie. 'What pills had you taken – or was it cocaine?'

Tamsin crashes to her feet, glaring at me. 'Did you tell her that? You told those lies?'

Suzie cuts in. 'He didn't need to. And they weren't lies. When I put you to bed you were high as a kite.'

'I'd been drinking. Sorry!'

'That as well? Listen honey, d'you think I lead a sheltered life? You think I never see junkies in the wards? Every weekend I see kids stoned.'

'I'm going upstairs.'

'I was wrong about one thing.' Tamsin pauses at the door to hear what Suzie has to say. 'You weren't on cocaine. It was some kind of hallucinogen, wasn't it? What's in fashion now – one of those with letters instead of a name: MDA, PCP, LSD?'

Tamsin tosses her head. 'XTC.'

'Ecstasy.'

Tamsin dithers in the doorway. 'It's quite harmless, you know.'

'It won't kill you, I suppose.'

'I'm going to bed.'

This time Tamsin does leave. Suzie stays in her chair, the prim ward sister. I stand up, walk across, and squeeze her shoulder. I ought to do something more. But I don't.

Slowly Suzie lets the air out from her lungs. She lets her head droop against my arm. Her hand reaches up to stroke my wrist. We stay like this, facing in opposite directions at her armchair. I don't say anything. Her fingers tickle the hairs on the back of my hand. I hear her breathing.

I sit down on the edge of the chair and put my arm around her. She feels warm against my side. After a while she says, 'What was I to do when Tom died – stop Tamsin singing? When he was alive, if she had to go somewhere that might not be safe, Tom went with her. Well, I let her carry on singing. Sometimes I went with her, sometimes I couldn't. I had to work. Perhaps I was wrong. Perhaps I should have told her to concentrate on school.'

'You did the right thing.'

'That's not how it looks.'

I stroke her blonde hair. 'She should have told you where she was, that's all. She probably didn't realise how long the party would go on.'

'This is not the first time.'

Sitting on the arm of her chair, I clasp Suzie's head into my body. It is quiet in the room. We rock softly to and fro.

Tamsin bursts in through the door. She wears pyjamas. 'Oops, I'm sorry!' she says archly. 'I should have knocked, I suppose.'

Suzie and I ease away from each other. We don't stand up.

'I came for a drink – if that's all right.' Tamsin runs into the kitchen. We hear her open the fridge. I am not sure whether I should stand up or stay close to Suzie. In the end, I stand up and move away. Suzie touches my fingers as I leave her. I think she would have preferred me to stay.

Tamsin appears in the kitchen doorway, clutching a tall glass of blackcurrant cordial. Her pyjamas are made of thin translucent cotton. She wears nothing underneath. I look away.

'I'm sorry about the party,' Tamsin says.

Suzie smiles. Relief drains the tension from her face. 'I know.'

'I should have phoned, shouldn't I?'

'I was worried.'

'Are we friends?'

Suzie holds out her hands. Tamsin skips across to her, kneels down, and kisses Suzie on the cheek. As she kisses her mother, she looks at me. Then she sits on the floor at Suzie's feet.

'Am I allowed to ask about the pills?' Suzie asks softly.

'No,' says Tamsin. She strokes Suzie's leg. 'They're not addictive or anything. They're not real drugs.'

'They're a start.'

'Let's not talk about it.'

'OK, honey.'

We all three stay silent with our thoughts. I move back to my original armchair and sit down. Tamsin smiles at me from Suzie's side. 'Am I sitting in your place?' she asks.

'No,' I answer easily. 'Your mother was a bit upset.'

Tamsin cocks an eyebrow. A shadow flits across Suzie's face. It is as if I had made a small betrayal. 'Your mother' instead of 'Suzie'. 'A bit upset' to put her down.

We all three sit in the warm front room, watching each other.

# 22

Ludo wants to make me a cup of hot chocolate. He says he knows what to do. I feel that he has been waiting for me to get home so he can demonstrate this talent. He wears an apron.

'It's the best thing to drink before you go to bed,' he says. 'It helps you sleep. Albie taught me how to make it.'

'Go ahead.'

Ludo strikes a match, turns on the gas, and holds the flame to it.

He shakes out the match and places the spent end on the work surface beside the cooker. Then he slides his saucepan of milk over the flame.

'The important thing is not to let the milk boil over. But I won't, I promise. I'll be careful, Floyd.'

'How much milk have we got?'

'I bought two extra pints. And some bread.' He beams at me.

'Well done, Ludo.'

'You don't put the chocolate in till the milk has boiled. That's what Albie says. Said. You sprinkle chocolate on top of the milk when it's in the cups. Three teaspoonfuls. Three for each cup. Someone phoned earlier.'

'Who?'

'He didn't say. He said he would phone again. And he did.'

'He phoned twice?'

'He wants to speak to you, I think.'

'Did he leave a name?'

'Do you want your chocolate in a cup or in a mug? A mug is bigger.'

'A mug. Did he leave a name?'

'Who?' Ludo leans over the saucepan and stirs the milk with a wooden spoon.

'The man on the phone.'

'Oh. No. He said he'd phone back.'

'He said that both times?'

'Yes. Well, I think he did.'

'If you keep stirring that milk it'll never boil.'

Just after ten o'clock, the phone rings again. Ludo jumps up. 'Can I answer it, Floyd? I did before.' I shrug.

'Hallo? Yes? This is the Carter household speaking. Yes. Yes. Floyd, it's for you.' He hands me the receiver.

'That you this time, Carter? This is Vinnie Dirkin.'

'And?'

'I gotta speak to ya.'

'You heard from Richardson?'

'I ain't gonna speak on the phone. Can you come out?'

'Why can't you speak?'

'I need to see ya.'

'You know where I live.'

'I can't come there. You know the Windsor Castle?'

'Of course I know it.'

'Half-past ten then. It's about your brother.'

'Which one?'

The phone goes dead.

We drive there in the Fiesta, arriving fifteen minutes late. I park a hundred yards away up the High Street. It might be wise to arrive on foot. Keep the car in reserve.

Of all the pubs Dirkin could choose, he would pick the Windsor. It is a small dive on the corner of Deptford High Street and Ffinch Street – the quiet part by the station, near where the railway bridge cuts at an angle across the street. Opposite the station is the Mechanic's Arms. The Windsor Castle is on the station side.

Sitting at the bar are several wizened old men and two blousy women hiding their age. They glance up dully when we come in. Then they look back into their glasses. They look as if they just heard bad news.

Dirkin sits alone at a side table. He stands up. 'Thought you'd never get here.'

'You know what thought did. You buying the drinks?'

'I know,' says Ludo.

'You know what?'

'I know what thought did.' He chuckles. 'Thought its bum was out the window so went outside to have a look.' Ludo laughs again. He is proud of his joke. Dirkin frowns.

'We ain't got time for a drink,' he says.

'I thought you wanted to talk?'

'Not here. Somewhere private.'

'This is private, Vinnie. People in here have been brain-dead for fifteen years.'

'We gotta go somewhere.'

'Sit down, Vinnie.' He hesitates, but he sits. 'Where d'you want us to go?'

Dirkin licks his lips. 'Not far. Honest.'

Ludo nudges me. 'He's playing a trick on us, I think.'

'You see? Even Ludo isn't fooled.'

Dirkin squirms in his chair. 'People are looking at us, Carter. You standing up like that.'

'What's the game, Vinnie?'

'Man wants to talk to ya. In private. About your brother.'

'I'm his brother,' Ludo says.

'Nah, the other one. Him that's dead.'

'Where do we meet this man of yours?'

'There's this flat in Childers Street. It ain't far. Come on.' Vinnie stands up.

'The last time we met,' Ludo points out, 'you tried to beat us up.'

I glance at him. 'You remember this guy, then?'

'Of course I do,' says Ludo. 'I'm not that thick. People think I don't remember nothing. Well, I don't forget a face. We aren't going with him, are we?'

'We can look after ourselves.' I catch Ludo's eye, and he stops arguing.

Vinnie wipes his nose on his sleeve. 'They don't wanna talk to both of you.'

'They? How many are there?'

Vinnie looks flustered. He glances down at the table, as if the answer might be written on a beer mat.

'Come on, Ludo,' I say. 'I wouldn't believe him, whatever he said.'

Which is fair enough, but why do we go with him? Why do we let him lead us out of the Windsor, along that murky little lane they renamed Ffinch Street?

Because I need to hear what Dirkin's man has to say.

Maybe it is also because Ffinch Street is such a dirty little alley it is not the place anyone would try to lure me down. It's too obvious. On a dark April night like this one, at around the time the pubs are turning out, most people wouldn't creep down Ffinch Street for a pee. If it looks that dangerous it *must* be safe.

Wouldn't you say?

The three of us pick our way across the pot-holes past a couple of lock-up garages into the patch of waste ground that leads to the blocks of flats. Above us to our left runs the railway viaduct, big and brooding in the night. Between it and us are two fenced yards, piled high with rotting rubbish. Puddles gleam dully in the dark.

Vinnie walks ahead of us. He makes a point of it. So if there is going to be trouble it will come from the rear. And it does.

Ludo and I hear it at the same moment. We both turn.

Two men have come up behind us. Each carries three feet of chain. The men's faces look familiar: they were with Dirkin on the night that we first met. I am disappointed. I had hoped for better than this.

When I glance back towards Dirkin, I see a fourth man coming to join him. He completes the original Dirkin quartet, back for a second performance. He too carries a heavy chain. Dirkin has a knife.

Ludo and I wait between the two pairs, watching them. They watch us. Dirkin's three friends are shivering. I suspect they have been out here on this cold patch of mud waiting since half past ten. I'm glad we were late.

Dirkin speaks first. 'I owe you one, Carter.'

I ignore him. The other three have not come for his sake. They have come to reinforce the message they left last time. Though first they would like to use those chains.

'You ready, Carter?' one of them asks. He is the talkative one: leader of the pack. Beside him stands the black guy.

'Brought the money, have you?' the spieler asks. He hopes I haven't. He wants to use that chain.

'It's all settled.'

'What you on about?'

'I talked to Richardson last night.'

'Oh yeah?' But his eyes flick toward Dirkin.

'Ask Richardson,' I suggest.

'He ain't here, is he?'

'Ask Dirkin. He took me there.'

Vinnie decides it is time he spoke. He sounds nervous. Maybe it is just the cold air that makes him sound that way. 'Yeah, well, Carter went round there, right enough. But the boss still wants his money. He phoned me today.'

Thank you, Tod Richardson. A man true to his word. The last thing he said to me last night: I still want that money. The first thing he did this morning: phoned Dirkin.

'Have you got it, Carter?'

'What if I haven't?'

'You get a beating, chum.'

Dark as it is on this patch of forgotten ground, I can see the eagerness in his eyes. I say, 'Show it, Ludo.'

And the dickheads stand there and watch us. They wait in the mud, stuck to their spots, chains in their hands, looking like cowboys challenging us to draw. Except that if they were cowboys they would be dead. Because Ludo and I drop our hands to where our holsters would be, and brush our jackets aside. But instead of guns, we pull out baseball bats. We had hung them down the inside of our trousers when we got out of the car. Now Vinnie will realise why we did not sit down in the pub.

If I was Wyatt Earp I'd have shot the four of them.

Ludo and I hold our clubs; they hold three chains and a knife. They can start it. The black goes first. Inching towards me, he suddenly lashes out. Like a whip in slow motion, the length of heavy chain curls towards my face. I ignore it. The man is too far away.

126

The end of his chain flicks harmlessly in the air. He moves closer to try again.

I grip the baseball bat with a hand at either end as I would grip the handlebars of a bike. I thrust it towards the lashing chain. The chain hits it. The links curl round the club and tighten. I pull, and the black guy stumbles forward. Then I release my left hand and swing the club hard at his face. The drag of the chain slows it but can't stop my club thumping against the side of his head. He reels backwards.

The other three close in on us. The spieler swings his chain. Ludo catches it on his club, as I caught the first one. But when the third chain comes clattering round my club, it smashes against my fingers like an axe. My fingers feel chopped off at the knuckles.

My scream of agony is like a yell of rage. I heave on the baseball bat, and wrench the chain from the big guy's hand. Then I leap at him, flailing the club. Vicious tongues of chain flick through the air. One catches his raised forearm. Another curls past his guard and cuts his cheek. He falls.

The black guy starts clambering to his feet while Vinnie dithers with his knife. He is not anxious to get involved. Nor is the spieler now. Ludo has just swung his club in a Boris Becker smash at the spieler's head, and I think I heard a bone break. He was a lucky victim: he got his arm up just in time. If Ludo's club had reached the spieler's head it would have caved his skull in. But all that happens to him is that he topples into the mud with his arm broken and his face bruised from where the broken arm was smashed against it. Yeah, he was lucky all right.

I go for Dirkin before he decides to use that knife. He makes a run for it. As he slithers across the mud I gain on him. My mangled left hand feels as if it is being eaten by a rat, but I have so much adrenalin surging through my body I could sail.

I catch Dirkin at the side of the waste ground. He turns on me, holding the knife out in front of him like a torch. I swing my club at it, and he jerks his hand back. As my arm swings past, he stabs feebly at it. We are now so close that his knife tangles in the material of my jacket and he loses it. I thump him in the ribs with my club. He totters backwards, and staggers through the dark opening into the patch of yard below the railway viaduct. He can go nowhere from there. The yard is piled high with rotting rubbish: boxes, bales of newspaper, two mattresses. A smell of decomposing food. Dirkin tries to climb the slippery mound of garbage, and I grab the waistband of his trousers. I heave him back. My left hand is now so hot with pain that it is useless. I used my right to haul him to me, and I use it again to punch his head. I do it three times. As he starts to crumple at my feet, I grab the front of his shirt and drag him upright. When I let go he slumps immediately into the pile of refuse. I pick him up again. I am shouting into his face but he isn't listening. So I push him backwards into the mountain of stinking rubbish, and he sinks down on it. He becomes a part of it.

I hear someone behind me.

My feet are tangled in old cans and cardboard boxes. I twist around. Looming before me in the darkness is my brother Ludo, a baseball bat dangling from his hand. 'Are you all right?' he asks. I say I am.

Out across the mud patch it looks empty. I ask if they ran off.

Ludo nods. 'Two of them ran away.'

'Two?'

He stands nodding, looking serious. I come out of the rubbish yard, pick up Vinnie's knife, and follow Ludo across the ground.

I sense what I will see before I see it. The body of the third man lies chest down in the mud, head to one side. The man's cheek is cut from where I caught him with the chain. It isn't bleeding any more. He has stopped bleeding for ever.

'He wanted to hurt me with a knife,' explains Ludo. The knife lies a few feet away in a puddle. I decide to leave it there.

'He hasn't moved, Floyd.' Ludo looks frightened. 'Is he dead, do you think?'

'You couldn't help it.'

'I'll get into awful trouble, won't I?'

'We won't tell anyone.'

Ludo still looks worried. He says that the spieler saw him hit the guy.

'He won't tell anyone, either.'

'Are you sure?'

'Certain. You saw him run off?'

'With the black man. I could have caught them. They weren't running fast. Should I have stopped them, Floyd?'

'No.'

'They saw what happened. I bet they'll tell on me.'

The pain in my left hand is such that I can hardly bear to look at it. My fingers have stiffened. Along the knuckles, my flesh gapes red and open. Ludo notices it for the first time, and asks what he can do for me.

'Don't worry about it. I got off lightly.'

Ludo frowns. 'I bet they'll tell the police.'

'Tell them that they waited in the dark for us?'

'It's a good job you made us bring those clubs, Floyd. Did you know they would all be here?'

'We just came prepared.'

Ludo and I stand a few more moments looking at the body in the mud. There is no doubt that he is dead. No one sleeps in that position.

'Should we bury him?' asks Ludo.

I shake my head.

'What about that other man in the rubbish dump?'

'Forget him. He'll slip away when we've gone.'

Across the high viaduct rumbles a late train. A cool breeze stirs my hair.

'What should we do?' asks Ludo.

'Get out of here.'

I sense it the moment we are inside the front door. I am not sure why: nothing is different in the hall. Maybe there was a draught from the window they smashed at the back of the house.

The rooms are a mess – drawers out, contents on the floor. Squab cushions on the carpet. Lids unscrewed from jars, boxes opened, books thrown off the shelves. Not too much damage. Upstairs, the beds have been unmade, clothes are everywhere. The panel has been ripped from the bath.

Ours is not the kind of house where you expect to steal jewellery and furs. Burglars would have taken the video. Kids would have made more mess. These guys were looking for something.

Ludo seems close to crying. He sits on his pulled-apart bed, holding his old brown teddy bear against his chest. They had thrown the bear into the corner of the room. Ludo shakes his head.

I ask him to come to the bathroom and help me tend my hand. He brings the teddy bear and sits it on the windowsill where it can watch us. Then we run tepid water and wash off the dried blood. Flakes of torn skin curl back from the wound like pith on an orange. With my hand under water in the bowl I try moving my fingers. They seem to work. I ignore the pain. It has become a part of me.

Maybe Ludo could have been a nurse. He smears ointment on a strip of lint and lays the dressing gently across my wound. Then he wraps a bandage firmly round my hand, making sure it is not so tight that my fingers cannot move. He fastens the bandage with sticky tape.

I help him tidy his room. We don't take time over it. We throw clothes back in their drawers and remake the bed. When I suggest we finish the work tomorrow he says that he won't be able to sleep yet, so he'll help with my room.

While we do it, I explain what the fight was about. He is entitled to know. I explain that Tod Richardson tried to do two jobs at once: one, have his boys reinforce the message about the ten thousand debt, and two, have another crew search the house.

If at one in the morning last night Tod had had his brain switched on, he could have had his minders sort me out there and then. But his brain was not switched on. Tod works on low wattage at the best of times. Besides, he would have seen last night as a meeting between two sides to an argument. There are rules about that. The rules state that you let a guy say his piece and you consider what he said. If you decide you don't like it, you show him later. You do not spill blood on your own carpet. You do not bring business into the house.

This morning, Richardson decided I still did not appreciate that he was serious about the money. He also decided that his usual debt-collection procedures would persuade me of that seriousness. He just had to let things run their normal course. Meanwhile, it was worth turning our house over to see if Albie had stashed the drugs inside. You never know.

Well, Tod looks to have missed with both his shots. Out in his Blackheath ranch he could even now be interviewing an empty-handed burglar, plus whoever dared turn up from Vinnie's gang. He will not be pleased with any of them.

I had better ring.

'You think you're fucking clever, Carter, don't yer?'
    'You cocked it.'
    '*I* cocked it? You're gonna wish you'd never been fucking born.'
    'One of your men is dead. Did they tell you that?'
    'What fucking men?'
    'The four you put on to me. Vinnie Dirkin's men.'
    'You fucking talking about?'
    'Don't try to smart-talk me, Richardson. You set Vinnie on me to get us out the house. You set someone else to turn it over.'
    'You're talking shit, Carter.'

I didn't think Richardson was the kind of guy who denied anything. I didn't think he would bother. But he *must* be behind what happened.

'What's your problem, Tod – you think your phone's tapped? Have your men reported back yet?'
    'Get off the line.'

'I beat you this time, Tod.'

'You couldn't beat a fucking carpet, you. You're in deep trouble, Carter, fucking deep.'

'One of your heroes didn't come home, Tod. He's lying dead on a patch of waste ground. And when I put this phone down, Tod, d'you know what I'm gonna do? I'll phone the law. I'll tell them a geezer is lying there, and he was killed by you.'

'You're off your trolley.'

'He's one of yours, Tod. The Bill can connect you. Especially when they are tipped that it was you who topped him.'

'What's with you, Carter – you a fucking nark?'

'And I'll tell you another thing for nothing.'

'Piss off.'

'There's a knife beside the body. The fingerprints on it belong to Vinnie Dirkin. And that's a fact, Tod: he had it in his hand. So the cops get this anonymous tip-off, right? It's from a guy who knows where the body is, and who knows exactly whose dabs are on the shiv. Why should that guy be wrong when he fingers you? You're in trouble, Tod.'

For several seconds there is silence, apart from his breathing. While he thinks about it, I am thinking too. I am wondering whether I have sussed this right. Richardson has denied everything so far. Maybe he is not involved. Maybe Vinnie has been working on his own. Maybe I'm wrong.

Then Richardson explodes. I hear a gush at the far end of the line, like steam bursting out under pressure. 'That fucking Dirkin!' Tod curses another full minute without drawing breath. I stand at my end of the phone line, grinning while he raves. When he finally pauses to suck some air, I say, 'Me not telling the cops is worth ten thousand quid, I reckon. It makes us quits. You just stay out of my hair, Tod, and I'll stay stumm.'

Ludo was supposed to be in bed. But when I put the phone down I find he has been standing in the doorway.

'That was the man who did this, is that right, Floyd?'

'Yeah. His name is Tod Richardson.'

'Will that end it now?'

'I hope so.'

'Floyd, did he say anything about – you know?'

'About what?'

'About the man I hit on the head.'

'Nothing at all. Go up to bed.'

'I'm not ready for bed yet.' Ludo shuffles his feet. 'That man – he was dead, wasn't he, Floyd?'

'Don't worry about it.'

'Did I really kill him?'

'I don't know. Don't think about it. Maybe he'll be all right.'

'Like when you play cowboys?'

'Yeah, that's it. Maybe he was just playing cowboys.'

Ludo considers this idea. He wants to believe it true. Then he gives up puzzling over it, and returns to my talk with Richardson on the phone.

'Those burglars he sent – you said they were looking for something. What were they looking for, Floyd? We haven't got much.'

'Something Albie had. Or something they thought he had.'

'What was it?'

'Nothing important, Ludo. We should get some sleep.'

'All right. Good night, Floyd.' He turns to leave. 'I thought you meant that smack of his, that's all.'

'Smack?'

'Yes, he used to keep it here. Is that what they wanted?'

I stare at him. 'You knew about the stuff?'

'I knew he kept it here. It was worth a lot of money, Albie said.'

'How come you knew about it?'

Ludo looks surprised I should ask. 'I just did. We used to divide it up together on the kitchen table.'

'You and Albie?'

'Yes. Well, Albie mainly. I used to wrap the bags up. Some were ever so small, Floyd.'

'I didn't know Albie involved you in this.'

'Well, I always like to help around the house. I *can* do things, you know, Floyd.'

As I am learning. In the last two hours I discover that he is a pharmacist, a male nurse, and a killer. Out on the waste ground is a guy with his head bashed in. Ludo swung his club at him with all that strength he hardly knows he possesses. Does Ludo now realise the man is dead? Does he understand what happened any more than when he divided heroin on the kitchen table? What goes on in Ludo's brain?

A thought occurs to him. 'Do you think they found the smack, Floyd? We didn't look.'

I pause a second. 'You know where it is?'

'I don't know. I haven't looked. Albie used to hide it, you see.'

'Where?'

*

If I had been looking, I might have found it. The giveaway was to stand in the upstairs hall outside Albie's old bedroom and examine the door. To look at the fingerplate above the handle. To look at the screws. There are glints in the grooves, a few rough edges, that show that these screws are often loosened. Two small scratches appear on the fingerplate itself, beside the screws, where the screwdriver sometimes slipped.

Ludo is conscientious. He bends closely to his work. He unscrews the plate and removes it from the door. Behind the plate is a chiselled cavity. Inside the cavity is a polythene bag. Inside the bag are several smaller bags. Inside each of them is a single ounce of heroin.

# 23

I should not be here. I should not have stayed. I should not have let the three days expire. Now one of Dirkin's friends lies dead beside a viaduct. Richardson wants the heroin returned to him, and I am in deep with Snake Carmichael.

Albie was less trouble when alive.

Carmichael frowns as I tell him what happened on the Island yesterday. I leave little out. I mention the white van I think was following me – it could have been his, checking on my performance. Whoever's it was, Carmichael will want to hear about it. I say that I don't know who the van belonged to, but it drove past when it saw me with the police.

'Could have been a Q-boat,' I suggest.

'What the hell is that?'

'Unmarked police car. We used to call them that.'

'You've been away too long.'

We are in his maroon and white office at the Parrot – Huey Carmichael, Dixie and me. Dixie and I are dressed up for the Island. I wear blazer and slacks, and my hand is bandaged. Dixie wears pale grey. Carmichael wears his beloved white linen suit, this time with a yellow sweatshirt.

We all three drink glasses of Lucozade. Huey thinks Lucozade will keep him healthy. All he has to do is drink a bottle a day, and he can skip lunch, keep late hours, loll around in his soft leather chair. From the look of him, he may be right. He is lean, hard, and his doggy brown eyes are bright as a terrier's. Lucozade and speed are all he needs. The only way *I* would like Lucozade is with a gin in it.

Carmichael is sending Dixie with me to the Island. I have some big deliveries to make, and after yesterday Huey prefers to have me kept an eye on. Dixie smiles apologetically. He would prefer not to come back on to my patch, and he has his own investments to look after in the City.

'What do you think, Dixie?' Carmichael asks from the chair behind his desk. 'You think we should lie low a few days, hey?'

Dixie scratches his chin. 'The day we hold off because some geezer may be watching is the day we should change our line of business. There is danger every day. That's the way it is.'

'Hey, Dixie, did you ever see this white van?'

'No.'

'Were you ever stopped by the police?'

'It could happen to anyone. Police are always stopping cars.'

I interrupt. 'These were not traffic police.'

Dixie shrugs. 'What's the difference? They were filling their quota. They need to book some motor violations so they can get a day off in court. Cops gotta do something on that island to justify the taxes.'

'Hey, this is some dilemma, Floyd,' says Huey, gazing at the ceiling. 'You have to make some big drops today. Now you come up with this. What do we do? To go or not to go, that is the question, hey?' Carmichael downs the last of his Lucozade and drums his fingers on the white leather top of his desk. 'What stars are you, Floyd?'

'Stars?'

'Yeah, stars, you know, your horoscope. What star sign were you born under?'

'Capricorn.'

'I'm a Capricorn too,' puts in Dixie, smiling. 'How about that, Floyd?'

'It's a small world.'

'Well, I'm a Scorpio,' says Carmichael. He is leafing through a newspaper, looking for the forecasts. I glance at Dixie, and he winks.

'Here we go,' Carmichael says. He folds the paper open and lays it on the desk. 'What does it say for me, hey? "Be on your guard against negative influences which may affect your professional and domestic life." What? I don't *have* a domestic life. Still, "don't be negative" means that I should go for it. Yeah. What else does it say? "Power games may be played out by others around you." Who wrote this stuff, hey? I don't want this psychological crap. I'm gonna change my paper. Where's the rest of it? "Confrontations and complex issues could show colleagues in their true light." What does that mean – I should stay in bed?'

'Well, you're a Scorpio,' Dixie says. 'Scorpio is all *about* confrontation, right? The sting in your tail.'

'They write this stuff for office workers,' Carmichael complains, peering at the newsprint as if it was written in a foreign language. 'Am I gonna have a good or bad day, that's all I want to know.' He plucks at the newspaper irritably, as if there might be a better forecast on another page.

'What does it say for Capricorn?' asks Dixie. 'We're the ones going there.'

'Oh yeah,' growls Carmichael. 'I'll read it out. Capricorn. "Don't lean too heavily on your lover, and try to avoid conflict with their family." Does that help?'

We shake our heads.

Carmichael continues. 'Get a load of this: "Your relationship with your boss is now extremely well starred." Well, fancy that. "Today you will need ingenuity and initiative. Don't be reckless or your plans may fall apart. Press ahead with self-control, and success will be yours." Hey, what more could you want?'

'You're making it up,' Dixie says. 'It sounds too good.'

'No, I'm serious. Look at it.' Carmichael hands him the paper. Dixie reads.

'Yeah, that's what it says,' he agrees. 'Don't lean too heavily . . . Relationship with your boss . . . How do they know about this, up in the stars?'

'Horoscopes are how the stars are interpreted,' Carmichael says. 'And yours are excellent.'

'What was that about confrontations?' I ask.

'That was *my* forecast, not yours. You just need – what was it? – ingenuity and initiative. Success will be yours.'

'Just send five pounds for details.'

'Don't laugh,' Carmichael says. 'There is truth in the stars.' He stands up. 'So we go for it,' he says.

He crosses to his wall safe. 'Look the other way, please.'

Dixie and I turn obediently away. It isn't necessary, because Carmichael shields the combination lock with his body. Not only does he believe in horoscopes, he thinks we two have X-ray eyes. We hear the door open. We hear him bring something out.

'OK,' Carmichael says. We turn round.

On the white desk he has tossed several wraps of cocaine. He holds others carelessly in his hands. I ask, 'How much have you got?'

'Just had a delivery from Spain.'

As Huey throws the spare wraps back into the safe, I glance inside. Some delivery. He must have several kilos there. If he paid between twelve and fifteen thousand pounds a kilo, Carmichael has a hundred grand inside that safe. And that's at import prices. The street price of that little lot, cut down into 40-milligram bags, would be half a million pounds.

That's how the police will value it. They'll calculate as if Carmichael sold the whole consignment to end-users and made all the profit himself. The police will ignore the distributors, like Dixie and me. They'll ignore the breadheads we sell to, who add their own hundred per cent markup. They'll ignore the little bagmen, adding another hundred per cent on top. The police will ignore all of that. They'll talk it big. When they announce one of their rare little hauls, they'll talk street prices, to make the figures really large.

Carmichael repeats our instructions.

When we make our rounds today, we are to shift as much stock as we can. The consignment in Huey's safe has to be moved out and down the line. He does not want to hold on to it. It is dangerous. And it is bad for his cash flow. We are to get the stuff out to the breadheads, and tell them to push it fast on extended credit. The whole consignment, Carmichael says, must filter down into as many pairs of hands as possible. It's what financiers call 'spreading the risk'.

Huey laughs at that. He thinks he made a joke.

If I was making a career of this I guess I'd resent Dixie coming with me. After one day on my own I am put back on trainee status. But I understand Carmichael's reasoning. He has to be sure of me.

Like I have to be sure of *him*.

To tell the truth, I can use an extra hand. Today I have to hit as many marks as possible, and Dixie can find them fast. He knows this island. He knows the cut-throughs and footpaths, the bridges, the temporary paths between building sites and brand new office blocks.

We are in the middle of the Island, at the top of East Ferry Road, at a pub where yuppies don't go. It is called the Queen. It is built of weathered red brick, and is V-shaped to fit a fork between two roads. The sign outside says it is 'The Friendliest Pub On The Island'. But that one painted notice is not enough to make up for the shabby doors, scruffy brickwork, and grimy frosted glass. Inside, the pub has dark wood, flock wallpaper, and a dense green ceiling. Its decor has not changed in two decades. For as long as ordinary people remain on the Island, this pub will not change.

The blonde behind the counter gives us two pints of John Bull, a smile, a plate of cheese and ham rolls. We move to a side table.

'Not a bad pub,' Dixie says.

'One of the old ones.'

'I like a pub where I don't meet my customers. They won't come in here.'

Looking more carefully at the people who *are* in here, I see that few are true locals. They don't live here. These men are working on building sites around the Island. They avoid the yuppie pubs and choose places like the Queen. It serves seven beers: Taylor Walker and John Bull – they're local, at least – then there is Tetleys from Yorkshire, Guinness from Ireland, Löwenbräu, Skol and Australian Four X. Even the video game comes from Japan.

'Are you gonna lean on your lover tonight?' asks Dixie.

I look puzzled.

'Huey's horoscope for us Capricorns. It said don't lean on your lover. Don't mix with her family.'

'You're Capricorn, Dixie. Does it sound true for you?'

He looks rueful. 'Only too true – that bit about not mixing with her family. Her mother's staying.'

'Does Carmichael believe in horoscopes?'

'Sure. He's a nut-case. Vegetarian too.'

'How about you?'

'This is a ham roll I'm eating, Floyd.'

'That shows you ain't Jewish, but do you believe in horoscopes?'

Dixie shrugs. 'They're nonsense but, you know, sometimes they seem to hit things right on the pin.'

Tacked to the wall above his head is a handwritten notice: 'The Strippers Are Back Thursday And Friday Lunchtimes 12.30—2.30'. In the bow-end of the V-shaped saloon stand rough wooden platforms, where the girls will come and strut. I doubt the pub will turn the lights down. Maybe someone will draw curtains across the frosted glass before they turn up the disco tape. Then a couple of women will clatter sweatily through a series of numbers, as close to the punters in the pub as their mum at the kitchen table. Lunchtime at the local on the Isle of Dogs.

Across from the Docklands Arena, East Ferry Street joins Lime-harbour and then widens. Opposite the Arena is a pub called the George. We don't go in.

Our mark stands by a white BMW. I guess it's his. He looks about twenty-one years of age and wears a mid-blue suit above a cream fly-fronted shirt. 'You're late,' he says.

Dixie says it has been a busy day.

'So what? I can't afford half an hour waiting for you to show up.'

'You eat lunch yet?'

'What's that to you?'

'You could have eaten inside the pub. Killed two birds with one stone.'

'I don't eat lunch. This the new man?'

I nod to him. He tells Dixie that he'll take an ounce. Dixie says the deal was for three.

'You think I can find three thousand quid just like that?'

'I gave you warning.'

'What d'you mean, warning? Don't give me warnings.'

The boy speaks cockily, but his voice trembles. Back in his office he is used to giving orders.

'In this game,' Dixie says, 'we all have to make sacrifices.'

The boy scoffs. 'Sacrifices! This is business. You sell, I buy. And *you* don't set the terms.'

'I set the price,' Dixie says.

'You *ask* a price. I don't have to buy.'

'You have an alternative?'

'There's always an alternative. Listen, I have a thousand pounds in my pocket. I'm in the market for an ounce.'

I speak for the first time. 'Perhaps you will tell us the name of your alternative?'

The boy looks at me coldly. 'That's my affair.'

'I would regard it,' I say pleasantly, 'as a special favour.'

Dixie narrows his eyes. He is watching the game I play.

'People come to me sometimes,' I continue, speaking quietly, with just the trace of an American–Italian accent – that shambling mumble that Marlon Brando used in the *Godfather*. 'They speak to me. They ask: will you do something for me, because you are my friend? I never refuse them. And then, one day . . .' Here I pause, to pick an imaginary sliver of oregano from my teeth, like Brando again, his cheeks stuffed with cotton wool. 'One day I return to these people, and this time I ask that they do a favour for me. You understand this? Return of a favour. It's how our family works. We help each other.'

The boy looks uncertain. Something about the words that I use, and the way that I deliver them, something about it strikes a low chord in his guts. 'What are you rabbiting about?' he asks shakily.

Dixie joins in the act. Gently, almost lovingly, he wraps an arm round the boy's shoulder. He places his mouth close to the boy's ear. 'Don't insult my brother,' he whispers. 'Don't even think of it. He would never forgive you.'

'My brother Dixie, he speaks well of you,' I say. 'He asked especially that I should meet you.'

'Why?' The question comes quietly.

I give a small but eloquent shrug. 'Perhaps you are not ready yet.'

'For what?'

'I will tell you this, my friend.' I still mimic Brando. 'I will take an interest in you. You will be special in my sight. Would you like to prosper in our family?'

For a moment nothing happens. He stands with his mouth slightly open, trying to follow the script. Then his teeth clunk together. His head nods. 'Yeah, I want to prosper. Sure I do.'

'I am glad to hear this.' I nod gravely. 'In three days I will visit you again. I will bring five ounces of cocaine. It is my hope that you will bring five thousand pounds. Do you think you can do this for me, as a friend?'

'Five thousand?'

I nod, and extend my hand. The boy is about to reach out for it when Dixie whispers urgently in his ear. The boy glances across at me. His eyes widen. Then he looks nervously about him, bows, and accepts my hand. He kisses my fingers.

For the first hundred yards we keep straight faces. Then, far enough away, we begin to chuckle. All our suppressed mirth escapes in little bubbles as we walk along the road. We replay the dialogue, improving on the lines.

'If we practise this around the Island,' Dixie says, 'we could make our own movie. Isle of Dogsfather, what d'you think?'

'It gave the boy a thrill. He thinks he's working with the Mafia.'

'We gotta do it again. Learn the words right, we'll get the whole island quivering in line.'

'If we had the words right, it wouldn't work. You need sponta-neity. That was a once-off.'

On our left is the big Asda supermarket where we parked the car. On our right, alongside but above the road, runs the Docklands Light Railway, bright and new. Little blue trains, each with two boxy carriages, glide up and down. They are Toytown trains; pretty in the architect's drawings, hopelessly crowded in the peaks of the day. The amount of people crammed into offices out here, they should have built longer trains.

Off the road to our left begins a grassy bank that will continue almost to the river. It is the edge of the Mudchute, a high wide wasteland of scrubby hills and valleys. Its tough pale grass grows on mud and clinker dredged up from the docks. Dixie and I climb the steps of its damp embankment to make today's final drop.

The Mudchute is still the same wasteland. These thirty-two acres have changed little since the three of us – Ludo, Albie and I – used to play here as kids. Even the inner-city farm is still here. When I was young, the farm was created by local action groups for schoolkids and anyone else who didn't know what a sheep felt like. Or a cow, or a pig, a goat or a pony. The farm had chickens and rabbits, and grew things. You couldn't eat what they grew: the soil was polluted, because at the bottom of this road there had been a leadworks. The lead stayed in the soil.

'That's the guy,' Dixie says.

The man leans against the gate two hundred yards ahead of us along the muddy path. He is waiting. Behind him, the path runs down into a fold of land that once had allotments. Families grew flowers and vegetables. In those days no one measured lead in the soil. Not round our way. Years ago, most of those allotments disappeared, because the Port of London Authority commandeered the land. They said they would expand the docks. Everybody was in favour of that. Our dad thought he might get his job back, but he should have known. The project never happened, plans were shelved.

As we stroll on the high path along the edge of the fields, Dixie explains about the man. 'He's new, but he built his network real fast. Surprisingly fast. We should watch him.'

'Maybe he brought his old network with him.'

'Maybe. A guy like this is either good news or very bad.'

'Bad as in dangerous?'

'Bad as in unusual. I hate things unusual. He's a big spender.'

'Just my type.'

'Big spenders have big ambitions.'

We are halfway there by now. The man has dark hair and wears a brown topcoat. He doesn't move from the gate.

'If you're worried about him, we should make him come to *us*. The land drops behind him.'

'He's the customer. We go to him.'

Moisture hangs in the breeze that drifts across the Mudchute. It could rain soon. On this damp cold ground, the grass is not like grass in picture books: it is town grass – tufty, unkempt, in patches of mud. The Mudchute is not a neat park, it is wilderness, in the guts of London. But it won't survive here. Not now. Land around here costs five million an acre. Already, around the edges of this open land, new money peers in: prim doll's houses along the west side, cranes on the northern skyline. Speculators will flatten these muddy green hillocks, bulldoze the few trees, and they'll build. Somewhere inside the thirty-two acres they will leave a landscaped formal garden. It is all that will remain of the Muddie we knew.

We arrive. The big spender asks if I am the new man.

'You can call me John Burns.'

'You look like a Carter to me.'

He doesn't smile. But he scored a point there – he'll be pleased with that. I check him over: square face, small eyes, black hair greased down, nose could have been in a fight. He doesn't look the city type. 'Do I know you?' I ask.

'Don't look like it.'

'Then how do you know me?'

'I heard you was back.'

'You're from south of the river?'

'I live on the Island.'

Not in the plush Cascades or the twee Cotton's Landing. I suppose he could live in one of the few old terraces not yet knocked down. He isn't saying. It's all right with me. I don't need his address.

Dixie asks the breadhead how much he wants. He says ten.

'Ten ounces?'

'That's what I said.'

'That'll cost you ten grand.'

'Less a discount for bulk.'

'First I heard of that.'

'You want to get rid of it or not? You're overstocked.'

I let them haggle. If the man is arguing prices, then he wants to do a deal. Down behind him in the straggly little valley, I notice that a few allotments do remain, after all. An old man works on one.

'OK, nine and a half ponies. Nine fifty an ounce.'

'I've heard better.'

'But we can deliver, can't we? We're always here, always pure.'

Behind me, out in the shabby rolling fields, a dozen brown and white sheep are munching the grass. Near our feet lie dead brambles. Not far away, in an old ditch called the Newtie, Ludo and I would come to catch tadpoles and newts. We took them home in jam jars.

141

Hardly anyone comes here now. Way over there, a man and his boy walk a dog. They keep it on a lead, away from the sheep. Down there, the old man potters with his cabbages. Across that fold of land behind him come two sporty types in joggers. They stop to chat by the gate on the other side.

'Not here,' the breadhead says. 'We're on the skyline.'

'We'll go down there,' suggests Dixie.

Down in that dip we will be completely out of sight. No one will see us. We won't see them.

I say that I will stay up here.

'What for?' asks the breadhead. He is already through the gate and starting down the slope. Even Dixie looks surprised.

'I'll keep a lookout.'

'The Muddie's empty,' the breadhead says.

'Almost.'

The breadhead doesn't like it, but Dixie claps him on the shoulder and laughs. 'We only need two,' he says.

I wait by the gate as they pick their way down to the slimy bottom of the dip. The dampness in the air becomes drizzle. I find I'm holding my breath. My stomach muscles are tight.

Dixie and the breadhead pause at the bottom, then turn to face each other. Dixie wipes a raindrop from his brow. Along the valley, the old man wanders off from his allotment into a small rickety shed. The two joggers resume their training run.

They trot lightly down the path on the other side of the dip. Dixie waits for them to pass.

But they don't.

Not both of them. In the bottom of the dip, one man stops beside the breadhead, the other jogs on past. It takes him less than five seconds to reach me.

'Down you come,' he says calmly.

He is a yard away from me across the gate. Just out of reach.

'I said, come on.'

I glance past him into the dip. The breadhead in the brown topcoat now holds a pistol in his hand. It is small and black. It pokes out above his clenched fingers and points at Dixie.

'Think I'm stupid?' I ask the man. I inch towards him.

He slips his hand inside the unzipped top of his jogger suit and withdraws it enough to let me see his gun.

'You won't use that up here.'

'Try me.'

I won't do that. The only witnesses on this whole soggy wasteland are the father and his son walking their dog. They're half a mile away. The old man is keeping dry inside his shed. It is as easy for the sportsman to shoot me up here as down there.

I open the gate.

He stands aside to let me pass. Down at the bottom, the breadhead covers Dixie while the second jogger takes Dixie's cocaine. Then he loosens Dixie's money belt. When he has taken that, he will go through Dixie's pockets. And find Dixie's gun.

I hesitate at the top of the path. 'Get a move on,' my jogger says. He moves a warning step closer, his hand snug inside his zip.

Coming down the slippery track, I stumble. Involuntarily I reach out my arm. I grab the front of his loose blouson and I heave at it. We crash to the ground and roll fighting down the slope. In one split second I see the brown topcoat and his jogger gape at us. I see Dixie ram his hand into his pocket.

But I have enough to do. This man does not wear a jogger suit for effect. He is fit. His fist crunches into my left cheek and drives my head against the ground. His other hand splays across my face to hold me down. He fumbles inside his blouson. Then a gun fires. I can't see whether it was Dixie or the topcoat. I wrestle with the heavy heap on top of me. He rams my head into the mud while he grabs his handgun. As it appears from his zip top I smack my right fist into his face. I can't grab the gun with my left, because my hand is still bandaged. I get my right to his gun. He smacks his other fist into my unguarded face, then tries to tug my fingers from his pistol. Twice I bang my bandaged left against his cheek, and feel the cuts re-open across my knuckles. I try to twist my body so I can jab my left elbow in his face. But he ducks, wrenches at my fingers, and pulls his gun hand free.

I force my forearm beneath his chin and thrust it upwards. Some of his weight lifts off my body. But even as I squirm free, I see his gun come round toward my face.

'Drop it!' screams Dixie.

He stands beside the topcoat's body. The other sportsman waits his chance. But my man fires his gun. The centre of Dixie's shirt caves in instantly, as if a hidden mouth inside had sucked at it and vomited blood. I heave the bastard off as Dixie falls. We grapple on the wet ground – both of us with a hand on his gun. He has it in his grip, but I control the way it points. His other hand clamps on mine and tears at my fingers. I try to thump him with my left, though my hand is a ball of pain.

He punches me. But I twist myself above him on the ground. I drag my knee in to his head and grind it into his face. I grind it deep for Dixie. The guy holds tight to his pistol but he can't make me move my knee. His left fist flails at me. He hammers against my ribs. But the blows are weakening. Suddenly I have twisted the gun out of his hand – but it flies away from us across the ground. I stab my finger in his eye. He screams with pain. I slide my knee to the side, grab his throat with my right hand, and squeeze. He rolls his head. He clutches at my fingers. I tighten my grip.

All this time his friend has been tugging at my shoulder. Now I see him scramble for the fallen gun. But I beat him to it. I am nearer. I dive across the mud, scoop it toward me with my bandaged hand, and take a hold of it. The jogger backs away. He stumbles against the topcoat's body. He panics.

As I clamber to my feet he starts to run. He slithers up the slope where he first came down. But I ignore him. His partner is writhing on the ground, about to rise. I take a kick at him. It catches the side of his head and he collapses. I kick again. The next kick he doesn't feel. But I have to do it.

Dixie lies so still and bloody that I don't need to touch him. There is no point. I become oddly calm. From my trouser pocket I take a handkerchief, and I use it to clean fingerprints off the gun. I work methodically. It's like a therapy. The gun is like a rosary to me.

When I have finished, I throw the gun several yards off into the brambles. I look at Dixie. His eyes are open but he does not move. His chest is obscenely red. Nearby, the man in the brown topcoat lies face down. He does not move either. I prod his body with my shoe.

Then I kneel beside Dixie and feel through his pockets. I don't know what I am looking for, and I don't find it. His gun lies in the grass. His envelope and money belt are with the runner who got away.

As I kneel in a kind of mourning, someone calls. The old man is hobbling across his allotment, shouting questions. I stare in his direction, hardly seeing him. He waves his fist in the air, and I realise that what he sees is three men on the grass, with a fourth going through their pockets. He will remember this. Blond man, blazer and slacks, one hand bandaged. Red on the bandage where blood has seeped through.

He is plodding closer. He thinks that I am the man who killed the others on the wasteland, yet he keeps coming. At his age, I guess he doesn't frighten any more. I shall have to go.

But which way? Back across the fields is the father and his son. And it's a long way to where we came in. The old man is ten yards away now. I stand up, and start to climb the opposite bank leading to the nearer exit. At the top of the grassy embankment I check the street scene outside. It looks normal. Cars with their wipers going. An old lady beneath an umbrella, carrying shopping. Several people over there, sheltering from the rain beneath the elevated section of the railway. Stairway up to the station. Man in a jogger suit halfway up.

He waits on a balcony where the stairs divide. We are no more than a hundred yards apart. As the crow flies. Two hundred yards on foot: down the slope, across the pavement, up the stairs.

He sees me watching him. He licks his lips nervously, but he doesn't move. He doesn't need to yet.

I start down the slimy path toward him. Behind me, the old man is still shouting. He has reached the bodies now. I keep my eye on the jogger suit. He keeps his eye on me. I get the ridiculous idea that as long as I walk normally and don't start running, he will wait there, to see what I do. But I'm wrong. The man turns and trots away from me up the right-hand staircase from the mezzanine to the station platform. When I glance to my left I see why.

Up from the river chugs a little blue train. The jogger intends to catch it. So do I.

I slither down the muddy steps leading off the Mudchute embankment. I stumble through the gate. I run between the concrete pillars holding up the elevated railway, on to the steep stairs. I have never used this model railway, but I saw which way he went. He took the right-hand staircase.

At the mezzanine where the stairs divide, a sign says 'Do Not Cross Red Line Without A Valid Ticket'. I hurtle past. On the final flight another sign demands: 'Have You Got A Valid Ticket?' They really care.

As I burst on to the empty platform, the train starts to pull away. It is moving slowly. I thump against the side of a carriage as it passes. People glance out at me from inside their cocoon. I run along the platform with the train, and thump again. A passenger frowns. A girl in light blue uniform waves her finger at me. The train moves on.

At little more than walking speed it glides away. I examine the track. It looks safe enough. This isn't like the Underground. The rails here are spread well apart on a concrete floor. Whichever rails are live, they have big gaps between them. I jump down.

I am not insane. I know the rails are electric, but the gap between them is a whole yard wide. I can run along the middle. At the speed the train is going, I will catch it at the next station. It is only half a mile away, near the Docklands Arena at the other end of the Mudchute.

The last notice as I leave the station reads: 'Warning: Automatic Trains Operating, Live Current Rails. Do Not Go On Or Near The Track'. I chase the train. From the rear window I am watched by a mother and her toddler child. The kid thinks I'm funny, but the mother shows no reaction. None at all.

The blue train is pulling away from me in the drizzle, gathering speed, effortlessly accelerating along its elevated track. My ribs hurt. They took a beating on the Mudchute. I am slowing down.

I stand gasping for breath, as I realise where I am: stuck on a strip of concrete railway within a pair of electric rails, twenty feet above the ground. Along the left side of the track is wire fencing. To my right is a three-foot central barrier, then the southbound rails.

I glance behind. If another train bore down on me, I'd have no room to stand aside. This track is not a public walkway. But no train is coming. I am quite alone.

No one can see me up here. The track is not overlooked. Down to my left are normal-sized houses. Across to the right is open land.

I trudge back to Mudchute Station. Nobody is on it. No passengers. No staff. No one walks the Mudchute on a rainy afternoon. I clamber up from the trackway on to the empty platform. It is an isolated world. The toylike character of this electric train set is emphasised by lack of people. I am like a lonely child, unattended in the attic. My toy station is blue metal and glass. The handrails are red. The electric advertising board has three-sided vertical panels, endlessly rotating to show repeating ads. Three for the price of one.

I trudge off the platform on to the exit gantry and look below. At the foot of the stairs is the old man. I duck back inside.

He didn't see me. He was telling his story to people sheltering from the rain. He was pointing across to the Mudchute, explaining what happened. Soon, someone will ask if the man he saw was a blond guy in a blazer streaked with mud. A man with his hand bandaged. Then they'll come up here.

A train is coming. I can hear the rumble. When I peer along the track I see that it will be on the track across from me, going south to the river. I need to catch that train. But I will have to cross the line.

To return to the mezzanine landing and nip up the other stairs would let them see me. I can't risk that. The only way I can get across is to jump down on to the track again. I do so. Through the central barrier there is no gap. So I run several yards to my left,

146

step on to a two-foot metal platform, straddle the barrier, and jump down the other side. But in the time it takes me to do this, the incoming train has reached the other end of the station platform. I am in its path. A hooter blasts as the train slows down. I hop across the outer live rail to haul myself quickly on to the southbound platform. A blast again. Two blue carriages shudder to a halt beside me, and the train doors open. I step inside.

On this damp day there are few passengers. And there is no driver. None at all. The train only has a guard. The guard presses a button for stop or start. He presses a hooter if he sees an idiot on the line. But that can't be right – no driver. It cannot work like that. Somebody must drive the trains by remote control, scanning the tracks by TV monitor. He must sit in his office, playing the Docklands Light Railway like an arcade game. It *is* a toy.

The guard is young, black and unconcerned. He shakes his head at me. I raise my hand. 'I know,' I say. 'I know. Let's not keep everybody waiting. Let's just go.'

I sit down hurriedly. He clucks his tongue. But the reason I have sat down so quickly is because the old man has just popped out on the northbound platform. He has people with him. I huddle in my seat, but they ignore me. They are all looking along the track to the north. Someone saw me running up that right-hand staircase, running for the train. He thinks I caught it.

Eventually the guard strolls off to press the button. We glide south.

Beyond Mudchute there is only one more station. Island Gardens is the end of the line.

The streets bring back memories, though the buildings here have changed. Nothing major – the odd warehouse and high wall, the swathe of railway at roof height. This is a corner of the Island not yet fully refurbished by development. Fifty yards from the station I recognise Island Gardens Park, looking out across the Thames. It looks as quiet and peaceful as it always did.

Any other day, I would visit the pie stall inside the park gate. If it's still there. I would take a coffee to the river wall, and gaze at Greenwich on the other side. I would admire the twin white domes of the Royal Naval College. I would squint across at the Cutty Sark and the never-absent cranes. I would watch gulls wheel above the Thames while brown water laps the river walls. I would gaze towards home.

But not today. At the park entrance is that familiar little rotunda. I nip inside. Rather than wait for the groaning lift, I use the stairs.

When we were young, we used to count them. Eighty-seven. Eighty-seven steps spiralling down sixty feet below ground level, into the Foot Tunnel beneath the Thames. The Greenwich Foot Tunnel is a long straight tube, about eight foot high, only seven in places, walls and ceiling tiled in white. No cars can use it – only people, walking. It is like a secret passage, bringing Deptford workers north of the river, taking them home again at night. It brought us kids under the river to the Isle of Dogs. Today its job is to drain the dregs from the battered Island, back to their houses in the south.

# 24

'We must get the car back,' Carmichael says.

That is the least of his problems, I'd have thought. He has lost his right-hand man, half a kilo of cocaine and around ten thousand pounds in cash.

I ask, 'Dixie's wife – has someone told her?'

'The police will do that.'

'Christ, we were talking about her, just this lunchtime. Her mother's visiting.'

Carmichael nods. 'That'll make it easier for her, hey? But you stay out of this. You don't go round there, right?'

I take a breath. He explains: 'The police will be watching Dixie's house to see who calls. You can't go there, you see that? We have to act like we never knew the man, understand?'

I nod.

'That's how it is. Casualty of war.'

Yeah, that's how it is. I understand. I ask, 'You got a drink in here?'

'Don't you like Lucozade?' He opens the wall cupboard, properly stocked, and pours a whisky, large. Just as he places it in my hand, he asks, 'Why today? Tell me that.'

'You mean how did they know that today was a big one?'

'That's right.' He keeps his hand on my whisky.

'All the breadheads knew it. They had to bring extra money.'

Carmichael purses his lips. He looks me straight in the eyes as he takes his hand from my glass. It feels light. 'You didn't talk to anyone?'

'No.'

He holds my gaze. 'Still, you did manage to kill one of them.'

'Dixie did.'

'So one of them suddenly got rich, hey? Did he look a user?'

'Too fit.'

Carmichael nods. 'You should have killed him, you know that?'

'Which one – the one that got away, or the one who shot Dixie?'

'Both. Why not?'

'There were two dead already.'

'You stop when both sides get one each? We play to win, not to draw, Floyd. You were on home ground.' He frowns at me, then shrugs. 'You better go get the car back.'

'Hope I'm not recognised.'

'What d'you think – the old man will hang around the supermarket? Of course he won't. Did those guys know where you parked, hey?'

'Doubt it. But the car has been there more than four hours. That's a long time to be shopping.'

'Cars overpark every day. What you cannot do is leave it overnight. But *you've* got to do it, Floyd. If you think you can't go on the Island in case you're recognised, then you are finished. Understand?'

'When you fall off a horse, the first thing you do is climb back on. I know.'

'It hasn't been a good start, has it?'

I don't take a gun. A gun didn't help Dixie. I return to the Island as if I was going on evening shift: catch a 188 to Greenwich Church Street, cross the harbour beside the Cutty Sark, slip under the river through the Foot Tunnel. I even use the Docklands Railway.

But I have changed my clothing. There is always the chance that those little blue engines are operated by a Fat Controller behind a monitor screen, and the Fat Controller might just recall the guy who chased a train along the track. I now wear a blue sweater beneath a navy anorak, dark slacks, anonymous. On my left hand is a clean bandage. No sign of blood.

The little train carries me two stops from the Island Gardens terminus to Crossharbour near the Arena. I linger across the road from the Asda, watching the carpark. The supermarket is still open: evening shoppers after work. I see my car.

Looking carefully all about me, I drift into the carpark. I shall be the only person returning to his car without a shopping trolley. Maybe I should pop inside and buy something. Then I shake my head. Just collect the car, Floyd, and get out of here.

*

By the time I park the Fiesta in Malpas Road, it is nine o'clock. I stay in my seat for the radio news. We are the third item.

'Two men died today in a shooting incident on the Isle of Dogs. At about three-fifteen this afternoon a group of five men congregated in the Mudchute, a park in the Cubitt Town area. It is believed that a scuffle broke out, and two shots were fired. According to witnesses two of the alleged assailants made their escape together via the Docklands Light Railway, while another made off across the park. The reason for the affray is unclear, though a police spokesman played down any suggestion of feuding between criminal gangs. At this stage, he said, it seems more likely that an attempted mugging went badly wrong. Police have appealed for witnesses, and ask anyone in the vicinity of Mudchute Station between three o'clock and three-thirty this afternoon to contact them as soon as possible.'

I remain in the car throughout the other headlines to see if I scored a double. But Vinnie's man with his head staved in on a patch of waste ground near Deptford Station does not get mentioned. His death is not remarkable enough.

What do the police think about the killings on the Mudchute? Maybe neither Dixie nor the topcoat had criminal records. Certainly the old man will have said he saw a man robbing them. But if the police really think those two stiffs were innocent members of the park-going public, why do they think villains gunned them down? Why did five men meet at all on the Mudchute in the rain? Why? Too many questions. The police are putting up a smokescreen. Someone has told them to play it down. Someone thinks he knows what is going on.

I get out of the car.

As I approach Jamie's house, I glance up at the first floor. No lights are on. I ring his bell. In my pocket I have the key he lent me, but if Jamie is not there I don't want to sit in the wreckage of his flat till he finally decides to show up from the pub. I'll go home to Ludo.

Halfway back towards the car I see someone standing there. It is Eva. She wears her usual dull black leggings, and for the cool April evening she has put on a black woolly top. She waits for me.

She says, 'Last time we met you had a key.'

'Don't you have one?'

'I don't live here. You have it with you?'

'Why d'you want to go in?'

Eva moves a step towards me. She keeps her voice down. 'This is urgent, man. Can you get us in?'

*

His flat is less of a wreck now. Jamie must have liked the way Eva tidied it, because he has not yet pulled the place apart. Maybe he does not pull it apart, maybe it just disintegrates.

Eva goes immediately into the bathroom. She wastes no time. She tells me that Jamie has been caught in a drugs bust at the Cross Keys pub. I groan. He and a dozen others are down at Lewisham nick, 'helping with enquiries'. If the fuzz follow their normal pattern, then at this very moment someone will be interrupting a tame magistrate snoozing in front of TV News to sign search warrants. Any of the dozen who was carrying will have his pad turned over. Anyone still in Lewisham nick *would* have been carrying. If they weren't carrying when they walked in there, they will be now. The Bill can fix that.

Eva emerges from the bathroom with several bottles of pills. 'I'll only leave his aspirin. Everything else goes.'

'You've got a packet of cough sweets there.'

'Victory V. Punks sometimes grind them up to mix with Iranian.'

'Does Jamie do that?'

Eva is in his bedroom now. 'He uses better stuff. But the filth won't care.'

'They can't charge him for possession of a packet of Victory V.'

'You've never been busted, have you, feller?'

Eva pockets Jamie's tin box of works. Inside will be any heroin Jamie has managed to get hold of, a tube and tin foil for smoking, plus needles for shooting up.

'Go through his waste bins,' she tells me. 'Find anything that should not be there – especially foil. You with me?'

'How long do we have?'

'It depends whose pad the police hit first.'


I drive Eva out through the west side of Deptford towards Bermondsey. Somewhere around there she can stash Jamie's things. I will not know where this hiding-place is.

I ask Eva what Jamie was caught carrying. She doesn't know. She shakes her head bitterly. 'I was doing so well with him, you know?'

'In what way?'

'You know, man. He promised me this time he really would stop cranking. He'd only smoke the stuff. He even gave me some needles – after that scare with the Soneryl, you know? I thought I had him straight.'

'You think you can get him clean?'

151

'Only Jamie can do that. But I tried to stop him shooting up, you know? To come down easy.'

'What are you, Eva – some kind of social worker?'

'Do me a favour! None of that official crap. We help our friends, you know?'

Quietly, we motor along Woodpecker Road. The drizzle has cleared, leaving the evening fine and cool. While I pull out to overtake a bus, Eva explains about the self-help group she belongs to. You can hardly call it a group – it is too loose-knit. It doesn't have a name. It doesn't really have members. But everyone in the group, association, whatever you want to call it, has been a user. Some still are. They know what it takes to maintain a habit. They know what it takes to come off.

'We don't preach, right? Don't make a judgement. Just try to help our friends – know what I mean?'

'D'you have much success?'

'Sure – if they're ready to kick it. But that's not all the group is about. We try to help friends through the bad times. Everyone has bad times, right? We look for clean supplies.'

'Are *you* supplying?'

Eva looks at me before replying. She shrugs. 'If we have to, we do, sure. In small quantities, clean, when the need is bad. Sometimes that's the best help we can give.'

We are in Trundley's Road now, slowing to turn right behind Deptford Park. Traffic is light. Driving is easy.

'Jamie says he has smack under control,' I say. 'Any chance he's right?'

'Junkies all say that.'

'He says it isn't smack that's the problem, it's buying it. If smack was on sale like cigarettes, he could survive forever. He'd live as normal a life as a cigarette smoker.'

'Junkies all say that, as well. Heroin is stronger than nicotine, man. I get out here.' She points with her ginger head. 'Heroin numbs the feelings. Junkies don't need to eat. They don't need sex. They don't give a lazy damn. The whole world may be against them, but they can't feel it. They shut everything out. D'you know what that's like?' She opens the car door, but pauses in her seat before getting out. 'It's like dying – slowly, beautifully, not a care in the world. A lovely way to go, don't you think?'

# 25

Tamsin opens the door and smiles. 'You came right on cue.'

I follow her in. She wears an enormous white sweatshirt so bulky that she could have had it from Ludo. She also wears skin-tight red pants. Her white sweatshirt is bunched up and tucked in at the small of her back, so her rear is exposed. In those pants I do mean exposed.

She flounces into the living room and holds open the door. The TV murmurs. We are alone.

'Where's Suzie?'

'On nights. She wants me to stay in.'

'She's worried about you. You're all she has.'

'I'm a big girl, Floyd. Hadn't you noticed?' The theme for the News starts on the television. 'You want this on?' Her hand reaches for the switch.

'Just the headlines.'

Tamsin remains poised by the set, ready to kill it. All we see are those headlines, and I have to hold my hand up to get the last one: 'Murder on the Isle of Dogs – muggers turn to guns.'

'That's local,' I say.

'And boring.' It goes off. 'Sit and talk to me, Floyd.'

She comes back across the room, punches me playfully in the chest, then flops on to the sofa. She curls up at one end, leaving plenty of room. I choose an armchair. She shrugs. 'I should hate you,' she says.

I raise an eyebrow.

'Dragging me off from that party. It's embarrassing. You were like a caveman collecting his bride.' She cocks her head. 'You know why they call it Ecstasy?'

'I can guess.'

'Because it's the Love Drug. I've still got some upstairs.' There is a devil behind her eyes. 'You're not going to tell Mummy?'

'No.'

'Oh goody.' She wriggles on the sofa. She is a little girl putting on a little girl act. She thinks she is a vamp putting on a vamp act. 'Now we have a secret between us, don't we?'

'Suzie didn't search your bedroom, did she? Because she trusts you.'

'You're beginning to sound like the older generation.'

'I am the older generation.'

'But so dishy with it.' She giggles. 'Some girls go for older men.'

She changes position on the sofa. Now she lies on her back, her head propped against one end, her legs bent, her bare feet flat on the cushion. 'I'm cold,' she says plaintively. 'Are you cold?'

'I'm going home. I thought Suzie was here.'

'And I thought you'd come to see me.'

She's a trier, I'll say that. When I smile at her, I try to make it a fatherly smile. I don't think I succeed. 'I'm too old for this, Tamsin.'

'I bet you're not.' Her head tilts.

'When your curfew is lifted, I'll come to the Parrot to hear you sing.'

'Don't strain yourself.'

'I will only have eyes for you.' I stand up. She lies watching me.

'Men are such patronising bastards,' she says.


I blow out so hard that I mist up the windscreen.

I must get my mind back to the here and now. Wipe off the windscreen. See clearly again. I put the car into gear and drive back to Jamie's flat.

I arrive just in time to run into the law turning the place upside down. They are searching the flat methodically, opening cushions, moving furniture, looking beneath the floor. I am interested to note that they have not unscrewed the fingerplates from his doors.

A police dog is whining in the bathroom.

My arrival depresses Jamie even more. He lights a cigarette from the butt of the first. He glares at me from beneath his eyelashes. A dog scratches vinyl in the bathroom.

The only person who looks happy is that smug cop, Kellard. One sniff of drugs and he is there. Sniffer of the Yard. He stands tall and thin, his eyes glinting, a tight smile on his face as if he is pleased to see me. He probably is. I can see what he is thinking: the pieces are falling into place. He doesn't know what they will build to, but as long as he keeps finding new pieces the picture will slowly become clear. The patiently plodding policeman: he should never have come off the beat. He looks wrong out of uniform. His plain clothes are plain. He wears an old-fashioned brown tweed jacket, looks like it has biscuit crumbs sprinkled all over it. Beige twill slacks. Heavy-soled brown shoes with laces. Green tie.

'You live here together?' he asks.

'You know where I live.'

'You came in with a key.'

I don't answer. It wasn't a question. It was one of those statements you feel you have to correct. He wants to hear how you'll do it.

'This is where the drugs are distributed, is it?'

That one *is* a question. I am supposed to say no. Then he'll stare at me silently, until I say more.

'Lost your voice, Mr Carter?'

'I'm not under arrest.'

'No, but your friend is. You ought to help him, if you can. Or perhaps anything you said would just make things worse?'

I shrug. A plainclothes man brings the dog out from the bathroom, into the kitchenette. I watch it stand on its hind legs with its snout on the worktop. The dog sniffs its way along. Jamie asks who is going to clear up when they have finished.

'It would be easier if you told us where the drugs are, sir. Then we could all go home.'

'There ain't no drugs,' Jamie mutters. He gives it no emphasis, doesn't try to persuade. His lack of interest adds plausibility. He must have realised that Eva has been in.

Kellard stands placidly in front of him. Kellard believes in the quiet approach: give enough rope. He would be the same in his interrogation room: no violence, no threats, just the quiet. Let an hour or two pass. Then some more. Stay with the man, watching him, waiting hour after hour, until eventually the man has to give in and say something to draw the whole thing to a close.

I ask what will happen when they have finished poking through Jamie's food cupboards.

'That depends on what we find, sir.'

'There's nothing here. You must know that by now.'

'How would *you* know that, sir?'

Good question. How *could* I know, unless I had moved the things out? I react as Eva would, and come back with my own question: 'What happens if you don't find anything?'

'Hypothetical, I'm afraid, sir.'

The man with the dog has come up behind me. His dog sniffs at my trousers. His handler coughs. 'Should this gentleman be searched, sir?'

Kellard considers.

'Friend of the accused, sir,' the man says. 'Had a key to his flat.'

Kellard looks at me quizzically. 'We've done you once already,' he muses.

'Try again,' I say, 'if it'll make you sleep better.'

Kellard gives me one more penetrating gaze. 'See what he's got,' he commands.

This time I do not have to lean against a wall. I stand in a five-pointed star position in the middle of the room while the dog-handler runs his hands along my limbs. It is a strangely impersonal experience. Even when his hands pat their way up to my crotch it is less embarrassing than having a tailor measure my inside leg. It is more embarrassing when the copper goes through my pockets. I have little in them, nothing that matters, but those few crumpled contents laid out on the table are my possessions. They define who I am.

They don't amount to much.

'Will you be staying here, sir, after we've gone?'

I shake my head.

'If we need to get in touch with you, sir?'

'I'll be at home. – Are you all right, Jamie?'

'Right as bloody rain. It was good to see you, mate. Thanks for everything.'

'Well. Anything I can do. You know.'

'Pop round tomorrow. If I'm not back, you better open the windows. Get rid of the smell.'

When I walk through my front door I hear the TV playing loud. Ludo has not gone to bed. I join him in the living room, where he is bolt upright in an armchair watching a video. Something about spacemen. The picture freezes on what looks like the underside of a vacuum cleaner, suspended like a novelty balloon in a clear night sky. Ludo has a shamefaced look. But the picture looks innocent enough to me.

'Don't try anything, Carter.'

Out of sight behind the door were two other men, two big men. One holds a pistol. We have met before at Tod Richardson's.

I don't give them a welcoming smile. 'Water pistols at your age?'

'Don't get smart.'

'Are you all right, Ludo?'

'I couldn't help it, Floyd. They tricked me.'

'Don't worry. You're not hurt?'

'Oh no,' he says, and he starts to stand up.

'Sit down.'

Ludo stops, poised halfway, thinks and sits down. He seems more puzzled than angry. The one with the gun speaks. 'You're coming with us.'

'Where?'

'Fucking find out.'

'What's he want?' I ask.

'Who?'

I close my eyes. 'Richardson, dumbo. Who d'you think?'

'Don't call me a fucking dumbo.' He steps closer.

'I'll call you what I like.'

He glares at me. If I can make him take another step he will come alongside Ludo. He's dumb enough to feel safe with Ludo. Ludo makes him feel smart.

'You punks mended that window yet?' I ask with a grin.

'Fuckhead,' he says.

'Come here and say that.'

He hesitates. His eyes narrow. They were little eyes in the first place. 'You're going on a ride, fuckhead. We're taking you in the car.' He does not come closer. He won't fall for that. 'You.' He turns to Ludo. 'You don't move out that fucking chair. You do, and your fucking brother is dead. Right?'

Ludo nods slowly. He is wondering how long he must sit in the chair.

Maybe Dumbo has done this before. I had hoped not. I had hoped he and I might snuggle in the back of the car while his mate did the driving. Big Dumbo would keep his gun on me, I would watch his hand. Somewhere on the journey would come a chance to make a grab.

But that's not how we do it. Dumbo puts me in the front passenger seat and seats himself behind. He jabs the gun barrel to my neck. 'Keep your head screwed front, and don't get fucking smart.'

Then we go. Part of the time I feel the point of the barrel jabbing at my neck. Other times it is at the back of my seat. Maybe there is a moment when Dumbo drops his guard, but I can't see him. So I wouldn't know. All I can do is sit in the front and wait till I see Tod Richardson.

What does he want now – the same ten thousand pounds? He can't be that short of money. The old Richardson family would have written it off as small change. But Tod is the last one left, clumping around his empty ranch with two minders and his Rottweiler dogs. I can imagine the man in the evenings, slumped in his armchair, a glass in his hand, brooding on how life has let him down. He is a spent force. His empire is gone. What income he has comes from heroin, extortion and other people's thieving. Small-time stuff, with small people. He can't live off that.

But what does he want with me?

Walking in through his front door comforts me, a little. It was possible we were headed for the marshes. Dark and quiet. A good place to leave a body. My worry now is that we meet at his house – before moving on. To the marshes.

We are in his front room. I notice his new window and the smell of fresh paint, but don't mention it.

'I fucking owe you one,' is how he starts.

'Why's that?'

'You killed my oppo.'

'Are you still on about that? There were four of them, Tod, with chains, and Dirkin had a knife. He was lucky it wasn't him that got stuffed.'

'I don't give a shit about fucking Dirkin. You're causing too much aggravation, Carter, you hear me?'

I nod, as if he gave me useful advice.

'You crossed me once too fucking often, Carter.'

I nod again, less confidently. I say that I thought we had already been through all this.

'When?'

'On the phone, Tod.' Tell him slowly, like a child. 'You would forget the ten thousand, and I wouldn't tell the law that you'd left a stiff behind the Windsor.'

'Fuck all that. I'm talking about this fucking afternoon.'

'This afternoon?'

'You fucking put a bullet in him, didn't yer?'

This afternoon. The Isle of Dogs. Me and Dixie on the Muddie.

'Those were *your* men?'

'Whose you fucking think?'

I stay silent for several seconds. I realise that the guy in the topcoat was not a loner, but a set-up staged by Richardson; that Richardson is not the no-hoper I had thought.

'Your idea, Tod?'

'Whose d'yer think?'

Richardson prowls around the room, stabbing his fingers in the air. 'What were yer fucking doing there, Carter?'

'On the Island?'

'Right.'

I ignore his question. 'Did you mean to kill Carmichael's man, or was it meant to be just a robbery?'

'What d'yer think? I went for his money and the drugs. Didn't

158

know how much there was of which, but who cares? I prefer the fucking money, to tell the truth. You gotta sell the drugs to make the money. So it's easier if the other fucker's done the work already, innit?'

He stands close, staring at me.

'What happens next?' I ask.

'Next?'

'Yeah. Why've you got me here?'

'Gonna fucking kill yer, Carter, that's why.'

'Unless?' I ask.

'Unless?'

'You'll kill me *unless* I do something. Such as what?'

He looks puzzled. 'What've I ever done to you, Carter?'

'What?'

'Why d'yer fucking muscle in? It was all set up. We take twenty grand from the nignog. We fuck his network. But then you fuck us up. You killed my man.'

'*I* didn't shoot your button man. Dixie did.'

'The fuck is Dixie?'

'The one they shot.'

'Who shot?'

'Your guys. Carmichael's man was called Dixie.'

Tod looks bewildered. I say, 'Dixie shot the button man. Then one of your runners topped *him*.'

He breathes out. 'Where do *you* fit in, Carter?'

'I was passing by.'

'Don't pull my tit.'

He has the look of a man whose cards are shot, so I try a finesse. 'You were right, of course, Tod. We should do it your way.'

'The fuck?'

'You sussed that I am in with Carmichael, and you want me to put the drop on him.'

'Is that right?'

'You're a shrewd bastard, Tod. I gotta hand it to you.'

I leave a pause. I want to hear the man deny that he is shrewd.

As if he would. 'Right,' he says suddenly. 'What's your game?'

'We take him out.'

'The Snake?'

'Who else?'

'The nignog. Right.'

A pause. What the hell, he thinks. 'How d'yer reckon we take the fucker out?'

I've got you, Tod.

'I'm inside Carmichael's gang, right? Like you sussed it. I know every move he makes.'

'I like it. I fucking do.'

'I find out when Carmichael takes his next delivery. I tell you. Then you come in and blast him out.'

Richardson frowns. 'Easy to fucking say that.' He is nervous. He shows me that he is nervous.

'*You* can take him, Tod.'

'So why haven't I done the fuck already? The nignog's got some clout, you know. It ain't that easy.'

'You got no ambition?' I ask.

'That fucking nignog? He can't fuck with me.'

'Not Tod Richardson, right?'

'Right! Fucking right.' His face clears. 'What's the plan?'

Oh, I have plans, Tod. Do I have a plan for *you*?

# 26

'Lucky? I'll say I'm lucky. What is it – seven years, eight? All that time I've used heroin, dikes, Palfium, you name it. I've even *drunk* morphine off a spoon, like a medicine. I've swallowed stuff, smoked it, snorted and cranked. And all they catch me with is a few DFs. Now that, son, is what I call lucky, bleeding lucky. No complaints.'

Jamie grins. DFs are painkillers. DF118s. They are so widely prescribed you may have taken them yourself. But then, knowing you, *you'd* have stuck to the proper dosage.

'What were the others carrying?' Eva asks.

'Mostly DFs. Coupla guys on dikes.'

'No H?'

'I told ya, we were lucky.' Jamie laughs. We are sitting around drinking coffee in his flat, but you would think we were drinking champagne. Morning sunlight burns through the grime on his front window. It glows on the carpet, and tries to join our celebration.

Eva wants to be sure of the facts. 'The charge was possession, right?'

'I only had six tablets.'

'That's just possession. Did you make a statement?'

'Yeah. I didn't want to look uncooperative in court. I said I didn't know the other guys, we just happened to be in the same pub. All the right words, Eva.'

'What about those other guys – what did *they* say?'

'Christ knows. I acted like I wasn't with them. In the end the cops had to let us out. Most of us, anyway.'

'Did you talk with any of the others later?'

Jamie grins – his little boy grin. 'We had a celebration, you know?'

'Where?' she snaps.

'Don't worry, the Bill was miles away. Some of us went round a guy's flat. A right little shooting gallery.'

'You prat, Jimbo, I knew you'd scored.'

'Did I say I hadn't? Jesus, Eva, I needed *something*. I can't walk out the nick a free man and carry on like nothing's happened, can I? Man's gotta let his hair down. Anyway, my nerves were shot. I needed a hit.'

He glares at us defiantly. We don't have to say anything, so we don't. Jamie drains his coffee and stands up. 'Fancy a drink?' he asks.

'On top of what?' asks Eva.

Jamie looks at her. He knows what she means. 'I only smoked some. I didn't crank it. A drink won't hurt.'

She studies the inside of her coffee cup. She doesn't say anything. I ask when his court appearance is. He says next week sometime. I nod. Jamie watches Eva. She keeps her eyes down. He crosses to the window, wipes the inside of the pane and gazes out. We are on the edge of a long silence.

But he breaks it. 'I said I was grateful, Eva. If they had found my works, I'd still be there.'

'They'll bust you again,' she says.

'Nah, they didn't find nothing here. Looked hard enough.'

'Their warrant's valid for a month.'

He frowns. 'They've used it now.'

'It is not an admission ticket, one time only. They can come back as often as they like.'

'Oh.'

'I suppose you want me to hold for you?'

'Yeah. Thanks.' Jamie is wondering when the police might call again.

'And they can renew it,' she says.

'Gotta have a reason.'

'They already do.'

Jamie sniffs. 'What, one offence? Handful of tablets?'

'Known To Consort With Other Users. Your card is marked, Jimbo. Did you have a medical?'

'Some doctor came. Gave us all a once over.'

'And?'

'My veins are clean.'

'But you inject,' I say.

'Not often. I only go in for skinpopping. It's mainlining that leaves scars.'

He and Eva glance at each other. Something was left unsaid.

'I should be all right in court,' Jamie continues. 'A year on probation, I expect. But I ain't going into no detox clinic, swigging bloody methadone. No thanks.'

His fragile good humour has faded. He kicks moodily at the carpet. 'Another thing – if I can't keep my works here, where am I gonna jack up?'

'Not at my place,' Eva says.

'Sodding public lavatories,' he mutters. 'Nah, I'll do it here. This is where I like it. Got a routine that I go through. It's important, that. Draw the curtains, make a space, lay the stuff out. Take my time. I mean, getting it ready is half the enjoyment, right? Calms me down before I fix. OK, it's a ritual – what's wrong with that? Not like fellers smoking a cigarette: just pull it out the packet, stick it in their mouth, don't think about what they're doing. Heroin is – what's the word? – something to be savoured. Know what I mean?'

'You've been lucky,' Eva says. 'You're still on top of it. And there's plenty of stuff around, not expensive. All that could change.'

That's right, Eva, I think to myself: now that Richardson has the market sewn, all that could change.

'There was plenty of stuff around when I was using,' she continues. 'I would buy an ounce and sell half. So I was out selling all day long. It was like a job.'

I nod. I don't ask what happened next.

'Then I lost my feller. We were both using, though even with selling the stuff we were short of cash. He started mainlining on barbies. Every week he needed more than the week before, and to get a *full* hit he had to inject. Anyway, he was no good with needles, and he made a mess of his veins. You know what happens to a mainliner's veins? They go lumpy and knotted, then they collapse. He had to keep looking for new places he hadn't fouled up. There's one in your groin, you know, the femoral vein? Don't look surprised, Floyd, I know what it's called. Close to the femoral vein is the femoral artery. He stuck the needle in that.'

'In the artery – what did you do?'

162

'Nothing. I was out scoring smack. I don't know what I'd have done anyway, because the jab sent his leg into spasm, cut off the blood supply, that was that.'

'Did it kill him?'

'You're too dramatic, Floyd. No, he's still alive somewhere. But he lost the leg. Had it amputated. He blamed me, of course.'

'Why you?'

'Had to blame someone. So, goodbye to him. Of course, I still had the kid.'

I didn't know she'd had a child.

'I used to take the kid with me, buying and selling. Good upbringing, right? I know. Well, one day I opened the door expecting a customer and there were three strangers. Tough looking. They threatened us – me and the kid. Screwdrivers and a bottle of acid. Took all I'd got. It scared me rigid. I needed a fix more than I ever thought that I could. But I was too scared to go out. For a while, anyway. But, you know, I had to live, so I *made* myself go out. I told my supplier – you know, I said I'd been done over, I had no money, no stuff. Could he drop me a few grams on credit? He was a cold sod, said he'd think about it. But I was desperate. He knew that. He said there might be one way, you know, I should think about it. An alternative arrangement.' Eva's eyes flicker. 'But then he gave me half an ounce on credit. I used some and sold some. I bought some more. Started paying off my debt. I really put my back into it, you know? Application. Hard work. Then the three guys came again. Same threats. They *threw* the acid this time – only at the wall, to burn the paper – so I could see it, you know? They started coming every week. Every time he heard a knock at the door, my little boy used to hide under the bed. Poor little bugger. He wouldn't come out till they'd gone.'

She stops. I ask, 'Wasn't there anyone could help you?'

'Such as who?'

Stupid question, Floyd.

'I moved to another pad. They found me. I moved again.' She pauses. 'Then I lost my little boy.'

She blows out noisily through pursed lips. Then she blinks, slowly, holding her eyelids together for three long slow seconds. When she opens her eyes, I don't know what it is that she sees.

We each find a different part of the room to stare at. Then Jamie coughs and offers more coffee. No one wants it. He leaves the window where he was standing, walks across to Eva and places his hand on her arm.

'I'm sorry, Eva. I don't deserve the help you're giving me.'

'People like us have to stand together,' she says. 'You aren't tough enough on your own.'

Jamie sighs. 'I don't even try to fight it, do I? I give in to it. I use smack to blot things out. Pathetic.'

'Don't start feeling sorry for yourself, Jimbo.'

'Ah Christ,' he says, leaving her and stomping round the room. 'I hate this life, you know that? What's the point? I oughta give it up.'

I glance at him, then I check Eva's reaction. There isn't one. She has heard him before.

'Nah, I mean it,' he says. 'I can easily give it up, you know.'

He waits.

'Yes,' she says flatly.

'Yes what?'

'Yes, you can. If you want to.'

'That's right. And I will.'

'But you don't want to.'

'Ah, come on, Eva.'

'You don't *really* want to, Jimbo. You think you do, at this moment. But you're not sick of it. You don't hate it. You're not heartily bloody disgusted by it. You don't want to purge it out your life more than anything in the world.'

'Yes I do.'

'More than anything in the world?'

'That's right.'

'Anything?'

'Yeah.'

'Absolutely anything I could name?' Eva faces him, holding him with her eyes.

Jamie hesitates, and tries to grin. 'Well, like what, for Christ's sake?'

'You see? You don't hate it enough, Jimbo. Not yet.'


'Well, well,' laughs Carmichael. 'So what are you telling me, hey?'

'You don't think this is a threat?'

'Threat?' He looks genuinely amused. He rocks forward out of his leather chair and walks from behind his long white desk. 'You think I'm worried, Floyd?' He rests both thumbs in the waistband of his trousers. 'I welcome it.' He laughs again, and crosses to his one-way window.

'I tell you what I really don't like,' he says, staring down at the club floor below, 'I don't like if I don't know who are friends and who are enemies. I don't like if I can't see what's on the cards. That's what I don't like. It's why I never gamble.'

Staying seated while he prowls around makes me uneasy, so I stand up and join him at the window.

'You sleeping with her?' he asks, pointing down. A group is rehearsing. Tamsin waits to sing.

'No.'

'You want to?'

I pause. 'No.'

'Not sure, hey?' His voice drops as he asks it. 'She's the one you were looking for, right?'

'That's her.'

Carmichael watches my face. 'Girl has not been here a few nights. I missed her.'

'She's back now.'

'I could have fired her, you know? But I didn't. I thought, no, she is Floyd's special young friend. His mistress or something.'

'She isn't.'

'Not even once?'

'No.'

'OK. She's pretty. A good singer too. I can use her, you know? Pretty girl with talent. But you're definitely not – you know, you can tell me, hey?'

'We're not.'

Huey drops it abruptly. 'OK then, this Richardson. He tried to steal my strip on the Island?'

'That's right. And it was his men killed Dixie.'

'You are managing that strip now, Floyd. What are you going to do about it?'

'Richardson wants to drive you out of all your strips. He's already frozen you out of Deptford—'

'He what? What's that man been telling you?'

'He says he undercut your prices and forced you out.'

'Did he hell! I let him sell some smack here, because it's peanuts. Deptford is a poor area, Floyd, you noticed that? Do you know what the smack market is worth in Deptford? About half what I earn from speed. Not a quarter what there is in cannabis. I can get more profit selling drink downstairs. Anyway, that Richardson sells smack so cheap he doesn't even make a profit.'

'He's a thorn in your side, though, isn't he?'

'He's not a thorn, he's a prick.' Carmichael laughs. He waits for *me* to laugh. 'Listen. He's welcome to Deptford. He *was* welcome.'

'His cheap prices don't annoy you?'

He shrugs. 'Of course not.'

'But you put pressure on his breadheads?'

Huey chuckles. 'Like your brother, you mean? You think I might have killed your brother because he worked for Richardson?'

'Somebody killed him.' Our eyes meet. I shrug and look away, as if it doesn't matter.

He breathes out. He takes his time about it. Then he says, 'Hey, look down there, Floyd. Your girlfriend's started singing. You want that I turn up the sound?'

I shake my head.

From up here, Tamsin looks like a teenager after school. She wears a long yellow sweater and light blue jeans. The sweater is big for her, but does not disguise the shape of her body. Huey and I watch as she cuddles the microphone, wrapping her mouth round it, almost swallowing it at times. Whatever words she is singing must be important. She concentrates on them.

'Tell me what you know of Richardson's plans.'


'The man cannot be serious, hey? He has a brain made of concrete.'

'He's serious.'

'But the Island is an upmarket area – a very upmarket area. Those people won't buy cocaine and designer drugs from a hulking great turnip like Tod Richardson.'

'He'll employ someone. A man in a suit.'

'Richardson wouldn't know cocaine from soap powder.'

'Does it matter?'

Carmichael collapses in his soft leather chair and rotates round in it moodily. 'Can you honestly see him making out on the Island?'

'Until a few years ago, the *only* ones on the Island were people like him.'

'The world has changed. We are talking about one of the most upscale markets in the country. That is the new City of London, man – millionaires and yuppies. My kind of people.' Huey grins, a vicious, hungry grin.

'Richardson thinks he can make them *his* kind of people.'

'It's preposterous. He is a small-time criminal. He does not belong.'

'His family goes back a long way.'

'He is a has-been, and you know it.'

'His family owned several square miles round here – *owned* them, Huey. They controlled the thieving, the gambling, the drinks and the sex. He is not going to give that up. He wants his empire back.'

'He wants the Parrot back. That's what it is. I gave him a fair price for it, and I have let him carry on trading in smack.'

'But you find him irritating, don't you, Huey? You want to shake him off like a wasp on a sunny day. But he won't quit that easily.'

'Then I'll have to make him.'

'You know how his family held on to their empire? Through fear, fear of violence. The Richardsons weren't sophisticated, didn't leave things to imagination. They just did it. If a girl stopped paying her percentage, they cut her face. If a guy tried to run out on them, they nailed his legs to the floor. I mean it, Huey. This family knows one way of persuasion: they hurt you bad. Really bad. They cripple you or they kill you. Nothing else, nothing fancy. They come along with something sharp and heavy and they swat you with it. It isn't clever. It won't please your rich folk on the Island. But it'll work. These are the men you'll be dealing with, Huey.'

'Yeah? Let me tell you the sort of guys I've been dealing with for years.'

Carmichael throws his head back. The lapels of his white jacket slide open to reveal his pink shirt.

'You heard of the Yardies, hey? Out where you've come from? In the West Indies, Jamaicans are called Yardies because people think we sit in our back yards all the time, thinking we own the Caribbean. Here in this cold country the word Yardie means a Jamaican gangster. You know why that is? Police can't tell the difference – a young male Jamaican is a young male gangster, simple as that. You see this gun?'

He produces the little black pistol he keeps stuffed in the waistband of his trousers, and he grips it snug in his hand. He points it upward, as if he means to blow a hole in the ceiling.

'You know what this is? Browning thirty-eight. A useful pistol. But you know what a Yardie packs – I mean a *real* Yardie? He packs a calibre forty-five minimum – maybe even a ninety. Those are huge guns. They are magnums, like for Dirty Harry. They blast a hole like a stake through your heart. If someone gets hit by a magnum bullet, he is dead. What I mean is that if he gets hit in the body anywhere, any place above his balls, he is dead, no dispute. There's no such thing as being wounded by one of those.'

'You don't carry that sort of gun.'

Huey smiles. Casually he holds his small pistol towards me, butt first, for inspection. I can look at it. But he does not bring it close enough for me to take a hold.

'Floyd, I'd be more scared of a man who carried this. A pistol like this can hit somewhere near its target. A magnum makes a lot of noise and a terrifying big hole, but might hit anywhere. That magnum has a kick like a field-gun. You gotta hold it with both hands, aim carefully, stand with both feet apart, and you have to be strong. Then maybe the gun won't jump out of your hands, hey? Maybe the bullet will go somewhere near the direction you aimed it. You see, the point about a magnum is that it is metal psychology: it scares the shit out of the guy it is aimed at, it makes the guy who holds it feel really proud.'

Huey stuffs his Browning back in his trousers. I say, 'So what are you telling me – that the Yardies swagger around with big guns they can't handle? Tod Richardson's boys aren't like that. They use things like a hammer and nails, a block of wood, even a saw. Those things don't sound fearsome – till you see them used on a man's body.'

Carmichael clucks his tongue irritably, and continues defending his team.

'Yardies can do all of those things. I was working a patch up in Islington once. There was a little breadhead called Innocent Egbulefu. Nigerian. He sold some Jamaicans a bag of fake cannabis. A mistake, but then, Innocent was not wise. Another of his mistakes was to live in a flat eight floors up. Yardies called by, smashed his door down, grabbed the man, threw him out through that eighth floor window. But the thing is, Floyd, they did it fast. When the police straightened out Innocent's body on the ground, know what they found in his hand, hey? The remote control for his TV set. He hadn't had time to let it go.'

'Just the sort of thing the Richardsons would do.'

Huey is not having that. He thinks we're into the big number from *Annie Get Your Gun*: 'Anything You Can Do, I Can Do Better'.

'But the Yardies know how to use guns. Listen. When Shankie Alfred was shot over Acton, it was in a club. Crowded. Two Yardies walk in – Danger Mouse Campbell and Sammy Dread Miller. Miller shoots half Shankie Alfred's head off. Literally, half his head, one shot. Everyone dives to the floor. You know what the witnesses said afterwards? Campbell and Miller were smiling, all the way through. You picture that, Floyd, hey? They come in carrying the shotgun. Smile. Hallo, Shankie. Smile. You had this coming to you, Shankie. Smile. Blam! Campbell and Miller look at the customers cowering on the floor. OK, folks, you can relax now, all our business is done. Smile. Leave the club. Smiling all the time. You see what that means, hey?'

'They were cocky.'

'They thought they would not be caught. *Couldn't* be caught.

168

Thought they could stand up in full view in a club crammed with people, *execute* the man. No one would testify. No one would dare. Metal psychology.'

'They were wrong.'

'They were caught. But it's how Yardies behave. Some of them think they are protected by magic, no one can stop them. They really believe they are Superman. Yeah. I used to deal with these guys. And you think I'll be afraid of Tod Richardson!'

Huey is supremely confident. When he says how the Yardies think they are invulnerable, he is not so different. That faint shine of sweat breaking out across his brown skin is excitement. He would welcome a fight.

'How did you handle the Yardies, Huey – outgun them?'

He smiles and shakes his head. 'That is not my way, Floyd. You know me better than that.' Back to the urbane businessman now. 'I talked to them, came to an understanding. London is a big town. Different areas, different products. Yardies like north of the river – Dalston, Acton, Harlesden. I like the south, and the river itself – the Isle of Dogs, the City. They are important to me.'

'You want to be Something In The City, is that it?'

Huey smiles his businessman's smile. 'There is a demand in the City that must be satisfied. It can't be satisfied by Richardson or the Yardies, so it might as well be by me. Why not? The City and I are right for each other. We can do business together. Don't you think?'

# 27

'I think Italians are right. They say you should only make love in the daytime. Sex in the dark is for peasants.' I turn on to my side in the bed and punch the pillow so I can see her. Then I grin. 'What do you think?'

She is lying on her back, looking up at the ceiling. 'Now I understand why they like siestas.'

'No sense wasting the best hours of the day.'

'Mm.' She stretches lazily. 'Maybe I should have found me an Italian lover.'

'English ones not good enough?'

She smiles with her eyes closed. 'Not sure yet. I'll sleep on it.'

'Don't count on sleeping while I'm here.'

'You still hungry?'

She shifts, so that she too lies facing me in the bed. We are so close that our hands lie against each other's naked body. There is one finger's length between our chests. We kiss.

'You *are* hungry,' she says.

'No secrets now. I can't hide anything from you.'

'Well, you can't hide that.'


Her tangled blonde hair fans across the crumpled pillow. Her mascara is smudged. Faint white lines leak out of the corners of her green eyes and splay softly across her face. In her skin, tiny brown veins lie like the criss-cross tracks of a spider on a dusty summer window.

She is beautiful.

In her neck are more lines. The hollow at the base of her throat contains slack skin. Her breasts have a mature ripeness, and when she lies on her back they slide slightly outwards and down, like melting junkets on a dish.

She is beautiful.

No normal woman can avoid a round softness below her tummy. Earlier, when she stood before me, that little pot belly hovered like a promised pregnancy. Now as she lies here, it is a soft pillow for my head.

She is beautiful.


In the bath we sit facing each other. To keep her blonde hair dry she has tied it in a hank above her head. Her skin glistens with wetness. She lifts her left leg and places the pink sole of one foot against my chest. I take the soap.

As I wash her legs, Suzie leans back in the choppy water and smiles at me. She is thirty-eight years old. She has cleaned off her make-up. She has nothing to hide.

'I didn't think you would stay,' she says, 'after the funeral.'

It is a simple remark, but hidden in it is a question: will you be here much longer? She doesn't ask that. It's too soon.

The tablet of soap slips from my hand into the water. I let it slither off beneath the surface while I lather her knee. 'I am responsible for Ludo now. I can't just leave him on his own.'

'Will you take him away with you?'

Her question is out: staying here or moving on? I say, 'Ludo could never manage German. It took him long enough to learn English.'

'Oh, Floyd.' Suzie reaches deep in the water to find the soap. 'Ludo isn't stupid. He's a little slow, but he's nice.'

I ask one of *my* questions. 'How did you and he get on together, when he stayed here the night?'

'Fine. In some ways I hardly knew he was here. He was like a dog, I suppose, sitting quietly in the corner, happy to share a room with you, wagging its tail when you show affection. Does that sound patronising?'

'Ludo likes dogs. I'm glad you got on.'

She frowns slightly. 'Would you like me to wash your neck?'

'That would be nice.'

Suzie shifts into a kneeling position, sending breakers of foamy water to rush along the bath. Her breasts swing before my face. As her warm hands caress my neck, she asks, 'Why are you glad that I like Ludo?'

'He needs friends. He might need somebody one day.' I kiss that pale plate of bone above her breasts.

'Why should he need somebody? Won't you still be here?'

Before she finishes washing my neck I run my hands along the damp sides of her body. 'I can't guarantee it, can I? Anything might happen.' I kiss between her wet breasts.

She laughs, a deep chuckle. 'Nothing's going to happen.'

'If something did.'

She leans back, still kneeling, and takes my face between her hands. She wants to smile, but isn't sure about it. 'Such as what?'

'Oh,' I say vaguely, looking away, 'I don't know. But if anything did happen, would you keep an eye on him?'

She gazes deep into my eyes. 'Floyd Carter, are you in trouble?'

'Trouble?'

'Yes, trouble. You've found a job that you won't talk about. You've had a couple of fights.'

'Fights?'

'You're like a little boy, Floyd, d'you know that?' Now she sits back on her heels, an arm's length away. 'Whenever you are being evasive, you start to mumble. You don't speak in sentences. You mutter one-word questions, repeating back what I ask you. What's going on?'

'Going on?'

'That's two words, Carter, but they're still not enough.' She sits waiting for me.

Suddenly I shiver, and start to rise. 'Getting cold, isn't it? Time to get out.'

She grabs my shoulder. 'Don't you dare walk out on me, Carter.

You're up to something, worried you might get hurt. Hurt! Killed, just as likely, leaving Ludo as a legacy. What kind of trouble are you in?'

She splashes close, and I grab her. We hold on to each other, damp and clinging in the bathtub, her face buried in my shoulder. She starts to cry.

I tell Ludo that he looks good in a tie. In the clothes he normally shambles around in, he looks like a boxer the morning after a bad fight. Put a tie and a clean shirt on him, he looks like a boxer the night before. There's a difference.

The tie that he wears is Italian. In Munich it cost me over fifty marks, so he should look good in it. He beams at himself in his bedroom mirror. 'Oh, thanks, Floyd, it really is fashionable.'

'If you want to be fashionable there's a load of clothes in your wardrobe you should throw away.'

'They still have some wear in them, Floyd.'

'Give them to the Salvation Army. Make an old tramp happy.'

'I'll clean your shoes for you, Floyd. To pay you back.'

'You'll get your shirt dirty.'

'I'm good at cleaning shoes, Floyd. I'll wear a pinnie.'

He'll feel better if he returns the favour. He'll feel proud. He wants to show that he can play his part around the household. When he carries my shoes downstairs he starts singing.

'What you fucking want, Carter? I'm watching *The Sweeney* on the box.'

'Looking for ideas?'

'Get on with it, Carter. I'll miss the programme.'

'I spoke to Carmichael.'

'Fucking nignog. What did he say?'

'You want the long or the short version?'

'Fucking short. Come on.'

'He'd like to meet you.'

'The fuck he would.'

'You got him worried, Tod. You topped his best oppo.'

'Fucking guy on the Island?'

'That's the one.'

'Well, that fucker topped mine. Makes us quits.'

'Carmichael wants a meeting. Face to face.'

'Fucking heat's on, that's why. He doesn't like it.'

'You got him running, Tod.'

'Fucking right.'

172

'You gonna follow up your advantage?'

'How?'

'Go and see the man. Tell him what you want.'

'Yeah . . . What's that, then?'

'A fair share of the areas. Half each.'

'Right on.'

'Strike while the iron's hot.'

'Right on.'

'I'll fix it up for you.'

'Right on.'

That's my boy, Tod. That's what I want to hear.

'I'll tell you another thing, Tod.'

'What's that?'

'About the drugs. He's had a delivery. When you meet him at the Parrot, the stuff will be in his safe. Several kilos.'

'How many is several?'

'I don't count the stuff, Tod.'

'Well, fucking several . . . Might be only five or six.'

'That's still fifty grand wholesale. Minimum. You'll get double that on the street. We're talking at least a hundred thousand quid here.'

'I dunno. I told yer I would meet the man, but . . . I dunno.'

He doesn't know? This is Tod Richardson, last of the terrible clan. I should have to hold him back.

'You lost your bottle, Tod?'

'You what?'

'There's a hundred grand there for taking, and you say that you don't know. It's waiting for you in his safe.'

'Which one?'

'I told you: in his office. At the Parrot. *Your* old safe, for Christ's sake.'

'*My* safe?' He thinks about it. 'Nah, that's no fucking good.'

'Why not?'

'He'll have changed the combination.'

My brain hurts. 'Well, blow the door open, Tod.'

'Fucking you can talk.'

'Where's the problem? You're invited, Tod, to his office. Where the safe is.' Lead the horse to water. Push his head down. Will he drink?

'Nah. Don't fancy it. Too risky.'

'Too risky?'

'Fucking smells to me.'

'It smells?'

'Listen, Carter, you know your problem? What you fucking do? When you don't like what you're hearing, you repeat it back to me. Like a fucking kid. Repeat the same words back to me. You fucking know that?'

'You're the second person to tell me that.'

'The second?'

'You see? You're at it now.'

But at least he has agreed to meet Carmichael. It isn't much. It isn't everything I had hoped for. I wanted to wind him up till he was determined to bust the place apart. In the meantime I would warn Carmichael. Then the two of them would meet, each of them thinking he could outsmart the other, and blam! May the best man win. It would halve my problems at a stroke. But now all that is sure to happen is that they will meet and talk. Knowing my luck, they could end up liking each other.

Knowing my luck. According to Carmichael and his horoscopes, I have the same luck as poor dead Dixie. Both Capricorn. 'Be reckless and your plans will fall apart.' Well, Dixie's did. His plans left him flat on his back in the Mudchute with his shirtfront stained with blood. Another funeral. I'll ask Carmichael when and where.

Still, that was yesterday. And I don't believe in horoscopes. Except that on an evening when I am off to watch the dogs racing at Catford Bridge, I might as well read the things. You never know.

'An exciting new romance could be marred by petty jealousies, and your high hopes could crash down in flames. An important business matter is balanced between success and chaos. You must look before you leap.'

So what are you saying, my fine gypsy friend?

I interpret you as follows: In the eight-thirty do not bet on a dog called High Hopes – it will 'crash down in flames'. A dog called Look Before You Leap would be guaranteed to win, if only one with a name like that was running, which it isn't. Nothing else is recommended. Gambling itself is not recommended. Everything around me is 'balanced between success and chaos'. Unpredictable. Like life.

So I do not bet on High Hopes, and the dog actually does stumble coming out of the trap, and trails along late in the pack. For 'look before you leap' the nearest I can find is Good Looker in the eight forty-five and Jumping Jack in the nine-fifteen. Neither does well.

But Ludo's stars are more helpful. 'A chance meeting may have a profound effect. Don't let sleeping dogs lie another day longer.

Remember: knowledge is power, and can be your passport to professional success.'

Which from a horoscope is everything Ludo needs. For his 'chance meeting', he backs Brief Encounter and Wotcher, scoring a first and a third. Wolf Hound and Scotty My Boy count as 'sleeping dogs'. What Do You Know is a cinch for 'knowledge is power'. And Passport Photo sounds written in the stars, except that it fades at the post and comes fourth.

Nevertheless, Ludo walks away sixty quid up on the evening *after* his drinks and cigar. He beams all over his face, pats his hair down, and straightens his Italian silk tie.

He is thinking of turning professional.


We stopped at the Mechanic's Arms and the Harp of Erin, and have been resting forty minutes in our own front parlour, toasting our toes at the gas fire, warming our bellies with Irish whisky, when we hear a rap at the front door.

Ludo starts up.

'Wait a minute,' I say. 'Let's check who it is.'

He sits down. I move the curtain and peer out into the night. At the door stand several dark figures. I can't see who they are.

'This place needs an outside lamp,' I mutter. 'Come out in the kitchen.'

Ludo clambers to his feet. He has his shoes off. 'What is it, Floyd?'

'Probably nothing. Come on.'

He follows me through the hall and into the kitchen. When we get there he whispers that he did try to persuade Albie to erect a lamp outside. 'I saw a brass carriage lamp in Greenwich. It would have looked nice.'

'Just wait here.'

I move back into the hall, flick on the light, and run upstairs. It does no harm to be careful. Whoever is out there will have seen the light come on, and will now be waiting for the door to move. The light will help me see them.

From the front window in the upstairs hall I take a squint. Two men and a boy. No, I recognise the boy. He is not a boy. He is Tamsin, dressed in yellow duster coat and jeans. The men with her are black. When one of them moves, I recognise *him* as well. I run down and open the door.

'Hey man, you in bed or what?'

Rufus and Des squeeze through the door with Tamsin between them. They are not what you'd call holding on to her. Not quite.

I call Ludo out of the kitchen and all five of us shamble into our front parlour. Des moves straight to the gas fire and squats before it, warming his hands. 'Oh, baby, I need you so much.'

Rufus waits by Tamsin. He looks at me, his face impassive. She looks at the wall. I ask her how she is. She moves her head but does not reply. I look to Rufus.

He is dressed in his comfortable navy tracksuit and white polo shirt, the same as he was the night they took me out to the riverboat to fetch her. Des is the snappier dresser. Instead of the loose suit he wore that night, he now wears a casual wool and suede top, bottle green, over dark slacks with sharp creases. Both men wear running shoes.

Rufus asks, 'You still looking after this girl?'

I nod.

'She your girlfriend, or what?'

'Daughter of a friend.'

Ludo coughs. 'Does anyone want a cup of tea?' he asks.

'Not now. What's this about, Rufus?'

'Last time when we found her, she using drugs, right? How d'you feel about that?'

'You know how I feel, Rufus. You helped me take her home.'

'You supplying?'

That's a curious question. He helped me drag the girl out from an acid party and carry her home to her mummy. He saw me play the decent citizen. Now instead of assuming that that's who I am, he jumps to the opposite extreme and asks if I am supplying. Why should he think that?

I switch to Tamsin. 'Ecstasy again?'

She doesn't answer. She stands with her head tilted, the weight of her body all on one leg, the sullen expression of a million teenagers across her face, her dark brown eyes staring at the wall.

'It wasn't Ecstasy,' Rufus says.

Deep in my stomach the muscles tighten. 'Tell me the news.'

'She moving up to crack. We don't like that.'

Tamsin flounces across to an armchair and flops down in it.

'Where did you find her?' I ask.

Des looks round from warming himself at the fire. 'Tucked up in one big bed, nice and snug. Right, girl? Six kids all together, keeping really warm.'

'Six of you?' I ask her.

Tamsin glares at Des. 'Get away from that fire, smart-arse. You block the heat.'

176

Des casually unfolds. He asks, 'You feeling cold again?' Then he moves away. He and Rufus wait for me to speak.

'Six in one bed?' I try again. She doesn't respond.

'Banged up on crack,' Rufus says.

'Dressed or undressed?'

'Some were dressed,' Rufus says.

'Having sex?'

Tamsin interrupts from the armchair. 'Hey! Am I not sitting here? Or do you like your sex third-hand, like a dirty story?'

'OK, Tamsin, tell me what happened.'

'What do you want to know, Floyd? What colour my panties were? How many times I got laid?'

'Tell it your way.'

'Sodding men. All you think about is sex.' She rests her forehead on the palm of her hand. Several seconds ooze past.

Rufus shuffles his feet. 'We better go, man.'

I meet his gaze. 'I'm grateful to you, Rufus. Is there anything else that I should know?'

'That's right,' scoffs Tamsin. 'Talk about me as if I wasn't here.'

I turn to her. 'Which do you want – they tell me or you do?'

'It has nothing to do with you.'

'OK, Rufus, what happened?'

'Oh, piss off!' she shouts. 'Just leave me alone.' She grinds her forehead into her hand again. 'Let me have a sodding drink or something.' She clears her throat.

Rufus glances at the ceiling. He wants out of this.

Ludo breaks the pause. 'Does anybody want some tea yet?'

'No, I don't!' she screams. Her shout starts her in a string of small dry coughs. Her hand slips to her neck. We watch her. No one moves.

'Yeah, crack do give you a sore throat,' remarks Des to no one in particular. 'Some people spit up blood.'

When Tamsin tries to snarl at him, she coughs again.

Ludo says, 'I'll get you a glass of milk.'

She shakes her head.

'I'll get water.' He scurries out the door.

'We leaving, man,' says Rufus. 'You and me have a word in your kitchen.'

Des stays in the front room with Tamsin. In the kitchen, Ludo asks if we think Tamsin might like lemon squash in her glass of water. We say no. He hurries back to her.

'What happens is this,' Rufus tells me. 'We hear there is trouble at a party – in a flat on the Pepys Estate. We hear it have crack. Well, you know what that means.'

'Police.'

'Yeah, and aggravation. We prefer to handle this ourself, you know? If we have the filth around, they roar up in a dozen cars, surround the block, bust into half the flats. Bad scene. A lot of people could get hurt.'

'And did the law come?'

'No, they didn't hear. After what the filth done on that Milton Court Estate, we keep them out. They hurt a lot of people, arrest some kids, fit them up. You remember that.'

'I wasn't here when that happened.'

Rufus looks at me. 'No. Well. For months we have the squad, the stake-outs, the journalists. Newspapers call it Crack City, all of that. A place like Milton Court, it have enough problems already, it cannot take that aggravation. Families get pushed over the edge, you know? The final straw.'

'But what about tonight?'

'Well, we sitting around. Some brother come on the telephone and tell us it have trouble at the Pepys. He tell us about the crack, so we get over there.'

'Who's "we"?'

'We got our own Flying Squad in Deptford. Anyway, we stop the fighting, we cool things down.'

'If people were fighting, how come Tamsin was still in bed?'

'Fighting was outside. It was because there not enough crack to go round. There never is. Anyway, up in the bedroom those children were not interested in fighting.'

'What was happening – group sex?'

'I don't think so, man. I just recognise who she is. We pull two kids out of there, take them home, and she was one.'

'Thanks, Rufus. How can I pay you back?'

'Be nice to the kid, you know? She needs help at this time.'

'What I meant was – how do I say thank you?'

'You just did.' He starts to leave the room, then changes his mind. 'Listen, I knew your brother, right? I knew of him. I don't know what you heard?'

'About what?'

'About what him did for a living.'

I pause. 'You mean, do I know that Albie sold drugs?'

'Uh-huh. Tell me, does that business run in your family?'

'Albie never sold crack.'

'He sold heroin. Him was a breadhead, you know that?'

178

'I heard.'

Rufus studies me for a moment. 'Heroin is bad news, man, but crack is worse. Heroin, if you get your supply, you OK. You in control. But crack, it have a ten-minute high, then phlut – you need more, right? Once you into crack, you got to keep scoring all the time. Fastest treadmill there is. That is why we will keep crack out of Deptford.'

'It's too late for that.'

'That's what a man say when he give up and die. We have a simple choice, Floyd. Either we let crack come in, or we get together and fight it. Together we win, you know?'

Tamsin screams.

It is more a yell of anger than of fear, but it is enough to pull us out of the kitchen fast. In the front parlour she squirms in Ludo's grasp. He holds her by the arms, her back against his chest. She is furious. But a girl her size, kicking against big Ludo, is as helpless as a butterfly in a robin's beak. She spits and snarls. Des circles round them like a referee in a wrestling ring.

'I think she wants to leave,' he says.

Huddled beside me in the front seat of the Fiesta, Tamsin looks like a schoolgirl with a cold. She shivers and stares at her knees. Each time that I stop at a traffic light I tense, in case she tries to leap out. But she doesn't. She has shrunk inside her yellow duster coat to brood.

When we arrive at the little street in Crofton Park it is past midnight. Behind curtains in the other houses, the lights are out. Neighbours are in bed.

I walk her to the front door, and stand beside her while she unlocks it. We step inside. I close the door. The hall is dark, lit only by starlight through the frosted glass. She turns towards me. 'What happens now?' she asks. 'You've seen me home.'

I wondered about that, coming over. If I turn on my heel now and drive home, Tamsin could be back out the door straight away. She could return to the Pepys Estate before I get home.

'What time is Suzie back?'

'Breakfast. She's on nights.'

Tamsin turns away and slouches into the kitchen. 'I need a drink,' she says.

'What of?'

'Water, Daddy, water.' At the sink she glances back across her shoulder. 'You can have a real drink if you want one.'

I shake my head. The stream from the tap splashes against the bottom of the steel sink while she drinks two tumblers of cold water. The third she pours away. 'Ugh. London water is disgusting.' She turns off the tap.

She leans against the sink, wipes her sleeve across her mouth, and watches me. I watch her. 'Now what?' she asks.

'You should go to bed.'

'What'll you do?'

'Stay down here.'

She tosses her head. Under her yellow duster coat she wears a crumpled white blouse. One side has become untucked from her jeans. 'Are you going to sit up all night?'

'I'll be OK.'

'You're seriously going to stay here keeping guard?'

'If I have to.'

'Jesus shit.' She turns her back and refills her glass.

'Quite a thirst you've got there.'

She spits water into the sink. 'My throat hurts.'

'You want to be a singer, so you burn your throat with crack.'

'Time for the bedside homily, is it, Floyd?'

'You wouldn't listen.'

'Yes, I would.' She opens her dark eyes, mocking me. 'I'd snuggle down in my bed beneath the cuddly duvet while you sat beside me and talked me to sleep.'

I scowl. 'Go on up.'

'You are coming, aren't you, Floyd? I might get scared, all on my own.'

She pushes away from the sink and flounces past the kitchen table. 'Of course, I don't wear a nightie or anything. But I can trust you, can't I, Floyd?'

'Just go to bed.'

'I'll be waiting,' she says.


Do you want to do the world a favour? Invent a sofa on which a man can sleep. When he stretches out, he finds that the arms are too high to rest his head on. They crick his neck. If he slides his body along the seat to move his head off the arm, then his legs dangle up and over the other end, cutting off the blood below his knees. He tries lying on his back with his knees bent in the air and his toes tucked inside the far end of the sofa, but he cannot sleep like that. So he turns on his side. Again, he keeps his knees bent, in a semi-foetal position. He finds the squab is just wide enough, provided he does not move. Lying one way means his face buries in the sofa back. Lying the other is tolerable, except his knees are still bent and he wants to stretch. Whichever way he tries to get comfortable, either his feet press against the far end or his head grinds against the top.

Then he feels chilly. He decides he needs a blanket.

Standing up in the middle of the darkened room, he gets a better idea. He takes the squabs from the settee and throws them on the floor. To gain extra length he adds another squab from the armchair. He lines them up. He lies on them. He stretches out. But now, on the hard floor, those cushions that on the sofa felt firm and supportive have become empty and thin. He twists around. One forearm lies restlessly along the floor. His fingers scratch at the carpet. He feels cold again. He stands up. He clambers to his feet. He walks to the door.

Standing in the lavatory, he decides he'd be better off in a bed.

I don't have to guard the front door all through the night. She won't creep out on me, not now. Anyway, if I'm in the front room sleeping, I'm guarding nothing.

I check the front door. It has both a Yale and a mortice lock. With the Yale she would only have to ease it quietly open and she could be straight out in the street. But to open the mortice she needs this key. I turn it in the lock, remove it, and slip it in my pocket. Then I creep upstairs, feeling secure.

On the bed in their spare room, I lie tightly wrapped in duvet, warming it through. I stretch and sigh. Sometimes my feet stray into pockets of cold sheeting, but now that the rest of my body is warm I allow my toes to probe and explore these cooler regions. I let my breathing slow.

Being a town-dweller all my life, I never got far by counting sheep. It doesn't work for me. What I do is visualise the stations on Underground lines. I remember them in sequence, off the map. Because I have been away so long, I start with the easiest, the Circle line. I rattle off the stations. The only place I pause is along the upper stretch, from Baker Street to Aldersgate. Farringdon, that's the one I miss.

When I have finished the Circle line, I begin the District. In the middle, it shares stations for a while with the Circle, but out in the suburbs it forks and divides into a choice of lines. There are the Richmond and the Wimbledon spurs, the Edgware Road, and then across in the East End, two more lines run out through Barking on to Upminster, and—

'What do you want?'

'You weren't asleep, were you, Floyd?'

'I nearly was.'

Tamsin comes further into the room and sits down upon the bed. She perches halfway along the side nearest the door, and looks down at me. In the half-light that creeps through from the hall I see that she has thrown on some kind of pastel-coloured nylon house-coat, drawn together by a belt at her waist. I suspect she wears nothing underneath.

'I can't sleep,' she says.

'Too full of crack.'

She giggles. She runs her finger along the duvet. 'But you weren't sleeping, were you?'

I grunt and bury deeper beneath the quilt.

'Is it warm in there?'

I breathe out heavily, as unseductively as I can. Then I sniff. Unseductively again.

'You're a naughty boy, you know that?'

I change position.

'Look, before you came to bed, you didn't hang your clothes up. You just threw them anywhere.' She pauses. 'You took everything off though, didn't you?'

'Go back to bed, Tamsin.'

'You're naked under there, aren't you, Floyd?' Her eyes laugh at me. They look huge in the night. The hand that has been stroking the top of the duvet slips underneath and feels for my body. I flinch away across the narrow mattress, and thump my left hand down on hers from above the quilt.

'Stop it. That's quite enough.'

She chuckles, and withdraws her hand. 'Well, well,' she says. 'Who's the sensitive one? Got something to hide?'

'Go back to bed.'

'I'm cold sitting here. Can't I come in for a little warm?'

'No.' I say this firmly, my tone responsible. The glance I give her is short and cold, as if she was a stranger who had stepped in my path. I pretend that I don't notice she is eighteen and beautiful, that she wears only that loose nylon coat, that her bare leg lies only one inch from my hand. I pretend I am made of stone.

She says, 'I'm choosy who I sleep with.'

'Yeah?' My throat seems gummed up.

'When those two friends of yours found me in the flat, we weren't having sex in that big bed.'

'They didn't say you were.'

'No? And we weren't undressed. We were just keeping warm. Having fun.'

I grunt.

'Is that why you won't let me come in with you?'

Her mood has changed again. She has grown serious. Her big brown eyes have stopped laughing. They burn into my face, forcing me to look at her, forcing me to look at her in a different way.

'I'm not like that, Floyd.'

One look could change everything. Her mischievous teasing might never have been. What she shows me now in this intimately dark little room is that she is a woman. Her next words will be adult. I have to stop her.

'D'you really want to be a singer?'

She blinks.

'Is that what you want to do with your life?'

She nods.

It is the one topic powerful enough. I could have jolted her: sneered, made a joke. But I couldn't do it. Or I could have grabbed her, torn that flimsy coat away, and pulled her into bed. I couldn't do that, either.

'You know I'm a singer, Floyd. What's this about?'

'Messing up your life.' She leans back from me. 'Crack will kill your singing.'

She looks away.

'You'll get more than sore throats. You know what that stuff is like.'

'Turn it off, Floyd.'

'All you'll want is your next fix. You'll do anything for that.'

'Don't give me lectures.'

'Then don't ruin your life.'

I am sitting up now, leaning on one elbow. In the dim light her face is closed and sullen. 'You're a hypocritical sod,' says. 'Working for Carmichael. Think I don't know what you do?'

I don't answer.

'You're pushing stuff, like your brother did. And you have the nerve to tell me how to live.'

'Who says I'm pushing?'

Her eyes are cold and lifeless. 'It's one law for you, isn't it, Floyd? Whatever you do is right. Like all sodding men.'

'What are you talking about?'

'Typical man. Did I discover your little secret? You are pushing drugs for Huey Carmichael – to anyone who'll buy them. But if I smoke one little joint at a party, you come over all virtuous.'

'Crack is not marijuana.'

'Oh, save it! I hate hypocrisy.'

Tamsin swings her legs off the bed and sits on the edge, staring moodily at the door.

'Where'd you get the crack?'

'Where'd you think?' She leans forward, hunched over her knees.

'Carmichael?' I ask it softly.

She sighs theatrically, a teenager again. 'He just gave us some to try. A little. Not even half a gram.'

'Who is "us" – the band?'

'Some friends of mine.'

'Girls?'

She turns on me. 'What are you – sodding cop or something? Why don't you ask him? He's your boss.'

'He is not my boss. Why do you think he gave you free samples?'

'You should know, Floyd. Isn't that the way it's done?'

'Not at his level. He wants dealers, not users. But if he starts a girl on crack, he gets control of her.'

She sneers. I cut her off.

'You think I'm joking? A crackhead will do anything for a fix. A crackwhore – you heard the word? – her pimp has the crack, and he holds the girl like a puppet on strings. He pulls, she jerks. For each rock of crack she turns a trick.'

Tamsin stands up. 'Not me, Floyd.' She takes a step towards the door, changes her mind, and walks around the base of the bed to the window. She pulls back one side of the curtain and looks out across the dark rear gardens. Then she lets the curtain drop back in place.

'You think I don't know about things like that? You think I haven't heard it all my life? Men have tried it on me since I was fourteen years old – if I want something I have to give them sex. An audition? Come to bed. A job? Sex again. But I don't fall for that male sexist shit. I never did. I'll tell you something, Floyd Carter. I have wanted to be a singer all my life. And I am heading for the top. I shall get there by singing, not by screwing. Christ, if you want to make money out of screwing, then be a whore – a high-class one – that's what I say. It must pay better than singing.'

She has come alive again. We are talking about her philosophy, her ambition. She even grins.

'You know something, Floyd? You still believe in the white slave traffic, don't you? You think Huey Carmichael will carry me off to the kasbah. You're out of date.'

'Only the names have changed.'

'You do believe it, don't you? Well, I can't be a white slave, Floyd, because I am black.' She hits hard on the word 'black' and lets it hang in the air like the final drumbeat to end a song. I ask how being black makes a difference.

'Being black always makes a difference. I am black enough to get all the rotten breaks that black people get. I'm not black enough for the perks.'

'Poor little Tammy.' I say it mockingly, and am about to continue when I see that she is giving me the kind of wide-eyed soulful look she wore when she first crept in. After a pause she says, 'My dad used to call me Tammy.'

She drifts back around the base of the bed and sits down where she was before. 'You remember my dad?'

'Of course I do.'

'It seems such a long time ago. I was just a kid then. Now it's like he didn't really exist.'

She picks at the edge of the duvet. 'I remember him, I remember hundreds of things we did together. I remember them well. But they don't seem real. It's like – I don't know – looking back into a different life. Like a TV serial you really loved, felt a part of, but which has ended. It's come off the air. I don't mean like after a dream – it's much stronger than that – but it still isn't like real life. I can't explain.'

'Old family photographs,' I say quietly. 'They're familiar – you recognise the people in them, but the people and places are not how you remember. They don't seem right. There's nothing in those pictures you could put your finger on and say was inaccurate. Everything's correct, yet it's wrong. So which is real – your memories or the photographs?'

'They both distort. The only reality is now.' Tamsin shivers. It is one of those big thoughts that a teenager dwells upon. 'On stage sometimes it seems more real than real life. That's the only place I am completely in control. I don't feel nervous when I am on. I create each moment. The audience looks up at me, watching me, listening to me. I don't mean they're captivated, held in thrall – not all of them, anyway.' She grins at me along her shoulder. 'But some of them are captivated, I can tell. Others, who seem to be watching me, may be thinking all kinds of things, imagining strange dreams about me, fantasising. I don't mind. I enjoy it. They pay attention, that's what counts. Whatever they're imagining, it's about me. I'm the one they're looking at, and I want them to just keep looking. Once they stop looking, I am nobody. Like when I'm not on stage.' She shivers again and when she turns to gaze into my face she has tears in her eyes.

I touch her arm. 'You'll never be nobody. Don't ever think that.' For several seconds we look deep in each other's eyes.

Then slowly, she lets her head drop to my shoulder, releases that long deep breath she's been holding, and starts to cry.

After a while she goes back to bed.

# 28

I don't react at first. Conditioning, I guess. You get used to the sound of your own doorbell, and a different sound makes no impact. This one does not ring: it is one of those two-note chiming affairs. Ding-dong. Or, if you keep your finger on it, deedaw, deedaw, deedaw, deedaw: like a kid's xylophone imitating the sound of a passing siren. Urgent, it says, get on your feet.

I slide out from under the duvet and reach for my trousers. As I pull them on, still bleary in the small spare room, I have difficulty standing on one leg. I lurch against the wall, hop away from it, and sit down heavily on the bed.

In the hall downstairs, Tamsin is shouting. Someone bangs against the door. Tamsin calls my name and runs up the stairs. We meet on the landing.

'Have you got the key?' she asks. 'It's not in the door.'

'The key?'

I remember. I took it out of the mortice last night to keep Tamsin in. It is in my pocket. As I hand it across to her the doorbell starts up again. Deedaw, deedaw, deedaw, deedaw. Tamsin runs down the stairs. I wait on the landing.

As soon as Tamsin has unlocked the door, Suzie stumbles inside. 'Why was this door locked? Who were you calling to?'

She stops short. From where she stands in the front hall we catch a good view of each other. Behind her, Tamsin closes the door. I say, 'Hi.'

She looks at Tamsin. She looks at me. She sees Tamsin naked under her nylon housecoat. She sees me and my bare chest. I start downstairs.

'Why was I locked out?'

'Floyd had the key.'

'Well, you sure stopped me bursting in. Did I arrive too soon?'

'Mum—'

'Did I, Floyd?'

'Cool down, Suzie—'

'Did you think you'd have time to slip out the back?'

'It isn't like that.'

'Well, look at you! Where are your goddamn clothes?' She wheels on Tamsin. 'Where are yours?'

'He stayed the night—'

'You're telling me! How could you, Floyd?'

'I slept in the back room. Nothing happened.'

'Nothing?' She turns incredulously to Tamsin.

'Nothing,' Tamsin says.

It takes another two or three minutes. The first to reassure her that Tamsin and I really did sleep in separate beds. The next to explain why I am here. Only when she has heard both stories through is she prepared to leave the hallway. Only then does she let me take her in my arms. She is bulky in her overcoat. It feels cold against my chest.

As I stroke her hair and soothe her, I look Tamsin in the eyes. She stares back. She absorbs the picture of her mother in my arms. Then she nods and walks away.

'I'll put the kettle on,' says Suzie.

'I better get dressed.'

'You think I'm stupid.'

'No, no.'

We break apart. As she walks away from me into the kitchen, I decide that Tamsin and I were right to tell the lie.

There wasn't time to prepare. We hadn't thought. I simply said that Tamsin had phoned me from a party, asked me to drive her home. She had been afraid to leave alone. It was late so she suggested I stay the night. I don't mention crack. It is a secret we share between us. It forms a bond.

Real families are like that.

As lies go, it becomes quite useful. It allows Suzie to insist that Tamsin go to less parties. Whatever Tamsin feels about the boat party, at this one she called for help. Even she must see she needs a line drawn. It is one thing, Suzie says, to work at the Parrot till midnight, but then to stroll off to sudden parties with God knows who – that has to stop.

'Yes, Mum,' Tamsin says.

Because she has to maintain the story that she phoned me, Tamsin can't fight what Suzie says. She doesn't try. She sits with us at the kitchen table, nodding reasonably, watching the two of us together. We're like a pair of new pets that have been brought into the house; something for Tamsin to be entertained by, something to tease.

'Are you giving up working nights?' she asks innocently. 'Hey, perhaps I need a chaperone at the Parrot, and Floyd could come. Or do you need him here? Actually, I was thinking: maybe I'll stay in the house all day today – if you don't mind?'

I suggest that Ludo would be delighted to escort her to the Parrot. She has only to ask.

'Don't make fun of Ludo. He's nice.'

'I'll pass it on.'

'Maybe there is something in that idea,' muses Suzie. 'Ludo would make an ideal watchdog. He looks so strong.'

'But he isn't fierce,' says Tamsin.

'Don't you believe it.'

They look surprised. 'Is he safe with girls?' Tamsin asks.

'He's very shy.'

'The shy ones are the worst. Can you imagine – with Ludo?' She giggles.

There is a pause. We feel we are sneering at Ludo behind his back.

'So,' says Tamsin, leaning back on her kitchen chair and regarding us. 'This is new, isn't it? Suzie and Floyd.'

Suzie smiles, cautiously. 'How do you feel about it?'

I wait for Tamsin's reply. She says, 'I saw it coming.'

We all laugh.


Eva brings the saucepan to the table and pours three bowls of steaming soup. It is the colour of apricots.

'Carrot and orange,' she says.

'Stone me,' mutters Jamie. 'This is carrying healthy living a bit far.'

'And wholemeal bread,' she says.

'With nowt taken out,' quotes Jamie. 'Not even the grit.'

'Soup's good,' I say.

'Yeah?' Jamie stirs it suspiciously with his spoon.

'Just eat it,' Eva says.

Jamie raises the spoon and sips. He winces. 'Too hot.'

Eva watches him as he toys with the soup. 'Are you in pain again?' she asks.

'I'll be OK.'

'What hurts?' I ask.

'Eat your soup.'

Eva watches us like a mother cat with her kittens. Over her usual black sweater and tights she wears a Bells Whisky pinnie. It belongs to Jamie.

'You should move in here permanently,' I suggest.

'Not a chance.'

'I already tried,' Jamie says. 'I could try again.'

'You'll get the same answer,' she replies. 'I'm not living with a junkie. Got more sense.'

'Ex-junkie.'

We both look at him, and he laughs. 'I gotta believe it, haven't I? I'll try my best.'

We laugh as well. We all make light of it. He hasn't a hope.

'He can't kick this on his own,' I say.

'Why not?' Eva shakes the soap suds off the saucepan and hands it me to dry.

'Heroin, Eva. You don't just give it up.'

She reaches into the sink and feels around for any last thing lying in the water. She finds a spoon. 'You think something magic has to happen? If you're gonna kick it, you just stop. That's how it's done.'

'It's not like giving up cigarettes,' I say.

'It's exactly like that.'

Jamie calls through from the living room. He asks if we are talking about him.

'That's right, Jimbo,' Eva calls back. 'Floyd thinks you can't give it up.'

'Thanks, mate.'

'Are you gonna prove me wrong?'

'Yeah, I've given up smack before.'

'You see?' responds Eva. 'Exactly like cigarettes.'

Squashing the dealers, she says, does no good at all. It just reduces supply and forces up prices. Either the junkie steals more before he scores, or he switches to chemicals.

'When do-gooders talk about stopping heroin at source,' she says, 'they mean tracing it back through the dealers and importers to Pakistan or Iran, right on to some little peasant grubbing soil in a mountain. Those peasants are not the source. The source is here. The source is Jimbo. People have the flow the wrong way round. It isn't heroin trickling all the way down from Pakistani mountains to Jimbo – it's his need, the fact that he'll pay for it, trickling all the way back upstream to those poppy fields. Jimbo is the source of the traffic. He's who they have to deal with. But the authorities don't want to admit that the problem is in *their* backyard. They blame the foreigner. He's out of sight. Jimbo is too hard to deal with.'

'You make me sound important, girl.'

'Don't get conceited.'

He grins. 'You saw how they wanna deal with me, didn't ya, Floyd? That cop who came.'

'Kellard.'

'Was that his name? Cops think if they come down hard on you, it'll make you quit. Couldn't be more wrong.'

'So what should Kellard do?' I ask. 'It's his job to bust you.'

Eva answers for him. 'It isn't just the cops. Everybody says "Don't go soft on druggies, whip them into line".' Turning to Jamie she says, 'How's your leg, Jimbo?'

'All right.'

I ask what he has done to it.

'Nothing. It just hurts.' Jamie yawns.

'It's called withdrawal,' Eva says. 'Not spectacular, but that's what it is.'

Heroin numbs by killing pain. If it can't find an existing pain to kill, it reacts on the nerve endings to create one of its own. Then it numbs that. Now that Jamie has withdrawn the painkiller, he can feel the pain it was killing. The next few days, Eva says, his pain will worsen.

'How long will it last?'

Jamie interrupts. 'A few days. Never more than a fortnight. I've handled it before. But it's afterwards that gets me – day after bloody day. That's when I go back.'

'And this time?'

'Who knows?' He grins at me. 'Could be another practice run. Every time I give up, I find something about myself I never knew before. The time ain't wasted.'

Eva says that the hardest time will be his court case. He will have stress, interviews with police and probation. He'll want a hit. 'That's when he'll need friends most.'

By the time the case comes up, she says, he'll be past withdrawal pains. He will have had the five-day flu, the diarrhoea, the cramps and shaking fits. He will be feeling anxious. He will be depressed.

'That's when the cures fall down,' she says. 'When he gets miserable and takes it out on his friends.'

'Even you'll walk out on me then, Floyd.'

'No, I won't.'

'Oh yes you will.'

# 29

'What d'you mean, we're invited?'

Ludo beams at me across the ironing board. 'It'll be nice.'

He concentrates on ironing the shoulder seam of his shirt. 'You, me and Suzie, to watch Tamsin sing.'

'She's not at the Parrot tonight. It's her night off.'

'It should have been.' The shirt puckers beneath the iron and Ludo frowns. This is the hardest part, flattening the shoulder seams. 'Some other band has got the flu, or their singer has, I don't know. Anyway they asked Tamsin's band to step in for them.'

'She can't sing tonight.'

'She can.' Ludo nods. 'She's got the evening free.'

'But it's her night off.'

'It's – well – quite convenient, really.' Ludo flicks the shirt over and begins ironing the front. 'Suzie hasn't got a night shift, and we weren't doing anything—'

'I am.'

Ludo glances up. 'Oh, are you? You didn't tell me.' He peers closely at the shirt as he works the iron between the buttons. 'Where are you going tonight?'

'Working.'

'In the evening? I'm sorry, Floyd. I said we'd go.'

'We can't.'

'Oh.' He finishes the button side and begins the other. 'I'll have to go there on my own.'

'No.'

He puts down the iron and asks, 'Why not? I don't have to get your permission, you know.' He stares at me, aggrieved.

'I'm sorry, Ludo. That's not what I meant.'

'I can – well, I can look after myself. I know where to go. I'm not – I'm not that dumb.'

'What I meant, Ludo, was that there may be trouble there tonight. It's best to keep away.'

'What kind of trouble?'

'Just trouble.'

'Well,' he declares, hands on hips, 'I will definitely have to go now, to look after the women.'

191

'*They* mustn't go either.'

'But Tamsin is singing. She has to go.'

I shake my head. 'She'll have to make an excuse. – You'll burn that shirt.'

He snatches the iron away and moves it to the side.

'Oh look.' He unpeels the shirt. 'I've got a mark on it. I've made it brown.' He wafts the shirt in the air. 'I think I've ruined it.'

'Let me see.' I brush at the burn mark with my hand. 'It's not too bad. You'll hardly notice it.'

'It's my best shirt.'

'I'll lend you one.'

'It would be too small.' He takes the shirt and holds it to the light. 'Oh, I don't know.'

'Don't know what?'

'Whether to wear this shirt or another. What do you think?'

'Wear that. It'll never show.'

Ludo thinks for a moment, then looks up with a grin. 'So I can go then, right?'

Their phone isn't answered till past six o'clock. They were out shopping together. Tamsin helped her choose a dress.

'It's only a nightclub, Suzie.'

'I should look a frump?'

'Listen, you're not gonna like this, but you can't go tonight.'

'What?'

She has spent half the day shopping with Tamsin, discussing colours and materials, full length or short, where is the best place to sit in the Parrot, what time to arrive, what songs Tamsin will sing, and Suzie won't wait till another night. This morning, when she suggested to Tamsin that she came to hear her sing, she was surprised how warmly the girl responded. Suggesting that she brought me and Ludo went down well too. It was as if they were starting over, the first day of a new life. Both women are now up on such a precarious high, Suzie will do nothing to knock them down.

'Word is there could be trouble at the Parrot tonight.'

'Rumours. D'you know for sure?'

Well, of course I do. But I can't tell Suzie. 'Carmichael may get a visit. It could turn nasty.'

'Is he expecting this visit?'

'Yeah, it's a meeting. Arranged.'

'Then he'll be prepared.'

She is determined to have a happy evening. She says she *has* to go, for Tamsin's sake.

And I must look after them.

We drive over in the Fiesta, but when we arrive you would think we stepped out of a Rolls Royce. As we parade across the car park we should have a canopy and red carpet. Suzie's new dress cannot just be kept in the wardrobe and looked at – it must be worn. Now. It is made of dark green flowing satin, low at the front, long in the leg, strapless. It swirls softly around her body like silk. It has no visible lining, no stiffeners, and looks as light as the tissue papers that it came wrapped in. To keep off the chill she wears a black velvet cape.

Tamsin wears a biscuit-coloured casual trouser suit, with a lightweight jacket so cut away you only see it from behind. Her white shirt is fastened with three little covered buttons that look too fragile to stay closed. Perhaps they have poppers underneath. I don't know.

Ludo carries the bag containing Tamsin's stage costume. He is dressed in that black formal suit of his that looks as if it shrunk in the cleaning. He wears his scorched shirt and my Italian tie.

I wear a suit.

The table we sit at is at the edge of the dance floor, near the stage. There was a reserved sign on it. I order drinks.

'I can't stay long,' Tamsin warns.

Before she leaves, Tamsin dances with big Ludo, while I dance with Suzie. Then Ludo sits looking pleased with himself. When I ask him to stay at the table and look after Suzie his eyes light up.

'Oh, I'll be delighted to. If that's all right, Suzie?'

'Sure it is. Where are you off to, lover boy?'

'Have to see someone.'

'Surprise, surprise.'

'I won't be far. You stay with Ludo.'

'You bet your life.'

'Don't worry, Floyd,' says Ludo eagerly, 'you can count on me.'

As I walk from the table, Suzie calls, 'Try to find a minute from your meeting to hear my little Tamsin sing.'

'I'll make sure of that.'

'I was watching you,' Carmichael says. He points behind him to the gaping one-way window. 'You've brought some friends along. That's good for trade.'

He beams a glittering smile. As he stalks around his office he rubs the heels of his hands together. His eyes dart from side to side as if he has just had his office redecorated and likes what he sees. He must have had a snort.

'What time d'you think Richardson will get here, hey?'

'Late. To make a point.'

'He better not keep me waiting. I'm a busy man.'

And your fix won't last forever, even though you are prancing around the room in your white suit, your white rollneck, and your light tan shoes. You could have stepped out of an ad for soap powder, Mr Snow.

'So the chump still hates me, hey?'

'He's the kind who sulks.'

'You'd think I *stole* the Parrot from him. I gave a good price. Well, quite good.' He laughs suddenly, louder than he usually does. I can see his teeth. 'And I gave him the kingdom of Deptford. What more can he want?'

'A bigger area. And to sell cocaine. He can't make money out of smack.'

'Not at his prices!' Huey laughs again. The thought of Tod Richardson waging a price war against himself fills the Snake with delight. 'I'll have to explain to him – this is a business, played to business rules. He'll understand that, Floyd, won't he?'

'Never has before.'

'Surely the man is a businessman? No, I suppose you're right. He is a cretin. You want a drink?'

'What have you got?'

'You know me, Floyd. I've got everything. I'm having Lucozade. You want some?'

'I'll have a whisky.'

With the panache of a cocktail waiter, Huey dispenses drinks from his low wall cupboard. He produces a bucket of ice from a fridge with veneer doors.

'I take it straight.'

But he doesn't hear me. I get two cubes of ice, plop plop in my glass. When he hands the drink to me I remove each cube between finger and thumb and, since ashtrays are not allowed in Huey's office, I drop them beside a potted Yucca tree. They'll do no harm. The tree is made of silk.

'So what gives then, Floyd – Richardson wants revenge? That's all history. No wonder his company loses money.'

'It's not his company he's concerned about, it's his family.'

'He's Italian?'

'He's concerned about his standing in the community. You watch that man while he's here, Huey. He wants to get you.'

'He won't try anything here.'

'You'd be surprised.'

'No, *he* would be. He'd never get out alive.' Carmichael has that spoiling-for-a-fight look again. 'I hope this is not a waste of time, Floyd.' He sits on the edge of his white desk and declares, 'Richardson better not come here and try talking tough. This is his last opportunity to do business.'

I put my glass down. 'And if he doesn't?'

Carmichael shrugs. 'I've handled trouble from the Richardsons before.'

'When was that?'

His snake eyes have clouded over. 'Recently. I expect Albie told you about it.'

'No.'

'It was the Richardson family's big idea – how they'd drive me off the streets.'

I wait for more.

'An old trick, you know? Not something they could think up for themselves. I was still handling heroin then. And there had been another round of supermarket blackmail stunts – you know, poison in the aspirin, glass in the baby food. The Richardsons thought they could do the same: put something in the heroin I was selling.' Huey smiles.

'What kind of something?'

'Powdered glass. The idea was that junkies would inject the stuff, the same as usual, and then they'd haemorrhage. Nice plan, hey?'

'Charming. So the results would be blamed on you?'

'Or on my dealers on the street. They'd have to run and hide.'

'Did the Richardsons go through with it?'

'No. They couldn't get into my network. They tried hard.'

'How did you find out?'

'Albie told me. One of the Richardsons tried to bribe him, then made some threats. But your brother was no one's pushover, was he? I confronted Richardson. I don't stand for that.'

A curious smile flits across Huey's face. 'That was a mistake by Richardson. He put his foot in it. You could say he put both feet in it.'

For a couple of seconds I do not react. Then I catch the sideways expectant look in Huey's eyes, as if he had made a quip which I haven't laughed at.

But I'm only just beginning to see the joke. 'Which Richardson are we talking about – you don't mean Tod?'

Huey shakes his head. 'No, of course not. I mean Frank.'

Frank Richardson. May he rest in peace. Three weeks he lay in a sack at the bottom of the river, his feet locked in a bucket of cement. And my brother Albie helped put him there.

No one knows that, says Huey. Frank's murder was blamed on the Miller boys, but neither the law nor brother Tod could make it stick. According to Huey, there is no way Tod could know that Albie blew the gaff on them. Albie told Huey, Huey told Frank, Frank told nobody.

But Albie was taken care of.

Tod Richardson certainly had a reason. Except that he does not know his brother was killed by the Snake Carmichael. Tod is coming here tonight to talk to him. He detests the man, but those grievances are about the price he got for the Parrot and the colour of Huey's skin. No more than that.

Though Albie was taken care of.

And Tod has had time to think. He will have thought hard. Surely he knew something of what Frank was arranging? He must have known Carmichael was the target. Except . . . Tod boasted to me that he and his brothers had driven Huey out of the area. He said Carmichael was confined to the Isle of Dogs. Therefore any rival Richardson had in Deptford would have to be somebody else. He knew Frank had talked to Albie before he died.

So Albie was taken care of?

Inside the door to the main clubroom, I pause to think. The band is pounding through some number that people dance to. There are coloured lights and clouds of smoke. But I am as detached from all of this as I was at Albie's funeral. People came up to me then, and shook my hand. They spoke to me and I answered. Nothing more.

I guess it has to be Tod Richardson. He knew Albie had been selected by Frank. He knew Frank had tried to bribe him. He knew the day Frank went to do it.

And then Frank disappeared.

Winding my way between the crowded tables I still feel that something does not fit. Something is illogical. When I join Ludo and Suzie at their table they don't notice that my face is set stone hard. 'You're just in time,' she says.

I stare balefully at the band before I recognise them. This is Tamsin's band: Pepys Dairy Crunch. Two guitars, two sax, a keyboard and the drums. Their tune seems to be thumping to its climax.

In the smattering of applause, Suzie turns to me. She seems excited. 'Tamsin should be on next.'

Ludo says, 'That was just the warm-up.' He nods wisely.

'You look grim,' says Suzie. 'Didn't things go well?'

She presses my hand.

I recognise the dress. It is the one Tamsin wore at the boat party, a little girl's party dress – white, lace-edged, stiff with gauze. Flounces and bows on the dress are echoed in her hair. Her eyes look huge, her arms slim and vulnerable. She sings in bare feet. Standing at the microphone in front of the big blacks in the band, Tamsin is like their mascot, a rag doll.

Her song is sexy and sad, the lyrics blue and intense. The bass guitar pulses like a heartbeat till the lead guitar bursts in. The saxophones growl. Tamsin stands aside. Although we sit just five yards away from her, she doesn't glance towards us. She doesn't look at anybody. She stands half turned away, thumb at her mouth, waiting to take back the song.

In its final verse Tamsin moves in to crowd the microphone, singing bitter defiance at love's tortures. The saxes burn, the guitars quiver, the keyboard sighs. Warm applause.

Before the clapping has subsided, Dairy Crunch moves straight into their next piece – faster now, an easier mood. Tamsin knows her audience. It can take one unhappy number, but then needs an upbeat. People come here to enjoy themselves. They don't want to share her pain.

In the instrumental break, Suzie leans across to ask, 'Are you staying now? Is work over for the day?'

'Not quite.' It has hardly begun.

Tod Richardson appears as Tamsin finishes her next song. He walks across from the main door, threading clumsily between the tables, ignoring the show. He has brought two minders.

They make straight for the big central bar. He hasn't noticed me. Tonight he has dressed to impress. He has a white evening jacket with a yellow flower in the buttonhole. The minders wear grey suits: Tod is boss.

When I rise from the table, Suzie and Ludo both look up. I make a placatory movement with my left hand, pressing downwards in the stale warm air three times with my palm. Suzie's eyes are questioning, but I smile and shake my head. As Tamsin starts to sing again I slip away across the floor.

Tod and the other two have their backs to me. I move lightly between the tables, my hands sweating, my lips dry. I am tempted to straighten my tie, but I don't. I have no need to check anything.

Tod senses that I have arrived. 'Wanna drink, do yer, Carter?'

I let him buy me an Irish whiskey. His two heavies stand looking at me. They remember the night I burst in through the window and blamed it on the dogs. They remember having to stay up half the night hammering boards across the window. They wonder why I was bought a drink.

Richardson hands the glass to me. 'Fucking prices here.'

'You can afford it.'

'Place got no fucking class.'

'Not like it was in your days?'

His eyes probe mine briefly. He is unsure if I am needling him. But my face shows nothing: I don't care what kind of club he ran. He may have had my brother killed.

'Got fucking nignog furniture.' He glares around the hall, resentment unconcealed. When he sips his drink he grimaces. He doesn't like that either.

'All fixed?' he asks.

'Upstairs.'

Richardson gives me his hardest stare. 'Is he gonna fucking try something?'

'He just wants to talk.'

'I bet he does.'

'He'd like to carve out the areas with you, divide territories. He wants you to sit in his office for a business discussion. That's the office with the safe in it,' I add quietly.

'I know which fucking office.'

'Then you know the safe.'

'I told yer, I'm not fucking interested in the safe. Be your age, Carter. He's got a building full of trigger men.'

'Some other time, perhaps.'

'Maybe.'

Richardson continues glowering round the crowded room. Every table is occupied. The place throbs with life and music.

'If Sambo fucking tries something, we'll burn this place.'

'Carmichael realises that. He knows who you are.'

Tod curls his lip. 'They let us in real easy, those fuckers on the door. They don't know who I am.'

'You're not banned from coming here.'

He leans toward me. 'I've got some people in, fucking planted.'

'People?'

'Yeah. I see the fuckers now.'

I turn my head.

'Don't start your fucking guessing. They're in here, that's what counts.'

'You need protection?'

'You better believe it. I don't walk in here alone.'

'I told you, Tod. Carmichael isn't gonna try anything.'

When I glance again around the tables, working out which ones he has his men at, I see Ludo staring across at us. I look away. I am at work now. I didn't want to do this while the three people who mean most to me are downstairs in the club, but it is too late now. If that other stupid singer hadn't gone down with influenza, things would not have been this way. Everything would have been as I planned.

'Let's get started,' I say.

One of his minders is left at the bar. I point out that Carmichael will not be happy if Tod brings even one man with him, but he shrugs it off.

'He can fucking lump it,' he observes. We are climbing the front stairs to Huey's office.

'I have to ask you if you're carrying guns,' I say politely.

'So what?'

'So are you?'

'That fucker hasn't got one, you telling me that? Listen Carter, he has one and I have one. That way we're both safe.'

'If you pull a gun you won't leave the building.'

'If he pulls one, nor will he.'

I guess it makes some kind of sense. Except I get the feeling these are two men who reach for pistols the way other men reach for cigarettes. They like the feel of the things in their hands.

Well, they can face each other with submachine guns as far as I'm concerned. They can blast each other down to hell.

I knock on Huey's door.

In his maroon-walled office he waits alone. He has combed his black hair. He sits at ease in his toffee-coloured executive chair behind his long white executive desk like a tycoon in the record business. In front of him is a ledger book with rows of figures. Carmichael closes it, replaces the lid on his inlaid fountain pen, then lays the pen carefully beside the book on his otherwise empty

199

desk. The idea is we should think we interrupted him at his work. We should hope he can spare a minute of his precious time.

Which runs off Tod Richardson like water from a hot boiled egg.

'You gonna sit and make us stand here?'

'Take any seat you like. Who's this man with you?'

'Fucking friend of mine.'

Carmichael shrugs, unbends from his leather chair, and stands up. 'One man each, hey? I suppose that's fair.'

Which places me firmly in Carmichael's camp. As he walks out from behind his desk, I notice the way his lightweight linen jacket catches against his hip. He has a bulge there, about the size of a silver-barrelled pistol, a cowboy gun with inlay on the butt.

While Huey mixes drinks I stroll over to his one-way window and look down to the cabaret floor. Tamsin is still singing. From the way she is moving I guess that this is another lively song, something powerful to climax her act. Sitting at the dance floor tables, some people watch her, others laugh and chat. When Tamsin first came to the microphone she held everyone's attention. But now they are used to her. They let her merge into the club background. There's a lesson here: the best chance you have to make an impact is the moment you first appear. Miss it and you're nobody.

Tod Richardson doesn't think so. He is about fifty years old and has had a lot of chances. Tod believes that any of those chances could pay off. He thinks if he keeps plugging away, one is bound to. One chance is all he needs.

Huey, on the other hand, believes he has already made it. He leans back against the front of his white desk, the fold of flesh beneath his bum comfortable on the desk rim, the inevitable glass of Lucozade in his hand. His eyes sparkle. His teeth gleam. His cocaine works.

I choose the chair opposite Richardson's minder. I lean back in it. Ill at ease in his own chair, the minder leans forward – his grey suit crumpling, his arms resting on his thighs, his glass of lager tilted in his hand. I look for a place where he might be carrying a weapon, but I can't see it. Maybe that's why the man leans forward. It makes the jacket hang loose, away from any holster, leaving the gun easy for him to reach. He contrasts with Richardson. When he came through the office door, the big oaf fastened his white tuxedo jacket as if he was coming for an interview. The heavy white material tightened across Tod's chest, making a bulge behind his breast pocket, just to the left of that silly yellow flower.

It doesn't worry me. I don't carry a gun, and have no weapon in my pocket, yet I don't feel naked. I don't even bother to sit close to the door.

'The idea is,' Carmichael begins, 'that we talk out our differences, open and frank.' The word Frank makes Tod Richardson wince. It reminds him of his brother.

Which reminds me of mine.

Carmichael seems unaware of it. The name Frank Richardson means little to him now. He has forgotten it. The record isn't filed in his office cabinet: it is shredded and thrown away. Carmichael also is the kind of man who can forget when he has killed someone. I should remember that.

'We have been foolish,' he says disarmingly, 'in the way we conduct our business. We work the same territory, in competition. We wage price wars. We poach each other's customers. We even kill off each other's men. Out on the Island we lost one man each. That has to stop.'

Richardson interrupts. 'You lost a top man, didn't yer? Fucking first lieutenant, right?'

Carmichael pauses, frowning. 'You think this is a game of chess? You think I lost a bishop to your pawn?'

'Sounds about right.' Tod sneers at him. He is winding Huey up. It surprises me. Maybe I have underestimated him. Maybe he wants to goad Carmichael enough to admit he also killed Frank Richardson.

But if that was his idea, it does not work. Carmichael flicks his head as if an insect bothered him, and continues with his pitch.

'All this is no way to run a business. For any businessman, the worst enemy is competition, hey? People beating down your prices, squeezing margins, giving customers a choice. That's *bad* for business. What we must do is create monopolies. We want a cartel here, don't we, hey?' He pauses for reaction.

'The fuck's that?' Tod asks.

'A cartel?'

'What fucking is it?'

Carmichael raises both eyebrows and chuckles – a condescending chuckle that narrows Tod's mean eyes. The two men watch each other. Then comes a tapping at the door. Their faces freeze. Three taps again. Nobody moves.

Carmichael's face has set like muddy clay. 'A friend of yours?' he asks.

Tod shakes his head. Huey stares at the door as if he could see right through it. 'You'd better open that, Floyd,' he says, and I stand up.

Even before I am fully on my feet I notice Tod's minder slip his hand inside his jacket. As I cross the room I see Tod himself loosen his front button. Behind me, Carmichael is waiting at his desk.

I open the door.

I hadn't thought it would be Ludo. But it is. My brother stands dithering on the landing, like a schoolboy pushed on stage who has forgotten his lines.

'I'm busy, Ludo.'

From behind me, Carmichael asks, 'Is that your brother?'

I say it is. The sound of three men letting out their breath is like a distant wave receding on a beach.

'Um – can I have a word with you, Floyd – in private?'

'Not now, Ludo. In a little while.'

'It's rather urgent.'

'Later. I'll see you downstairs.' He looks uncertain. I say, 'I'll be down in a few minutes,' and I close the door.

I am halfway back to my chair when Ludo knocks again.

'You'd better humour him,' Carmichael purrs.

This time when I open the door I place a hand on Ludo's chest to restrain him. I step outside and close the door.

'Ludo, I'm in the middle of a very important meeting. I told you before we came, I have to work tonight.' I make sure he sees me check the time on my watch.

'I'm sorry, Floyd, but this is important. It really is.'

'Suzie all right?'

'She's at the table. That's – um – that's not why I came up.' I wait for him. 'That man in there, you know? I've seen him before.'

I nod impatiently.

Ludo tugs nervously at his tie – my Italian tie – and coughs. He licks his lips. 'You know that man, Floyd?'

'Which one?'

Ludo frowns.

'Which man?' I ask. 'Someone in the room?'

'Yes.'

'What's he wearing?'

'Well, a white – um . . .'

'A white suit?'

'Yes.'

'You mean the black man – sort of brown?'

'No, he's white.'

'You mean the white man in the white jacket?'

'Well . . .'

'A white jacket and black trousers. A big man. A white man.'

Ludo wrinkles his face. He frowns at the wall behind me. 'Oh dear, Floyd, I can't remember his trousers. But he's got a pretty flower on.'

'A yellow one?'

'And a white jacket. I told you.'

'That's Tod Richardson.'

'Oh.'

'What about him?'

'That's him.'

'That's who?'

'That's the man who killed Albie.'

I stop halfway through a breath. For five seconds I stand on Huey's landing with my mouth open, like a waxwork singer. I begin to hear background noises floating up from downstairs – music, laughter, people talking. And I hear a noise like a distant drumroll. It could be the blood pounding in my ears.

'How d'you know?'

'Well, I saw him, didn't I? He was in the car.'

I stare into Ludo's earnest face. 'You *saw* Albie's killer.'

'Well, yes. I saw him in the car. I got a good look at him.'

'Why didn't you tell me?'

'I tried to. I told the police, too. But nobody listens to me.'

'Jesus.'

'When I saw you talking to him downstairs, I thought – um – well, you know.' He looks at me admiringly, the brother he can rely on. 'Are you going to tackle him, Floyd?'

I nod my head.

'Um – can I – do you need me to help you?'

'I can deal with it.'

'Will you be all right on your own? Are all those men in that room on the same side?'

'No. Go back downstairs.'

'I helped you before, didn't I?'

'You did a good job. But just now I need you downstairs to look after Tamsin and Suzie. There may be trouble down there soon.'

'But the men are up here.'

'Don't worry about that. Go back downstairs.'

Ludo is reluctant to leave. He says, 'Albie was *my* brother too, you know.'

'Please, Ludo.'

He gazes at me like a dog refused a walk. Then he nods abruptly, turns on his heel, and sets off downstairs.

\*

Back in Carmichael's office the mood has darkened. Richardson has lit a cigarette. He sits in a low chair flicking ash on Huey's carpet and blowing smoke into his clean air. The smoke haze and the way they are glowering at each other make it look like the air temperature has risen ten degrees. Richardson puffs on his cigarette. Carmichael strides around his office lecturing on price strategies and cost efficiency. The grey-suited minder stares at the carpet.

I drift across to my seat and sit down. Carmichael keeps talking. Now I can see how Richardson thinks. His brain only handles one thing at a time. When he first decided that somehow Albie was involved in Frank's death, he lashed out. Albie was dead before Tod's anger had cooled. Only afterwards did he remember that he'd given Albie ten ounces of H. That he had just lost ten thousand pounds. That he wanted that heroin back. Up to now, when I thought that Richardson would not kill a man just because he refused to pay back ten thousand pounds, I was right. Sort of right. He didn't kill Albie for that. He killed him for Frank. But as he said the other day when I met him: being dead doesn't write off your debts. Your creditors still have to be paid back. I look at my watch. Before long I will have to act. I slip a hand in my pocket.

Richardson interrupts. 'Fucking words you use.'

Carmichael stops.

'What the fuck they mean? "Segmentation." "Market share." Can't you talk fucking English?'

Carmichael disguises his disdain. 'Let me put it this way.'

I take my hand out of my pocket. They're not watching me.

'Fucking English this time.'

'I'm speaking English.'

'Teach us how to speak our fucking language? What you mean, nignog, is *you* want all the rich areas, leave me the shit. Think I'm fucking stupid, don't yer?'

The strain shows on Huey's face. His cheeks look as if they have been highlighted with white make-up. 'I am giving you Deptford, New Cross, Brockley, Ladywell.'

'The fucking shit. Run-down areas.'

My hand drops nonchalantly down beneath my chair, leaves a package on the floor.

'Run-down areas?' Carmichael queries. 'I thought you lived in them. This is your own manor, hey?'

'Me, live in fucking Deptford? No, I'm from Blackheath, a touch of class. Something you don't fucking know about.'

'So what do you want, then, hey? Blackheath as well?'

'I fucking live in Blackheath. It's mine already. I want the Island.'

'The Isle of Dogs?'

'Too fucking right.'

I ease into a more comfortable position in my chair, my fingers laced in the 'intellectual at prayer' position below my chin. It's to show I have nothing in my hands. Huey, now, has stopped pacing round the room. He stands ominously beside his desk, the fingers of his right hand flexing by his side. Inside his white jacket, six inches above those flexing fingers, he wears his silver-barrelled shooter. I wonder if he watches cowboy films.

'I have worked that island, Richardson, for three long years. I have tended it like a farmer works his soil. The people on that island are my kind of people. They belong to me.'

'Fucking yuppies. City types.'

'Exactly. I speak their language. *Your* language is spoken here in Deptford. That's why I give it you. It's the place where you belong.'

Huey is beginning to lose his cool. Richardson never had any he could lose. 'Where I fucking belong – what's that supposed to mean?'

'You said you lived here. So it's where you belong. In dirty Deptford.'

Richardson is about to jump out of his low chair. Both feet are positioned to help him rise. 'What's fucking dirty about it?'

'You called it shit. They were your words, hey?'

As Richardson starts clambering to his feet the telephone rings. He stares at it. While he sways above his seat, uncertain what to do, Carmichael snatches the receiver. 'Yes?'

I glance below my chair to check my package is out of sight.

Whatever Carmichael is hearing on the phone has driven business out of his head. 'What?' he snaps, his cold eyes fixed on Richardson. 'What sort of gang?' He listens another two seconds before slamming the receiver down and pointing at Richardson. 'What are you playing at, hey?'

But he doesn't wait for a reply. He darts to his one-way window and glances down. 'Jesus Christ!' he yells.

Now the minder and I are also on our feet. The minder stands flummoxed while I dive across to Huey. I look through the window too.

There is mayhem there. Everyone is on their feet, rushing around. Chairs have toppled over, crowds are surging. Through the sheet of one-way glass it's like a panic scene from a silent movie.

Beside me, Carmichael spins round to face the others. He has his

205

pistol in his hand. 'Get your hand out of your jacket,' he yells to the minder. 'I mean *out*!'

Richardson stands astounded, both hands showing, an unfinished drink sloshing in his grasp. His minder is frozen against the far wall, his eyes on Huey, his hand lost inside his grey jacket.

'Last time!' Carmichael calls. 'Pull your hand—'

The minder dives to his left, his right hand slipping out from his jacket to jab at us. He holds a gun, black and squat. When it fires I haven't moved. But as the sound crashes around me I hit the floor. Carmichael fires his gun, quieter than the minder's. Both shots have missed. Plaster dust falls from the ceiling on to Huey's shoulders.

'Stop!' yells Richardson. 'No fucker move!' He has his own gun now.

All three men pause with guns pointed. Richardson and his minder aim at Huey. Huey aims at the minder. I lie on the floor and wish I had brought a gun.

'The fuck's going on?'

'You brought your gang in, Richardson. You're trying to bust us up.'

For a man with the odds against him, Huey plays it cool. He keeps his silver-barrelled gun trained on the minder, and holds his left forearm between himself and Richardson, as if that arm bore an invisible shield that could protect him from Tod's gun. Hanging in the air is a fine cloud of plaster dust.

'What fucking gang?'

'Down there!' Carmichael gestures behind him with his left hand. His right does not waver. 'You staged this.'

The frown on Richardson's face is like that on Ludo's when he reads a paper. Even a kid could see he doesn't know what is going on. I move into a crouching position. 'Let's put the guns down,' I suggest. No one moves.

'What we'll do,' I say, carefully standing up, 'is I'll count to three. Everyone lets their gun dip when I get to three.'

'Fuck off,' says Richardson.

I ask if he has a better idea. He says he has. He has realised that in their stand-off he is free. Carmichael and the minder train their guns on each other, so they cancel each other out. Richardson is left with the floating gun. He turns to point that gun at me.

'I say what fucking happens,' he declares.

Well, if Richardson holds the ace here, I know who holds the deuce. The only thing that can be said for the game now is that from the viewpoint of a disinterested observer, things have improved. The way things were, when both he and the minder were

trained on Huey, Richardson only had to squeeze his trigger and
the game was won. He would scoop the pot. So when he aimed his
gun away, the disinterested observer would say that Richardson
missed a trick. But the disinterested observer does not have Tod's
pistol pointing at his stomach. And I do.

The minder fires.

The shock of the gun blast makes me jump like a startled frog.
Richardson and Carmichael fire as well.

Carmichael's shot hits the minder in the face, and the man falls
backwards. Richardson's slug thumps in the wall sickeningly close
to me. The minder's final bullet hit the glass behind Carmichael's
head. The window quivers in its frame. Then, like a shattered
windscreen, it turns opaque.

I am reaching down for the minder's gun when Tod's pistol fires
again. So does Huey's. The room goes dark.

'Don't touch it! Keep your fucking hands off!'

I stop moving. Across the gloomily lit room Tod Richardson
points his pistol at me. The electric light has gone. Someone's shot
has smashed the bulb.

It must have been Carmichael's. He is in a half-seated, half-lying
position beneath the shattered glass window. There is blood all
down his shirt. Above him through the window creeps the only light
we see by. I keep expecting Carmichael to do something. But he
doesn't. Then he moves. His head flops forward to rest upon his
chest, then he doesn't move again.

'You tried to trick me, Carter.'

I must keep Richardson talking – not let him fire that gun.

'You know me better than that, Tod.'

'You fucking got me here.' He raises the gun. I talk fast.

'There are police down there, Tod, you know that?'

'Police?'

'We've been busted by the Bill. Carmichael thought you'd set
him up.'

Richardson peers at me through the feeble light. He does not
lower his gun.

'They'll be up here any moment, Tod. We'd best get out.'

'The cops?' He shakes his head.

'Look down through the window.'

'Like fuck I will.' He thinks a moment. 'Get over by Carmichael.'

I stand up and edge towards Huey's body by the window.
Richardson joins me. He keeps the gun aimed at my heart. After
one quick glance through the crazed glass window he steps backwards, thinking. He isn't used to thinking. Down there in the dance

hall he sees blue uniforms. Up here in the dimly lit office he sees two corpses and the only living witness.

'I can get you out,' I say.

He stares at me. The expression in his eyes is like I'm already dead.

'I can show you a way out of here.'

'Fuck off, Carter. I used to own this fucking building.'

'Don't use the stairs, Tod. They'll be waiting for you.'

He hesitates. Keep your right hand relaxed, Tod.

'There ain't no other way out.'

'There is one. Come on.'

I start for the door. I move there confidently – as if I knew any more exits than he did. I simply have to get us out of this closed room.

'Where you fucking going, Carter?' I freeze. He lurches past me. 'Don't you get no smart ideas.'

Standing with his left hand on the door knob, he waves his gun like he'd wave a finger at a naughty child. Then he opens the office door. He turns to go through it. But he can't. Because Ludo is waiting in the door frame. And Ludo hits him.

He is a big man, Tod Richardson, but Ludo is a bigger one. The thump that Ludo gives him sends Tod back three steps into the room. He sways on his feet. He swings his gun towards Ludo, but as he completes the move Ludo grabs his wrist, forces his arm up in the air, and crashes his fist into his ribs.

The man buckles. With his right hand stuck up above his head he tries to use his left to claw Ludo's face. He tries to kick him, and loses balance. Ludo thumps again. Each blow he thunders in weakens Richardson's grip on the gun. But he will not drop it. Even if he can't use it, he won't drop it. I come in behind and try to twist it from his hand, but I can hardly reach it. Richardson cracks his elbow into my face. Then he tries to pull Ludo to the floor. But Ludo simply hoists him up again, then suddenly ducks and straddles the huge man across his shoulders. Keeping one hand firmly locked round Richardson's gun, Ludo totters forward. He lumbers across the room like a gigantic wrestler about to deliver the last fall. I couldn't stop him if I wanted to. He staggers across to where Carmichael lies slumped beneath the broken window, then he hurls the struggling Richardson through the glass.

The big one-way window had been weakened by the minder's bullet, but the sheet of fractured glass had stayed in place. It doesn't now. Richardson strikes it feet first and goes through. He and a thousand shards of glass sail out above the dance floor. As his flying body twists in the air above the startled people, he fires his pistol. He fires another time as he falls. Before he hits the ground he has fired it twice. Splinters of broken glass fall round his body like a shower of rain. I peer down through the darkness at three hundred faces lifted towards us, then I pull Ludo hastily out of view.

'We'd better go,' says Ludo, his grasp of the situation remaining firm.

But on the way to the door, I make a detour. From beneath the chair where I was sitting, I slide out the little package I had planted there. I wouldn't like the police to overlook it. So I rip open the envelope and shake out the contents. Small cellophane packets of Albie's heroin scatter around the room. They fall upon the carpet, the armchair, and Huey's desk. Then I thrust the empty envelope in my pocket and follow Ludo quickly out the door.

# 30

'Carter, sir, a customer. Nothing abnormal in his possession.'

'Thank you, constable. That will be all.'

The policeman leaves. When the door closes behind him, the room is quiet. The police have transformed a backstage stockroom into the kind of interview room I have seen in a thousand movies: cream walls, harsh lighting, crude wooden table and hard chairs. There are only two people in here – me and Sergeant Kellard.

He indicates the chair opposite him at the table. I sit down.

'Sorry to have kept you so long, Mr Carter. We had a lot of people to interview.'

'I noticed. Seems like you arrested everybody in the club.'

'Arrested? We don't arrest innocent bystanders. No, it's been statements mostly. Brief ones. Names and addresses, that sort of thing.'

'You know my name already.'

'We've caught several people in possession. Nothing much. Small stuff, you know?'

'And?'

'The only real find was yours, upstairs.'

'Mine?'

'No-one's listening, Floyd. I can call you Floyd, can't I?'

I nod slowly.

'Don't worry, there's no tape recorder. You set this up for us very efficiently. Two gang leaders, as you said. Drugs all over the place. Some just lying on the carpet. Then when we opened Carmichael's wall safe we found a large supply of narcotics. As you predicted. You've given us a very nice haul here, Floyd.'

I grunt. 'How many cops did you bring?'

'A hundred and twenty. Unnecessarily large, as things turned out.'

'You could say that.'

'No one will mind. The end justifies the means. After all, we couldn't be sure what we'd run into, could we? According to your information, there was to be a meeting of two gangs to divide their latest narcotics delivery. Our experience suggested that those gangs might turn very nasty indeed. They have a tendency to. We anticipated firearms, and firearms we found.'

'Your men had guns too.'

'Just as well, as things turned out.'

'Shoot anybody?'

'We never like to do that, sir.'

'I said you'd find the dealers *upstairs*. You didn't need to bust the whole place.'

'That was your opinion, Floyd. As it happened, we made a number of arrests downstairs as well.'

'Small fry.'

'From little acorns, oak trees grow. Downstairs we arrested four men with firearms, not to mention seven people for possession, three for supply, eleven for assault and obstruction. Quite a reasonable haul in itself.'

'Three for supply – of what?'

'Cannabis, I believe.'

'Cannabis,' I sneer.

'Come on, Floyd, we're on the same side, aren't we? These little dealers don't matter. What made the raid worthwhile was the guns and the class A narcotics upstairs. We're very grateful to you for this. What can you tell me about the deaths?'

'Deaths?'

'There were three deaths, Floyd, weren't there? Everyone witnessed one of them, when Richardson fell from the window. But you saw the other two.'

'Me?'

Kellard brings out his 'reasonable man' smile again. It doesn't suit him. 'Your brother Ludo did his best to confuse us, but . . . He's not very bright, is he?'

I don't reply.

'Don't worry, Floyd, we'll honour our agreement. The police do not break their word, despite what some people say. But I do need to know what happened. You were in the office when the murders took place.' He pauses. 'Relax, Floyd. No one will know that you were up there.'

'What about those two cops who met us on the stairs?'

Kellard lifts his eyebrows. 'The officers don't seem to have recorded that meeting in their notebooks. As far as the official record goes, you were found downstairs with all the other customers. I dare say your two lady friends would bear that out?'

'Did you ask them?'

'There was no need.' He leans toward me across the table. 'But unofficially, Floyd, off the record, I have to know what actually happened.'

'They quarrelled.'

'And shot each other?'

'Yeah.'

'After which, Tod Richardson, being the last one left, felt guilty and jumped out the window?'

I shrug.

Kellard says, 'Overcome with remorse, your Honour. Couldn't live with the shame. You see my problem, Floyd? Someone had to be left alive.'

'Maybe Carmichael killed Tod Richardson first, then he and Richardson's minder both shot each other?'

'Do you honestly think the public would buy a story like that?'

I shrug again.

'Richardson's minder, eh?' muses Kellard. 'Is that who he was?'

I nod.

'Come on, Floyd, give me some help. Was there a fourth man, apart from you and your brother?'

'No.'

He examines the table top. 'Awkward, isn't it?' He sucks on his teeth. 'You know what I think must have happened? I think Tod Richardson killed those two men in a fit of blind rage. Then when he realised that the police had very cleverly got him cornered, he made a last desperate attempt to escape. But he slipped. Fell from the window. How does that strike you?'

'Sounds thin. But the press always believe what the police tell them.'

He comes as close to a laugh as he ever will. 'If only that were true, Floyd. Fortunately, this time, Richardson's death forms a small part of a bigger and more dramatic news story.'

'Such as?'

'Rival gangs with guns. Our biggest drugs haul this year. A quarter of a million pounds sterling.'

'As much as that?'

'Give or take a bit – at street prices.'

Didn't I tell you? The police always talk street prices to bump up their haul.

'In Carmichael's safe we found three kilograms of cocaine, worth between a hundred and eighty and two hundred *thousand* pounds. Scattered around the office was a further quantity of heroin – worth perhaps another ten thousand pounds. On top of that, we have all those little dealers you tipped us off about, out on the Isle of Dogs. We scraped another half kilo from them, worth perhaps another thirty thousand pounds. So all in all, talking the kind of round numbers the press prefer, the whole night's work netted a cool quarter of a million pounds.'

'It sounds impressive.'

'Exactly. A good night's work. You and I know that in London, three and a half kilograms of drugs hardly scratches the surface. But I shan't emphasise the weight. I shall talk money. I shall talk success. The death of three known villains will add to our success.'

'You should make Inspector after this.'

'I wouldn't count on it, sadly. Though it's nice of you to think of me. No, for an exercise this big I had to bring in bigger brass. Most of the credit will go to them. I may get a mention, if I'm lucky. Nothing more.'

I meet his eyes for once. 'There's no justice, is there?'

Well, well, you are thinking, so that was it. Carter was a stoolie all the while.

No, not *all* the while.

When I first went to see Huey Carmichael, it was because *he* sent for *me*. I went because I had a brother recently murdered, and a town full of people waiting to see what I would do about it. It's a small place, Deptford. Somebody would know who had killed Albie. Somebody would talk. Whispers would reach me, if I just opened my ears.

Carmichael sent that message: he would like to talk to me. We met. I played along.

Then there was Vinnie Dirkin. He said I had inherited a debt left over from Albie. A piece of unfinished business. Dirkin led me eventually to Tod Richardson, and bingo! I had found another bigshot. Another who could have killed Albie. Or known who did.

Carmichael or Richardson: they ran things round here. I was sure one of them must know.

Out on the Island, I made Carmichael's drops – peddling excitement to yuppies, cocaine to rich young businessmen. If those guys needed snow to support their fancy lifestyles, that was OK by me. People who lived on that island had had their lifestyles desecrated by executives. Why should I care if a few executives fouled up their own lives?

Kellard walked on to the right spot, at the right time. Though tonight he went over the top. I guess cops do. Busting into the Parrot with a hundred and twenty cops – plus a team from the D11 firearms unit – is obscene. Kellard says he could not prevent it. He says the system took control. Nowadays, he says, the bobby on the beat has been transformed into a hit squad for bureaucracy.

But the day he stopped me on the Island was opportune. He couldn't pin anything on to me, but he was sure I was dealing in drugs. I wasn't sure about anything, but I realised that Kellard could be useful. We could both help each other. When I dreamt up the scheme to take Carmichael and Richardson in one hit, I didn't know which of the two was responsible for Albie's death. But I was pretty damn sure it was one of them. So I phoned Kellard and told him I would lure the two men together into a place laced with class A drugs. Kellard could bust the joint. He would catch two notorious villains red-handed. They would get seven years inside. I would have revenge.

We all got more than we bargained for.

Outside in the carpark most of the cars have gone. The little Fiesta stands over at the far side, beneath a street-lamp. Perhaps the car is mine now. After all, Carmichael is dead: he won't need it. I guess it is listed somewhere in his company assets. One day in a month or so, some auditor will pause at an entry in his books. Fiesta, one: whereabouts unknown.

As I walk towards it in the dark I see Suzie through the front windscreen. I raise a hand. Behind her in the back seat sits Ludo. They have been talking. They look cold.

I open the car door and slide in behind the wheel. 'Told you they'd let me go,' I say. 'Where's Tamsin?'

'Over there.'

Against the side wall of the Parrot, Tamsin stands talking to a man in an overcoat. He has his collar up. Occasionally as they talk, he writes a line on his notepad.

'Another cop?'

'Reporter. Are we finished now?'

'Yeah, it's time for bed.'

'I'm too tired to sleep,' Suzie says. 'My body thinks it's on night shift.'

Ludo speaks up from the back seat. 'I could sleep, no problem, if I wasn't so cold. When we get home I'm going to put a hot water bottle on, straight away.'

'Here comes Tamsin,' Suzie says.

When Tamsin arrives she squeezes into the back beside Ludo. She had been waiting till I came out. I start the car. It takes two tries. As we drive away I ask if that was the only reporter. She says there were two more, but they have left. She waves at the last one through the window. He smiles and puts his pad inside his pocket.

'What were you talking about?'

'About me and Huey Carmichael.'

We are cruising down the dark empty street. 'You and Huey – what's to tell?'

'Oh, I let the reporter drag it out of me.'

'Drag what?'

'Of course, he could see I was upset. But eventually I admitted it.'

Suzie interrupts to ask what on earth the girl is talking about. Tamsin laughs. 'I told the guy I was Huey's mistress.'

'His mistress?' I glance back across my shoulder.

'Why not?'

I shake my head, and concentrate on my driving.

'It'll make a good story, won't it? I let another man take my photograph.'

'For God's sake!' Suzie says.

'Well, who will know the truth of it?' asks Tamsin. 'Carmichael's dead. He can't deny it. I've given the papers a nice human angle, you know? Silent Grief Of Gangster's Sweetheart. Sexy Singer Mourns Her Man.'

'You don't need that kind of publicity,' snaps Suzie.

'She Was Sex Slave To The Snake,' continues Tamsin. 'The Snake Who Squeezed Me. What d'you think?' She laughs again.

Ahead of me, the traffic lights turn to amber and I cut across. I chuckle too. 'Come on, what did you really tell them?'

'What I said. That I was his mistress. That I was awful sad. But I didn't give them a load of sexy confessions. I couldn't. It didn't seem right, so soon after he died. Mind you, if the story runs, I might consider it. I could release a few more details, perhaps next week.'

'They'll pillory you,' Suzie says. 'You've no idea the filth those papers dream up.'

'Just count the column inches,' Tamsin retorts. 'I did tell them one thing about "our relationship". I said Huey was like a father to me. I said he hired the Crunch and me because everyone knows we're the hottest draw south of the river, and he wanted to keep me his exclusive property. But, of course, now he's dead, I said, we're available again. We'll be a hell of a draw, I said, wherever we play. I hope the paper prints all that.'

'You should go far,' I say.

'Bet your life. But I couldn't miss a chance like that, could I?'

Beside me, Suzie relaxes her shoulders. 'I must be getting old,' she says. 'I haven't got your "grab it as it passes" attitude. The new realism.'

Tamsin leans forward to kiss her cheek. 'D'you forgive me?' she asks.

Suzie strokes her daughter's black hair. 'Of course, of course.'

As we glide down the deserted Brockley Road, we are snuggled warm and cosy in the friendly little car – Suzie and I in front, Ludo and Tamsin squashed in the rear like grown-up children. For a while no one says anything. We are comfortable with one another. There's no urgency to speak. We can lean back in our seats, watching silent night-time houses through the car windows. We can think back on the evening, and work out what it meant. Then Ludo coughs. He says, 'Um, I'm sorry, Tamsin. Really I am.'

'What about?'

'Well, Mr Carmichael. I didn't realise you loved him—'

We laugh.

'No, honestly,' he insists. 'It wasn't Floyd and me that killed him. It was Richardson. If I had known he was a friend of yours—'

Tamsin explains the truth to him. Before Ludo starts feeling too foolish she kisses him, in that same open and easy way that earlier she kissed Suzie. 'I'm glad you came, Ludo, to protect us.'

'Oh—'

'And you saved my life,' I put in. 'Richardson would have killed me.'

Ludo is embarrassed. He squirms in the corner of the car. 'I did it for Albie,' he mumbles. 'Richardson killed him. I know he did.'

'You avenged him,' I say. 'You were the hero tonight, the only one.'

I pull the car off Brockley Road into the small side street by Crofton Park, and I stop. Suzie opens her passenger door. 'Come on,' she says. 'I need my bed.'

Tamsin, clambering out, tells Ludo to get out too.

'We can't,' he explains. 'You only have that one spare bed. So we're best to go home.' He looks at me and chuckles. 'Because I'm not sharing a bed with Floyd,' he says, and he laughs again.

Suzie and Tamsin hesitate on the pavement. I can see them wondering when we're going to explain to Ludo.

'He's right,' I say. 'It's best we just crawl into our own beds tonight. I'll call round tomorrow.'

'Bring Ludo,' Suzie says. In the back of the car he is still chuckling at his joke.

Tamsin leans her head down to my window. 'We can all read the papers together,' she says. 'Who knows? It could be the best break I ever had.'

Ludo says that he will buy all of them. 'We can spread them out on the table like rich people do on Sundays. That'll be fun, I think.'

As we cruise away, Ludo says, 'I hope you and I aren't in the papers, Floyd. That would not be good.'

'Yeah, you're right. You've been right all evening. You're getting pretty smart in your old age, you know that?'

He chortles to himself in the back of the car, pleased as a puppy who has found a new bone.


Eva is disgusted. 'Two hundred cops,' she says. 'Guns and everything. And for what?'

I don't answer. I don't correct her two hundred down to Kellard's one hundred and twenty. I don't tell her the part that I played.

'They're so proud of themselves,' she spits. 'Get a few kilos of cocaine and they call it a major drugs haul. They got nothing.'

'That's all right then.'

'They stamp all over us.'

'Police are paid to bust drugs rings,' I say quietly. 'They can't do it by pussyfooting.' Although I keep the casual, indifferent tone, I feel that I have to offer some kind of defence. I can't dissociate myself from what happened.

Jamie looks up. 'Waste of money, though, innit?'

He is slumped on his wreck of a sofa, pale and unshaven, wearing a dark rollneck sweater which makes him look like a sailor the morning after. Beside him on the carpet stands a chipped mug of cold tea.

'Bloody harassment all the time,' he says. 'That ain't gonna help.'

'They were after the big boys.'

Eva cuts in. 'They never catch the big boys – just middle men and users. A complete waste of time.'

'Richardson. Carmichael. They weren't middle men.'

'Of course they were,' she sneers. 'Local distributors, that's all. They should ignore the bloody dealers, and work on *him*.' She points to Jamie, who looks indignant. 'They should help the junkie kick his habit. Cure the customers, kill the trade.'

'Dead right,' agrees Jamie, sitting more upright on his untidy sofa. 'They can find two hundred cops to bust the Parrot, but there ain't one to help guys like me.'

I smile, close my eyes, and lean back in his shabby armchair. Let Jamie have the last word. I don't know what to say anyway. The thought of Floyd Carter working with the police leaves me bewildered. I certainly couldn't explain it to these two. I feel as if I have changed sides, a secret agent against my friends.

Deep inside, of course, there's that indignant little voice: you've done nothing to be ashamed of. You have not betrayed your friends. You took action against the villains. You paid them back for killing Albie. That's a noble motive, isn't it? Honourable. Yet I don't feel proud.

It's strange that I feel dirty from having worked with the forces of authority. But I do. I guess it is that word Authority – they who must be obeyed. And it's the image I have of cops. Round here, we've had them push us around. We've seen them punch, wrench and kick. We've seen them arm themselves with guns. And we know what happens in their concrete cells. The thought of co-operating with men like that makes me squirm. It's against everything we were brought up to.

'Am I boring you?' Jamie asks. 'Or have you fallen asleep?'

From our separate chairs, Eva and I blink open our eyes and dredge up polite smiles. Jamie sits huddled on the edge of the sofa, watching us. He shivers, then brushes a lock of dark hair away from his face. 'I'm fed up with clean living already,' he says. 'D'you know what I'd really like?'

'Yes,' we say.

'If I popped out, I wouldn't need five minutes and I could score. Just a little one, you know?'

Eva stretches and says, quite equably, 'I've wasted two days on you so far, Jimbo. You're nearly halfway through the worst. So you can damn well sit there while I make another cup of tea.'

'Just testing,' he says. 'To see if anyone was there.' He gives a tired smile. 'You two are gonna clean me up despite myself, ain't ya?'

Eva smiles.

'God help me,' Jamie says.